What Readers are Saying About *Alex and Amirah*

Ms. Gardner has written an extraordinary tale that is both brilliant and could all but qualify as historical fiction. It is a timely commentary on racism and trending values. By holding up an unflinching mirror and illuminating the age-old intrigue of new love, we are treated to a journey into the minds and hearts of two distinct national types. I enthusiastically recommend this book to be both entertaining and offering a deeper look into their lives. Gardner's mission to serve the world with a slice of life leading to peace and harmony gets a huge "Yes" from me.
~ Rev. Colleen E, Brown

It is a love story. It is a thriller. It is a learning of the fight of interests that moves the world, with the religious beliefs behind the scene. And if terrorism has taken the front line since the beginning of the century, you will catch some of the strings of the history. Set in the beautiful city of Paris, once you start reading, it will not fall from your hands. ~ Maya Selva

Kathryn Gardner has written a fascinating novel that tells a story of mystery and international intrigue. Through the eyes of Christians, Jews and Muslims, she gives us a glimpse at the desperate circumstances of the Middle Eastern crisis that plagues Europe. The story considers answers that the world needs. I invite you to join the journey of the characters in her book and especially the spiritual awakening of Amirah. Enjoy!
~ Mike Farien

I hope my reading of this book in 24 hours says a lot about my enjoying it! The author has a sharp mind, and has studied and traveled widely! I enjoyed the detail in the descriptions of scenes. Amirah is a good example of fleshing out a character; I feel that I know her. ~ Dr. Earl Davis

The captivating love story of *Alex and Amirah* is full of mystery, art and romance. After reading the sensational descriptions of the city of love, I am ready to stroll down the Champs-Elysées and taste the French cuisine. As an artist I found inspiration from Amirah's use of painting as a means of coping with her painful past as well as preserving the memories of the Syrian city she loved. Ms. Gardner gives a beautiful perspective on different cultures and faiths as she ties together historical and modern events. ~ Georgianne Daws, Artist and Pilates teacher

Alex and Amirah provides suspense and intrigue, while giving readers a sense of what it's like to be a refugee. As Amirah navigates a fresh start in Paris, the life she left in Syria is never far from her thoughts. Just like the past haunts Amirah and other expatriate characters, their story lingered in my thoughts long after I finished the book.
~ Beth Gooch, Romantic Suspense Author ~ Beth Gooch

Alex and Amirah

From Darkness Into Light

Kathryn Gardner

Alex and Amirah

Dedicated to my son, Jay and his wife, Tonia
and my grandchildren,
Anna Elizabeth, Alexander, and Olivia Kate

and

the workers of Life In Messiah, International

Prologue

At 6:30 A.M., three times a week, Doctor Alexander Winston laces up his running shoes, grabs his I-phone and sunglasses and leaves for a morning run.

He knows the Paris neighborhoods well. He passes the stately *appartement* building of his godparents, Philippe and Maya Dalle in the sixteenth *arrondissement*, when he hears the sirens and the primal scream of the emergency ambulance. Quickening his pace, he instinctively turns toward the sound.

It leads him up the hill to the *Palais de Chaillot.* This area is a favorite for many North African and Middle Eastern refugees who hawk Eiffel Tower keychains, silver coins, and knock-off designer bags. Crowds are forming quickly. Obviously, there has been a casualty. The curious observers try to get pictures of the ominous scene while the sun rises through the platforms of the Eiffel Tower and Parisians enjoy their *petit déjeuner* and *café au lait.*

Dr. Winston approaches his friend Lieutenant Fournier of the *Préfecture de Police* and then sees the body. A young woman, most likely Middle Eastern, wearing a stained, torn black *hijab* lies dead at his feet.

Chapter 1

The Painting

Friday morning, the first of April, a month before the murder, Paris's famous Left Bank was bustling with activity at seven in the morning.

Artists were setting up their easels and displays, hoping the tourists would purchase their art. This atmosphere was a dramatic and colorful world outside Dr. Alexander Winston's clinic at the *Salpêtrière*, where he treated his patients. These cosmopolitan scenes and charming culinary delights of his adopted city had changed so much since he and his parents lived here years ago, but he too had changed. Now he was the adult working in the international hospital where his parents had served. His had been a fortunate childhood and yet, with all the international moves the family made from country to country, the adjustments had been hard for him.

The aromas from the *boulangeries* captivated him. He darted in one and chose a rich roasted coffee with thick cream and a *roulé*, a rolled flaky pastry filled with praline rose. Finishing his coffee, he walked by the stand of the old Syrian Nanian, who sold books and prints. "*Bonjour, Nanian, Comment allez-vous?*"

"*Je vais très bien, Docteur.* Take a look at this." Nanian handed him a small exquisite painting of a raging sea.

"Excellent. Who painted this?"

"A talented young refugee from Aleppo, Amirah Hassan. Have you never seen her? Well, I guess not, though she often paints on the Left Bank of Paris. She will be famous one day, I am sure."

"I don't doubt you, and besides, I like it. How much?"

"Twenty euros. Shall I wrap it for you?"

"Sure. *Merci.*" Alex took the painting in exchange for the money.

"And you too, *Docteur.* By the way, I saw you on television yesterday. Your advice always helps me."

Alex acknowledged Nanian's compliment and continued his walk along the Left Bank.

He was looking at his purchase. Even though it was small, the raging sea and the small boat with tiny figures crowded together on it had a paralyzing effect on him. He immediately paralleled it with all the photos he had seen of refugee boats in dangerous waters about to splinter into pieces in the powerful seas of the Middle East. Looking up, he noticed a very similar, but larger painting on an easel, and a young beautiful woman with paints spread on a blanket in the morning sun. He thought what she was painting was as impressive as she was attractive. He didn't know she had noticed him every day he passed by, but this morning they glanced at each other simultaneously.

Alex was recognized in the *arrondissements,* because he appeared on "*Parlons Santé,*" a popular local television program, where he provided honest answers and useful information on health issues. He wondered if she had seen him on the television program or perhaps been a patient in his clinic. His mind turned to work as he glanced at his watch and hurried to the hospital.

Chapter 2

Life or Death

Later Friday morning, Alex arrived on the cardiac floor and greeted his nurse with a friendly good morning.

"Good morning, Dr. Alex. Here's a note for you. The Chief of Staff would like to see you after work. I think they have more work for you. You can't relax, can you?"

"Not much, I'm afraid. Maybe I'll work less when I take the assignment to *Médecins Sans Frontières.*"

"I doubt that. But, why go to the refugee camp in Greece with that organization, when you have plenty of refugees to treat here?"

"I know, but I have to go. I feel God's calling."

"Honestly, Dr. Winston, I just don't get that faith and certainty you feel about God calling you. You have everything here in Paris, but excuse me, that's none of my business."

"That's okay." Alex looked at his schedule. "What's on tap today?"

"Five caths and follow-ups, plus Houssain al-Jabar, a patient in room 212, who kept everyone busy last night."

"What happened?" inquired Alex.

"He was brought in having chest pain, but it improved with nitro."

"Did it go away?"

"No, he's still having pain but not as bad."

Alex, flipping through the chart, said, "Troponins and CK-MB both rising. Hmmm, that's not good. I'd be concerned he has an unstable lesion. He needs a catheterization as soon as possible. Let's get him set up-first thing."

"Right away, but I should mention that the two men who brought him, claiming to be relatives, were very rude."

"Rude?"

"Yes, they ogled the nurses and made everyone, including the patient, extremely nervous by their loud talk and complaints."

"Do you think they're a threat?"

"I don't know, but I notified security to come to our floor just in case. I hope that's okay."

"Fine. You did what you thought best. Let me see the scanned charts and lab reports. Houssain's thirty-years old, young for this medical condition. You and I know the heart reacts as a spiritual and emotional organ as well as a physical one. I don't want anyone upsetting the patient before a procedure."

He swigged a cup of coffee and headed down the hall to room 212.

After tapping on the door, he entered and recognized one of the men at bedside as Ibrahim, a shop owner in the *Marché Aux Puces.*

"Good morning, Mr. Al-Jabar." Houssain glanced at his two visitors but said nothing. Ibrahim spoke, "Excuse us, Doctor. We will leave Houssain in your good hands. But tell us what you're planning to do with him."

"He needs a catheterization."

"What's that, Doctor, and is it absolutely necessary?" asked Ibrahim. "We don't like hospitals or doctors in general."

"Many people may agree with you, sir, but as to the catheterization, yes, it's a necessary procedure to properly diagnose and treat cardiovascular conditions."

"How safe is that, Doctor?"

"Complications are rare, but we need to see the exact extent of his heart damage."

Houssain roused, "Will I be okay, Doctor? I've never been in a hospital until now. I've never even been sick. I thought heart problems were for old people."

"I think you'll be fine, Houssain. All ages can have heart issues. Are your visitors relatives?"

Ibrahim spoke, "No, we're not blood relatives, but Houssain is like a son to me and a brother to Abdul. Houssain works in my shop."

"Don't you own a shop in the *Marché Aux Puces*?" Alex inquired.

"Yes, and Houssain is one of my assistants. I hope I haven't pushed him too much, but I'm sure with your special training you can fix any health issue in this excellent hospital. Isn't that right?" asked Ibrahim.

"I don't make that claim, but we do our best," Alex said, wanting to end this conversation.

But Ibrahim continued, "I'm worried about him, so you better take good care of him, Doctor Alex. Just so you know, we would be very unhappy with you if anything bad happens to him. How long will he need to stay here?"

"That depends on the results of the cath. We'll know right away if a stent or other procedures are needed, but usually the patient can leave in a day."

"That would be most excellent. Houssain, Allah is with you.

We'll be back to check on you later. What time may we return, Doctor?" asked Ibrahim. Abdul said nothing and stared at Houssain the whole time.

"Probably early afternoon. The nurse or I can call you if you'd like. Did you leave a number?"

"No, no, we didn't. No need to call us. We'll just check later." Ibrahim glared at Houssain and warned him, "Keep quiet and rest." Ibrahim went over to the bed and whispered something in his ear, before turning to the door. He and Abdul gave the doctor a nod and said, "*Masalama,*" to Houssain as they left the room.

Alex walked to the bedside. "Houssain, how are you feeling? I heard you had a restless night."

"Yes, Doctor. I am scared. My father died when I was very young."

"I'm sorry. Was it a heart attack?"

"We never knew because there was only one doctor and a small hospital two hundred miles from my home in Syria. We couldn't afford to get there or pay a doctor, but my mother thought it was a heart attack. He was very young like me in his thirties. I think I'm going to die."

"No, Houssain, I don't think so. I'm going to give you the best medical attention I can. You know, you've been brought to one of the finest hospitals in Paris. You relax and this procedure will be over soon and you'll be able to get back to work."

By late afternoon, Doctor Alex returned to Houssain's room. "The procedure went well," You have two stents in your heart that should keep your arteries open and allow blood to flow freely."

"I'm still worried I may be like my father who died early."

"I can't tell you if you're like your father because we have no family records. I can tell you risk factors, if you want?"

"Yes, tell me."

"Do you smoke?"

"Not much. Now and then."

"That needs to stop completely, Houssain. It's harming your other arteries. I can see you're under stress, and that's not helping you either."

"I don't know how to live without stress. Working with Ibrahim, the slave driver, stresses all of us."

"Well, your heart has been damaged. Maybe it's not all Ibrahim's fault. Is that possible?"

"Everything has worked against me since I tried to leave Syria. I was beaten and robbed by the smugglers I hired to get me on a boat out of Syria. They did terrible things to my sisters and I could do nothing to help. I see it over and over every day and my dreams haunt me every night. I've even been robbed at knifepoint, since I got to Paris. Ibrahim said he would get my sisters out of the refugee camp and pay me decent wages, but Doctor, I've been working for him a year and nothing's changed. I'm afraid of him, too---and all his work."

"Houssain, I hear what you're saying. You've had major stress factors, but the hospital staffers are going to help you in any way they can. With diet, exercises and counseling, we'll get you on a road to recovery. Maybe you need friends other than Ibrahim and Abdul."

"I wish I had even one of my old friends from Syria, but here, I don't speak the language well, and Ibrahim works me so hard that I don't have much time for friends right now."

"You have a job and a place to stay. I know it's miserable now, but it takes time. You're going to make it. Trust me. I'm giving you a prescription for a blood thinner and an aspirin a day for your physical condition. Next, take this advice for your emotional and spiritual condition. I have a good friend, Doctor Reza, who volunteers at the International Church, helping refugees like you get settled and meet people. It would be great if you'd talk to him."

"Oh, no, I could never go near a church. Ibrahim would not approve and I cannot go against him. Thank you, Doctor Alex. I'll take the medicine, but I'll deal with the stress myself."

"Well, if you ever reconsider, Doctor Reza speaks often at a dinner for internationals here in Paris, hosted by Mr. and Mrs. Hertz, who are really fine friends of mine. It's a great time to get together, share your stories and enjoy dinner. They also offer French as a Second Language in classes. Why don't you try it sometime? You might like it."

"Thanks, Doctor. Maybe I will."

"Houssain, I want you to stay here for a couple of days and come back to see me in two weeks. Rest all you can. If you change your mind about talking to someone, here's Reza's card."

"I hope I don't need to come back to the hospital after that two-week check-up. I'll never forget you. You're a good man, who has saved my life."

"It's all in a day's work. It was nice meeting you."

"It was nice meeting you, Doctor. You are the kindest man from Paris I've ever talked to. Thanks."

Alex walked down the corridor. He hoped Houssain would call Reza. Alex knew Houssain was under Ibrahim's control and sensed that was a major problem for him and maybe other refugees working for him.

The day was long and stressful, but the meeting with the Chief of Staff was a complete surprise. He asked Alex to consider staying with them at the *Salpêtrière* instead of taking another assignment and made a quite generous offer. Alex had thanked him and said he would think it over. Leaving the hospital, he walked to Victor's, a small café near his *appartement* and ordered a duck breast, a glass of Chablis and a light salad. His mind returned to the artist he had seen painting that morning, and he planned to say hello if she happened to be there tomorrow. He watched the glittering lights of the *Eiffel Tower* as he walked home. He slept soundly that night.

Chapter 3

Romance

Saturday morning, walking his same route, he saw her — the young artist sitting on her blanket, painting. He stopped at a newsstand and thumbed through *des journaux*, pretending not to notice when she looked up and watched him for a minute. After checking his watch to be sure he had time before rounds at the hospital, he went to her and with naïveté said, "Your painting grabbed my attention yesterday. I can see you are very talented."

"Thank you. I noticed you walking by."

"Did you think you recognized me? Have you been one of my patients at the *Salpêtrière*?"

She was embarrassed and felt a pink-tinged blush edging up her neck. She took her time answering, but finally said, "No, I don't think we've met, because I am an *émigré* from Syria and I don't get out much. Fortunately, I've never been sick enough to go to a hospital."

Wanting to alleviate her anxiety and his too, Alex said, "I did not mean to embarrass you."

"Please, it's okay. I'm a little shy sometimes, but I'm learning to speak up."

"Do you know the French as a people cannot be embarrassed? Nor should you. I will tell you a joke, which is all too true, if I may."

Amirah gave him an elusive smile and nodded yes.

"The joke is – when God created France he made it the most beautiful country in the world. However, to prevent all the world from moving here, he populated it with Frenchmen."

Amirah laughed at the joke and recognized the sensitivity of this handsome young man. "Well," she said, "I was staring at you and I do apologize. The truth is, you reminded me of home in Syria. Every morning the local herbalist would walk past the window of my father's shop. He had the same stride, the same tilt of his head and the same purposeful expression on his face as you. I'm sorry, I do not mean any disrespect."

At that moment, Alex was smitten with unusual interest in this young lady. Maybe she didn't even know who he was, which was all the better. "Oh, forgive me, let me introduce myself. I'm Alex Winston, visitor to Paris from Canada, and you?"

"My name is Amirah Hassan from Aleppo. *Enchantèe, monsieur.*"

"*Enchantè.* From time to time I walk by the cafes here on my way to work and have a pastry and coffee. Forgive me, if I seem too forward, but one day, perhaps, you would join me for coffee," he suggested.

Amirah said, "You're very kind to ask, but I would have all my supplies and I could not leave them here, but perhaps you could bring coffee here and sit one morning."

"Well, then, would it be too bold if I ask about tomorrow morning? Would that be good for you?" Alex looked around at the surrounding cafes and pointed to one nearby. "Do you think they make *un bon café* and *un petit déjeuner* at that one?"

"Most likely. I'm sure they have great coffee. I've had it a couple of times. *À quelle* heure?"

"Eight o'clock?" Amirah nodded agreement. "See you then. Here is my card, should you need to make a change of plans." He continued his walk to the clinic, but turned his head to see Amirah and said, "Looking forward to seeing you again, *Mademoiselle Amirah.*"

And so began the first of several early morning coffees and chats. Although he did not know why yet, Alex was attracted to Amirah by a force he had never felt before. Something about her dedication to her art and her quiet seriousness appealed to him, but she was also exotically beautiful with an interesting accent.

Chapter 4

International Church

Three weeks later on a Sunday morning, Amirah decided to go to the International Church. Although she had been in Paris almost two years, worship on Sunday still seemed strange. Friday is the Muslim holy day and Amirah often worshipped in the Mosque. The service connected her with happy memories of a lost time that would never come again.

Fauziah, her Muslim friend from Malaysia, attended with Reza, and they had invited her many times. Fauziah had taken her under her wing and played big sister, substitute mom and close friend rolled into one, and Amirah was grateful for her friendship. Although she knew the Christian faith was important to Alex, the thought of it made her nervous and uncomfortable. Nevertheless, she gathered her courage and decided to visit.

Hurrying down three flights of stairs at the *Bonne Nouvelle* station, Amirah waited for the next train. It was easy to get around on the Metro on Sunday mornings, she thought — no delays, no crowds. On weekday mornings it was packed and stuffy. Remembering the nights of bombing in Aleppo when she hid in the basements caused fear in Amirah that the train would stop underground and she would be stuck in the dark with hundreds of strangers for hours. She controlled her fear with steely determination to endure the Metro ride until she arrived at her destination.

This morning her fears were somewhat allayed because a talented trio of Romanian musicians played folk and pop songs while the train rolled. The ensemble reminded her of peaceful times in tourist hotels in Aleppo when rich, American tourists listened and danced to Syrian musical entertainment. The trio was comprised of a female vocalist, an accordionist and a fiddle player, dressed in their national costumes. The woman wore a full Roma skirt and princess bodice and a bright red embroidered headband that accented her long dark hair and luminous brown eyes. The men wore Romanian ethnic embroidered shirts tucked into white pants with matching hats and belts. Soon she arrived at her stop.

After a brief walk, she stood in front of the imposing International Church. It was not like the magnificent cathedrals, nor was it like the ancient mosques in Aleppo and Damascus. It featured rounded arched windows all along the sides of the church. The façade had three small arches under a single larger arch and there were smooth wide steps leading to the rounded outdoor space in which a memorial fountain flowed continuously. She noticed more arches at the top of the campanile tower to the right. The architecture of the building was a combination of French and Byzantine. Yet it was open and fresh like modern architecture without being cold and hard. The beautiful design was warm and welcoming. Amirah would sketch that one day.

She walked around it a few times, summoned courage, and ascended the smooth church steps. Pausing to listen to the bubbling water fountain and admire the terra cotta designs surrounding the ceiling, she opened the iron square glass door and entered. She was startled by loud voices and the accompanying band. This was not the kind of music she expected to hear at a Christian worship service.

She wanted to avoid speaking to people loitering in the vestibule in order to observe and listen, so she walked to the sanctuary doors and peeked inside. The interior was designed like a huge theatre with lattice work surrounding the stage. At the back of the stage was a huge painting of a man dressed in white in a river or lake, but actual water was in a basin at the foot of the painting. This was a most unusual place. Elegant lights hung from the ceiling sparkling throughout the auditorium. She spotted Reza and Fauziah and quickly turned away from the door. She would tell them she visited, but she wanted to enjoy the art and architecture of the building on her own.

Was she disobeying Allah by even being here? She thought she should leave, but she wanted to stay and learn more, so she could know more about Alex's upbringing.

Chapter 5

New Friend

A man wearing a name badge approached her with a friendly good morning. "I'm Bill Hertz, one of the elders here, and what is your name?" he asked.

"I'm Amirah."

"Welcome, Amirah. Would you like a cup of coffee?"

Amirah noticed a large serving table in the center of this foyer with five or six coffee urns. On another serving table were sugars, creamers and chocolate mints. She had never before been inside a Christian church and was surprised to be offered coffee. In her country one did not drink coffee in a mosque. "Yes, that would be lovely. Thank you very much."

As Mr. Hertz walked with her to the coffee table, she remembered the name. This might be the Mr. Hertz Alex was to meet soon in the *Quartier Latin* but she didn't want to ask him. "Your church is magnificent."

"Thank you, Amirah. It was my first job after my official retirement. I was the architect on the project. Are you visiting Paris or do you live here?"

"I'm a refugee from Syria. I've been living here almost two

years." She chose hazelnut flavor and Mr. Hertz filled a cup for her. "You are an amazing architect. The church is a magnificent structure."

"Thank you. We're very pleased with it."

"It is glorious. I've never seen anything like it."

"Thank you, Amirah. Please look around." She noticed big screens in the lobby showing various ethnic groups singing together inside the larger room.

She heard people clapping their hands and even saw people dancing. Stranger still was the fact that girls and boys, women and men were sitting together. "This is very interesting music," she said, although she thought all of it was a bit peculiar.

"Yes, this is the contemporary service. In addition to this one, we have a traditional service earlier at 8:00 A.M., which you might prefer. We have a guest speaker this morning from the persecuted church in Uganda. His bio is in the bulletin. I will get it for you. He suffered greatly for his faith. One night a Christian witnessed the Gospel to him and he began to read the Bible. He told his parents he wanted to go to a Christian church. They threatened him with death, but he became an itinerant preacher there. We have been sponsoring his work in Uganda for about eight years now and once a year he reports to us. Our regular pastor is on a mission trip to Greece. Just a minute, I'll get you a bulletin with information about the service and the church." He walked to a different table.

Amirah wondered where the pastor was in Greece. Could he possibly be near Lesbos, where her mother and brothers were in the refugee camp? She would like to talk with the pastor another day.

The music did not seem reverent to Amirah. Jazzy music blasted all over the building She expected the worship of Jesus to be formal and strict. Still, she was curious and wanted to learn about this man Jesus. She believed she had seen Jesus on the Aegean Sea the night she and Yousif escaped. Was this a regular church worship service or was it some kind of festival to honor Jesus? She could not grasp it. There was a definite joy and a spontaneity in the worship — very unlike her mosque.

Mr. Hertz returned and handed her a bulletin and a small book *La Chambre Haute.* "This bulletin will explain the order of service today — the hymns to be sung by the congregation, an outline of the sermon and announcements for the week. This little devotion book is for your daily reading if you're interested. I like to read something from the Bible, a short devotion and prayer each day. If you're interested in knowing more about Jesus or the Bible, *La Chambre Haute* could be a little guide."

Amirah hesitated to take the material. "Is there a charge?"

"Oh, no. Help yourself to any of the materials on that table over there. Would you like to join the service?"

"Thank you for the coffee, bulletin and book, but I would prefer not to go into the service today. I'll just listen a little longer. Thank you for being so kind."

"That's fine. Do what makes you comfortable. I have an invitation for you, however. Mrs. Hertz and I host Wednesday night dinners for international students and friends, young and old. These *soirées* in our *Montmartre* apartment once or twice a month have become a highlight of our years in Paris. Not only is the cuisine exceptional, but also there are extraordinary refugees, internationals and locals with amazing stories of their homelands and their new experiences here. We make new friends and enjoy food from around the world. Here's a little flyer about that and you are welcome to come any time and bring a guest. I think you would enjoy it and I know we would enjoy getting to know you."

"You are too kind, Mr. Hertz. Thank you very much."

"Mrs. Hertz and I were in Damascus many years ago. I had

always wanted to see the eighth century *Great Mosque of the Umayyads*, built on the site of an Assyrian sanctuary and certainly the UNESCO site was magnificent. Mrs. Hertz shares my interest in architecture, so we have traveled to many wonders of the world, and your ancient country brought to life cultures older than the Bible. Did you go to the *souq* in Damascas?"

"Yes, my parents took me there, but I'm actually from Aleppo where we had an even more extraordinary *souq*. It was closed down and now it's destroyed. Her eyes filled with tears. Forgive me for getting emotional. Thank you again. I must go now."

"I'm sorry I brought up a sad memory for you."

"No, please, do not feel bad. I've enjoyed visiting with you."

"Thank you, Amirah. I hope we see you at the dinner and come again any time to the church." Mr. Hertz walked her to the door.

Chapter 6

Riot

It was near noon, when Amirah left the church. She decided to enjoy a walk on the *Champs-Elysées* before her meeting with Fauziah and Maleeka, the Imam's daughter. Some Indian ladies in lovely saris walked in front of her as well as some men she recognized as Orthodox Jews by their *kippahs.* She was processing her short visit to the International Church, and although it had seemed strange, she appreciated the kindness of Mr. Hertz. Since Reza, Fauziah and Alex attended services there, she decided she would visit again and stay for the service.

She had almost reached the Eiffel Tower when she saw a large group of people gathering nearby. People were driving down the boulevard, yelling out the car windows, "Go home to your promised land. We don't want you here!"

One car almost ran into the Jewish men and screamed in their faces, "We are sick and tired of you Jews killing our Palestinian children, blowing up their schools, and stealing their homes." People were coming on bikes, scooters and walking from everywhere. Before Amirah could change directions, she found herself in the middle of a French protest. She was terrified. Would she be their next target? She spoke French well, but she could not understand all of the angry words.

Cars stopped on the avenue and a mob of protesters quickly formed. They carried placards and signs reading, "Go home, Jews." "Get out of Paris." "Jesus-Jews." She understood enough. They said, "France is better off without you and your money. Don't expect peace in Israel, because you have stolen our land." Amirah tried to push her way in another direction when a skinhead yelled at her, "Hey, you little head-scarfed girl. We don't want you here either. You want some special treatment?"

Amirah was shaking and could not think of enough French to reply to the skinhead who pursued her. He was reaching for her scarf when a gypsy lady appeared on the street, put her arm around Amirah and introduced herself. "I am Sylvana, the mighty gypsy prophet. Do not be afraid."

The gypsy called the skinhead by name, "Lothario, the spirit is strong within you. You are possessed and you know it. I will not deal severely with you today. As for us, let us pass. You have already caused yourself more trouble than you can handle."

"Shut up, old woman. Your spells and curses don't frighten me."

Sylvana stuck a long bony finger in his face and said in an ominous croak like the creaking of a tomb, "Shadow of a man, feeble imitator, you repeat the words of your old commander Raymond." And then in perfect street slang she said, "Like boils all over you."

The thug's jaw dropped in amazement, his eyes widened, and reflexively he pulled back. "Crazy old woman," he announced loudly as he turned around and walked the other way and continued mumbling, "I'm not afraid of you, Old Lady," but he kept walking away.

The gypsy lady asked Amirah, "Who are you, child and

daughter, and where are you going?"

"I'm Amirah and I was just walking to meet my friends at a café near the *Trocadero*, when protestors started swarming on the street near the *Eiffel Tower*. Cars came from everywhere. What a mob!"

"Don't worry, Amirah. I am Sylvana, your savior today, and you are coming with me. I will take you to your friends on my motorcycle. You should have been warned. The French protest all the time. It could be the Metro workers, government workers or teachers. Everyone here is protesting something hourly. Lately, protests have turned violent and hate-mongering hoodlums join them."

Amirah was reluctant to go with Sylvana. On the other hand, she had rescued her from the despicable man. "I think I'll be okay. Thank you for your help."

"No, Amirah, you will be safer with me. I will take you to your friends. This protest has been planned. We must get out of here. Listen to me. Come now."

Amirah climbed onto the back of the motorcycle and they roared off.

Chapter 7

Meeting

Sylvana roared up in front of the *Café Pour Vous* at 3 *Place Trocadero* and stopped by the parked motorcycles and scooters outside the busy restaurant. "You must go meet your friends, Amirah. *C'est tout pour nous*," she said, and gestured rather impatiently for Amirah to hop off.

"Please join us. I would like to introduce you to my friends as the woman who may have saved my life today."

"Thank you, but I have done my deed. Now you have important business. We may meet again. Run your race well and let your light shine. *Au revoir*." Sylvana rode away toward *Rue de Passy*, never looking back.

Amirah stood stunned for a moment or two. Beginning to feel the festive atmosphere of the *al fresco* diners on this sunny day, she meandered through the crowded outside tables and entered *Café Pour Vous* through wide doors. She spotted Fauziah and Maleeka, waving to her from the back of the restaurant, but did not recognize the petite blond girl with them. Papers and materials were spread over the table.

Fauziah greeted Amirah as she approached them, "Who

brought you on that motorcycle?"

"Her name is Sylvana, but that's all I know. She appeared out of nowhere and rescued me from this monster on the *Champs-Elysées* trying to pull the scarf off my head, and I don't know what else he would have done. It was scary."

"Did he just run up to you on the street and start harassing you?"

"Yes. I left the International Church and decided to stroll to meet you here at the restaurant, but along the way, a riot erupted. People were driving recklessly, shouting curses, and jumping out of their cars. Others ran out of *cafés* and from street corners and joined them. They blocked the streets, broke windows, threatened people and carried hate signs against the Jews. And there were no police."

Maleeka said, "No police? What did you do? You said the racist was trying to pull your *hijab* off?"

"Yes, I didn't know what I would do, if that Sylvana had not come to rescue me."

"You know, the Parisians are always protesting and these were mainly protesting the Jews, because they want them out of the country."

"Jews, I think, but it must have been Arabs too, since he was after me."

"You poor dear."

"No, it's okay, I think he saw me and hated that I was wearing the *hijab* or he was mad about all internationals pouring into his city. I'm fine. Let's move on with our meeting."

Maleeka said, "Oh, Amirah, excuse me for not introducing you to Olivia. She is a psychologist who works with abused women and I invited her to join us in our new service outreach. Olivia, Amirah is an extremely talented artist who has been recognized by the art community as a rising star here."

"Olivia, she's exaggerating, but I'm charmed to meet you."

"And it is a pleasure to meet you. I'm very privileged to be invited to work with you on this project," said Olivia.

Fauziah spoke, "I just thought of something Reza was telling me this morning, when you said no police were on the scene. Reza said that the police have been understaffed, since they received so much criticism for their handling of recent protests, saying they were too severe on criminals and rioters. They can't be as effective any longer."

Amirah spoke, "Indeed. The police here can do better, but the military of Syria was brutal. Our policemen were hit squads. The French people don't understand what police in our countries did. The protestors here should be sent to countries where they can see real police oppression. Then they might understand the Paris police position better."

Danger lurks everywhere," Fauziah warned. "You had a guardian angel by providence this morning."

"Anyway, thank Allah, I am here with my friends now, but let's not talk about me anymore. I've been wanting to ask you why you left Malaysia," said Amirah.

Fauziah replied, "I love my family and I was almost a perfect daughter." The girls laughed. "I mean it, and if truth be known I suspect you all were too. It's the way we were reared. We respected our parents and our elders and were very sheltered. We did what we were told. We studied and fortunately for us we were allowed an education. I knew there was more in the big world. When I arrived at the University of Memphis, Tennessee under a special government grant to learn English, it was my big opportunity to live my dream. I have never regretted going to school in the US or this move to Paris."

"Wait a minute. Here comes the *garçon* again. Tea, everyone?" asked Maleeka. "Shall we have a bite of lunch too? It's on me, ladies. With all your help, it's the least I can do. I know they have delicious *Quiche Lorraine* here with a green salad, divine onion soup, *omelettes mixte jambon et fromage. Fais ton choix.*"

The girls glanced at the menu and decided on a green salad and the *omelettes mixte jambon et fromage* and Maleeka ordered when the *garçon* arrived at the table.

Fauziah said, "Tell us about growing up in Paris, Maleeka?"

Maleeka began, "Well, you know, Paris is my home. I was born here, but with the imam as my father, growing up in Paris was still growing up in a Muslim family with all the Muslim traditions. I had a lot of opportunities, but not the freedom of girls born into Christian families. As you know we were closely guarded as teenagers. Some of my Muslim girlfriends felt trapped and were very afraid to mingle with anyone outside the Muslim community."

Their tea arrived and it was pleasant to all.

Amirah spoke up, "At home with my father, I am free, but my father is exceptional. Some Muslim fathers are merciless with their daughters. It's so sad."

Maleeka responded, "You're right. You've been blessed with an incredible opportunity to study at one of the greatest art schools in the world. I don't think all Muslim fathers would allow their daughters to study at a western university, even if they were fortunate enough to be accepted at the *Sorbonne.* You would never have had this opportunity if you weren't in Paris. You've had great teachers, plus you've made great contacts and you've been helped more than a Parisian girl would have been in an Arab country."

"Regrettably, I agree with you, although before this horrible war, Syria and many Arab countries welcomed foreigners," countered Amirah.

"Well, a lot of them didn't. What have ISIS, HAMAS, and AL QAEDA done for foreigners in Arab countries? I'm saying the Parisians have opened the doors of freedom to us," responded Maleeka.

The *garçon* brought the salads and *omelettes* to the ladies and they enjoyed the delectable meal with each other.

Chapter 8

Women Plot

"We have a lot to do," said Fauziah. "Our work today concerns our Muslim sisters, who are struggling with abuse in their own families, whether it's from their fathers, brothers or even mothers. I think it's remarkable that you're going to help us too, Olivia. Your experience in counseling abused Muslim women will surely raise their consciousness, making them aware of their human rights and dignity. People of different backgrounds working together will expand the outreach and perspective of us all."

Amirah chimed in, "We are committed to help you with your project, Maleeka. I know Muslim women living in this city, who are trapped by their families and the social restrictions of Sharia law. Little by little we can make a difference. Tell us your plans."

Olivia spoke up, "I want us also to address the issue of female genital mutilation, because many of the immigrants have already been subjected to this trauma in their own country by their own mothers. Their lives have been scarred in two ways. They've been mutilated personally in a very intimate and embarrassing way and the trust that girls need to have in their mothers has been permanently damaged. Something this traumatic lasts the rest of their lives, unless they get help working through it."

Fauziah said, "I had an older cousin who had a miserable marriage and life because she always felt inferior and unfit for social and work situations. This betrayal controlled everything she did."

"We will raise the self-esteem and confidence of these women so they can make their own plans and live free from the bondage of tradition," said Fauziah. "How are we going to locate the women who need our help?"

"I want this business to appear as an adjunct counseling center where women learn more about homecare, healthcare, et cetera, so they will not be embarrassed to come for our services. Once we meet the ladies, we'll find opportunities to talk with them about other issues of concern," said Maleeka.

"Now, where are we going to work?" asked Amirah.

"I've found an old building in the second *arrondissement*, where many Muslim families live. I've talked to Adrian, the realtor, and she says we can rent an office floor for next to nothing. That's amazing for Paris. I will set up my office for my regular law practice but on the same floor, I intend to provide a place to talk with these women who need help. Our work must be as discreet as possible," Maleeka confided.

"Of course, we know how a traditional Muslim man might react. He might harm his wife if he learns she's talking to us and our involvement could jeopardize us too," Fauziah said.

Maleeka agreed, "We will keep a low profile and maybe we need a contact in the police department who could refer abused women to us."

Fauziah said, "My friend Reza works with so many refugees at the International Church and through his university job. He encounters people who need help every day, and he often says that he wishes he could refer them to resource people."

"This is really coming together. What do you need me to do?" asked Amirah.

"Actually, it's simple, Amirah, I hope you will design special cards and flyers to be distributed discreetly. Also, I was wondering if you could do some art therapy with the ladies who have suffered the female genital mutilation and domestic violence. I know it could help them to visualize the traumas that they might not be able to talk about, and the making of art might be a first step to healing."

"I'm on it. I'm so excited to use my art in this new way to help people here." Amirah began sketching and designing cards and flyers while Fauziah and Maleeka were setting a schedule of events.

Maleeka said, "As you know, Olivia, I will turn to you for advice for our psychological counseling. We need to know which day you will be able to help us. We understand you have an extra busy schedule with Levi, your family and regular work, but we appreciate any time you can give us."

Olivia said, "I am only too glad to help. In addition to my regular counseling, building bridges between Christians, Muslims and Jews is part of what I do with my husband. I think Thursdays would be good."

Fauziah said, "It's almost 3:00 P.M., and I told Reza I would help him with some of his office duties this afternoon, so I need to hurry. I think we've accomplished a lot, plus it's been great reconnecting with you, Maleeka. Please let me pay for my lunch."

"No, I told you ladies this was on me." Maleeka straightened her back and squinted her eyes while she held her stomach as if she were in pain.

"What's wrong, Maleeka?" asked Amirah.

"Oh, it's my back from an old accident. Sometimes it flares

up at the oddest moment. It's nothing really."

Fauziah looked concerned. "Maleeka, what's going on? We haven't seen you much lately and frankly, I've been worried about you. I know you were working down in *Aix-en-Provence* for a while and then you said you could no longer do it. Were you injured down there? What happened?"

Maleeka sipped her tea and shook her head, "No, I wasn't physically injured down there, but I have been having some back pain. I haven't told anyone, but I am under some extra pressure from that job in *Aix*. Don't worry about me, and please keep this strictly confidential." The girls promised they would.

Fauziah took Maleeka's hand. "You can trust us. I've always been here for you since I met you. Amirah is like a sister to me and now we have Olivia as another true friend. What's troubling you?"

"Fauziah, you know that I studied art for several years against the wishes of my family, but at the same time, I was attending law school. That won out as a career choice, but I keep my hand in art in various ways."

"I had no idea. You never talk about it," said Amirah.

"No, no, I don't," said Maleeka, "but I do have a very good eye for brilliant paintings. I don't have the raw talent you have, Amirah. My skills are more in the area of identification and classification. I became interested in techniques to examine the authenticity of pieces of art."

"Fascinating," said Amirah. "What made you decide to study the recognition of forgeries and the ability to authenticate the art?"

"I was attending a small art show of several new artists and mixed in at the gallery were several famous pieces of art. I could not believe that this small gallery could actually own some of these paintings, so I studied the brush strokes for starters. I was thinking the brushstrokes had too many fine points of contact with the paint to have been made by a pre-modern brush. I told no one what I was learning. I began to research artificial intelligence and discovered the existence of a machine with the ability to detect a forgery or an original every time."

"This is beginning to sound very technical. Where are you leading us?" asked Fauziah. "I'm captivated."

"Well, I saw a Rembrandt that I suspected was a forgery, and a friend of mine verified an isotope in the vermillion orange of the alleged Rembrandt. The Nazis stole thousands of paintings from victims of the Holocaust. They were and are the world's best record keepers. They fingerprinted, photographed and documented every stolen painting. The chain of possession from looting to storage to post-war ownership is often clear. The forgeries occurred after the originals reached Paris. In many cases the evidence indicated that forgeries replaced the originals on the walls of the families who received them. I think this practice is very lucrative for the criminals involved."

"Are you saying we could be surrounded by forgeries in Paris, and dealers could be selling them as originals?" asked Amirah.

"Absolutely," Maleeka responded.

"But," asked Fauziah, "what is the pressure you are under? What is bothering you?"

"Several things. In the shop where I was working in *Aix*, there were people I suspected of selling forgeries. I've had some implied threats from the owners, although no one has accused me of being aware of their nefarious activity. I think they wonder if I have informed the police. I'm very nervous and I don't know what I should do."

Before the girls could continue their conversation, Maleeka saw a very handsome man standing in the doorway, looking their way. "There's Jonathan," she said, waving at him to join them.

"Don't say any more about this. I don't want him to worry. He and I have enough problems ourselves."

Jonathan walked back and greeted the ladies in the European manner. After a few brief words, Fauziah, Amirah and Olivia left, and Maleeka and Jonathan sat down at the table.

Fauziah and Amirah walked together to the Metro. "Who is Jonathan?" asked Amirah.

"He is Maleeka's boyfriend, but I don't think her family knows about him, especially that he's Jewish."

Fauziah was reluctant to say more, so they walked on simply enjoying the sunshine and the beautiful weather until they parted ways at the station.

Chapter 9

Homesick

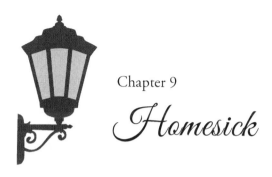

Monday, Amirah strolled along Paris's Left Bank past bookstalls, smart restaurants and *les petits bateaux* as she approached *Notre Dame.* More than eighteen months after she arrived in Paris the cathedral had been ravaged by fire, causing the collapse of its spire and dreadful damage to the windows and vaulted ceilings. It reminded her of all the suffering and devastation to Syria. Here the historic glorious symbol of the French people was destroyed in a few days. Her city, Aleppo, Syria, was reduced to rubble in a few years. The houses, the souks, the shops, the people themselves were destroyed intentionally and mercilessly with deadly force. Her city was older than *Notre Dame* which perhaps would be restored. Aleppo would not likely ever return from its ashes.

She had never heard cathedral bells ring until she heard them from *Notre Dame.* In Syria she had been drawn to the Arabic sonorous calls to prayer by the emotional and compelling tones coming from the mosques on loud speakers. The religious councils decided to cancel those calls and Friday prayers because of the brutal war on human life. As a refugee in Paris, she was surprised at how much she liked the cathedral bells. Both *Notre Dame* and Aleppo's mosques were silent now. She listened to the bells of other Paris cathedrals like *Saint-Chapelle and Saint-Sulpice* and continued to pray to Allah for the restoration of *Notre Dame* and Syria.

Strolling along the Seine, she inhaled the fragrance of the dogwood and peach blossoms. She delighted in the glorious colors of the blooming jacaranda and cherry trees. Normally, on the Left Bank she was laser-focused on her painting, but today her thoughts kept leaping ahead to her dinner with Alex in her humble apartment tonight. She wondered what he would think of the way she and her father Yousif lived, but she knew unpretentious Alex would understand.

She had met Alex only a month ago, but deep feelings were emerging for both of them even with the extreme differences in their backgrounds. Their world views were built on faith that men could raise themselves and create strong, beautiful lives. Alex worked with patients and she worked with art. Yes, she thought Alex had his life together. He was kind, polite, and respected for his medical work. How amazing that their paths had crossed in this city. Yet if he would be leaving soon, for what reason had they met?

She smiled and greeted her old friend Nanian the bookseller on the Left Bank.

"Would you like to buy this one, Amirah?" Nanian asked. "It is by Ulfat Idilbi."

"Yes, of course. She is one of my favorite authors. I would love to buy it, but I can't afford it right now. Thank you so much." She leafed through the book, pausing to read and admire several passages.

"She is my wife's favorite author too. Did you ever see 'Sabriya: Damascus Bitter Sweet' on television? No, it was before your time in the eighties, Amirah."

Nanian frequently seemed to answer his own questions, but she loved this trait in him. She had often wondered how the old man and his wife had managed to get to Paris, until she learned that their sons had arranged through bribes to get them out of Syria. Later both sons were tortured and killed in the early Syrian conflicts. Now Nanian and his wife were in their 60's. They brought nothing with them from their home or from the bookstore Nanian had owned in Aleppo. He worked on the Left Bank every day in a little shed, selling books, magazines and some art, while his wife, a talented seamstress, earned a little money doing alterations at a dry cleaners. They were survivors. The Syrian War was not their fault, nor was it Amirah's. They refused to call themselves victims.

"Amirah? Are you okay, Dear?" she heard Nanian ask.

Drawing herself back into the conversation, she said, "You're right. It was several years before I was born, but I've heard my parents talk about it, and I read it for one of my classes."

"Ah, good classes and a good teacher you must have had," he said. "Amirah, I'm concerned about your father. How is he?"

"He has adjusted to his job of carpet salesman instead of owner of one of the finest carpet shops in Aleppo. He makes enough money," she said. "He misses Aleppo and the White Helmets he led in battles for Syria's independence, but he never mentions that part of his life now. I'm also very worried about my father. He has visitors late at night and I have heard conversations about paintings I think. I'm not sure what he's involved in, but please tell me what you know."

Chapter 10

Revenge In His Heart

"It will get better, Amirah, but you must be careful. Sit down with me a minute. I wish to warn you about a few things."

"Not all the Syrians in Paris are like us. Some of them want to be our judges. They want to punish disobedience and they do not always know the difference between Allah and themselves. They place great value on their own authority — too great perhaps. Take Mr. Ibrahim, for instance. I don't like him, but he has power. Did you know your father and Ibrahim played together when they were boys?"

Amirah blinked in surprise and stiffened her neck. "Father has never mentioned that," she said. "I don't think he sees him very much, but sometimes they eat at *Café de la Lumière* or in the *Marché Aux Puces.* He makes me uncomfortable, and I avoid talking to him if possible."

"I see some of his friends around here from time to time. Just be careful, Amirah. You're a very beautiful young woman, and they'll try to marry you to some old *Batrak.*"

Her thoughts flew to her past. It had already happened once

before and she didn't intend to suffer those consequences again. It was disastrous. "Tell me what else you know about my father and Mr. Ibrahim when they were young."

"I was thinking about them this morning. People change so much, Amirah. Your father and Ibrahim played all the sports together and competed in everything in Aleppo. Your families were related. They were both smart and competitive, but your father seemed to always have the edge on Ibrahim in school, in business and then once they saw your mother, they both were determined to marry her."

"Really? I wonder what my mother thought about that. She has never mentioned another man in her life to me."

"No, I don't suppose she has. They both wanted her, but your mother loved Yousif from the beginning. Ibrahim had no chance and he never got over that. Oh, he married and reared a family, but he always resented Yousif and carried revenge in his heart."

Amirah looked puzzled. "Do you think Ibrahim is a threat to my father?"

Nanian replied, "That's what I wanted to tell you. Yes, Amirah, I think Ibrahim is involved with a very dangerous group of art thieves. I have seen them around the left bank with him. They sometimes harass me in my little art business. They are very shrewd and evil in their intent to sell paintings for quick cash to buy arms. They cannot be trusted and they want your father to help them in some way. I don't know exactly what it is, but I think maybe you should warn your father that I have heard news on the street about these men. I don't want to frighten you. Please be careful."

"Enough about this now. We are here with the sun shining, and you are like a sunbeam to an old man like me. Did you bring me any paintings to sell?"

"Yes, I have a couple," she said, taking them out of her satchel and handing them to him.

"Amirah, as I am standing here, I tell you, one day your paintings will hang in the *Louvre.* Do you believe me? Yes, I know you must. How much do you want for these?"

"I don't know. Whatever you think you can get for them. I trust your judgment, Nanian."

"Okay, but you know I cannot get you the money your paintings are worth. They take me back to Aleppo. I am an old man, and I will never see it again, but you--you with your paintings, will always keep it captured for us. What a beautiful homeland--what a history--what a life we had created there in Aleppo. Oh, for Aleppo I weep, but you have it in your soul, in your art, my dear child. Okay, here's what I will do. I will pay you ten euros for each one and hope to sell them for twenty euros apiece. If I do, I'll give you five more euros on each one. Fair?"

"Of course, thank you."

"Now, here's a bit of advice from an old man. You could make postcards and notecards, and I can get them printed for you and sell them here. Then you continue painting the large canvases for the art world, Amirah. Here," he said, handing her the Idilbi book, "you keep it and read it this week. Just bring it back next week or whenever you come."

"Oh, no, you need to sell it. I couldn't take it."

"Of course, you can. I insist. I will hear no more. You'll bring it back. I can sell it another day. Now, go and enjoy your walk and your painting. I know you love the bells and the *Quartier Latin* on Sundays. *Salaam.*"

"*Ma'aasalaama,*" said Amirah, and continued her walk.

Perhaps Nanian was right about some of the Syrians wanting to marry her to a *Batrak.* Thank God her father and husband were more progressive than Sharia law had allowed. She had been granted a divorce and was welcomed back into her father's home.

She hoped never to see her former mother-in-law again, or hear the vicious rumors and curses she spread. But today, she would not be depressed. No. It was a gorgeous day and her vivid imagination wanted to capture something mystical that happened to her on the night she and her father fled on a boat on the Aegean Sea.

How could she express on canvas what she felt when she realized her life could have ended that night? What she had seen she did not understand, but it often returned to her mind. She remembered a man walking toward her on the water. He came near and touched her shoulder and said, "Come to me, Amirah. Do you want me to save you?" and she said, "Yes," but she didn't know to whom she was speaking. Was she so tired, hungry, seasick and scared that she was delusional or had she actually encountered a being who held the power over the wind and the sea and who touched her? She could not answer these questions.

Nevertheless, the storm did cease, the waters calmed, and the boat sailed on safely to Greece. She had to paint the image of that touch today. The cathedral bells rang softly.

Amirah found a shady spot on the Left Bank and sat down to begin painting her impression of that night at sea, not noticing two men, Ibrahim and Abdul, watching her from a distance.

Chapter 11

Robbery

Monday Morning around nine, Alex left his apartment and walked to *Café de la Lumière.* He entered the restaurant. "*Bonjour, bonjour,* Dr. Alex," said Hilba, the Sudanese waiter. "It is a good morning to be alive. You don't know, Doctor, but today is the third anniversary of my arrival in Paris from Sudan, praise God. It is the second year I am working here at the restaurant."

"*Bonjour,* Hilba and congratulations. You are a blessed man."

"Yes, Doctor, I pray for the two million South Sudanese brothers every day who fled or were driven from their homes all over the world. There's only one world and one more, don't you know? But now, what may I bring you?" Hilba asked.

"I'll take *un café au lait,* a bacon, egg and cheese on a croissant with honey," Alex said, handing back the menu. "How is your wife?"

"She is very well these days, Doctor, thanks to you. You treated her diabetes and like magic, she is better every day. You helped make a miracle. I'll be right back with your order."

Alex mused about Hilba's Sudanese cronies who for a few

measley euros spent each day selling trinkets, handbags, and miniature Eiffel Tower keyrings on the steps of the *Trocadero.* Yet, they were thankful to be out of the wars raging in the Sudan. Hilba and his friends were fortunate to be a continent away from the destruction and genocide of their country.

"Here you are, Doctor," replied Hilba, presenting breakfast and the check. "Let me know if I can get anything else for you."

"Thank you, Hilba. Give my regards to your wife. Also, thank you for the note that Ibrahim and Houssain would be coming to the hospital, but I didn't see it until I had already seen and treated Houssain. I'll keep an eye on them."

"Good, I tell you Ibrahim treats his workers in the worst way. Just watch him."

Alex ate quickly and handed a generous tip to Hilba. He left *Café de la Lumière*, walking toward the Dalles' *appartement* building.

He noticed in the distance the peculiar, stoop-shouldered, unsmiling Mrs. Pilon, the manager of that stately building, talking with a man he thought he recognized. Noting the man's dark skin, extra weight and long beard, he thought it was Ibrahim Soliman, the Syrian who had brought the refugee Houssain to the hospital. Why was he talking to Mrs. Pilon?

As Alex witnessed two figures rush from the *belle epoque* building and knock Mrs. Pilon to the ground, broom and all, Ibrahim seemed to disappear into thin air. The figures disappeared as swiftly as Ibrahim had done. He saw Mrs. Pilon struggling to get up. Alex ran to help her. Arriving at the front of the *appartement*, he checked Mrs. Pilon's pulse, ankles and legs.

"I'm fine," she said. "All this fuss is not necessary. I can walk. I am fine." He helped anorexic Mrs. Pilon to her feet. The lines in her face and her gray hair in a tight, neat bun created a caricature. Alex was amazed that the fall on the hard concrete had not seriously injured her. She was alright.

Alex opened the door for her. "What was their rush? What's going on?"

"I have no idea. I'm doing my usual morning work and boom, I'm run over by two men. I suppose they were men. These days, who can tell?"

Mrs. Pilon shut and locked the door behind her, as she and Alex entered the *appartement* building.

"Wasn't that Ibrahim Soliman talking to you?"

"Who? I have no idea. You mean that man who was asking for directions to some street. I don't know him."

"If you will promise me to rest, I'm going up to the Dalle's *appartement*, Mrs. Pilon."

Alex got into the elevator and pushed five. It groaned as it rose, as most of the Gilded Age lifts did in the older Parisian *appartement* buildings.

Alex's mind returned to Houssain. He planned to return to the *Marché Aux Puces* to look around, check on Houssain and see how Ibrahim was treating his hired men. Plus, he loved *Café La Vie*, the famous restaurant located inside. Maybe he would take Amirah there to enjoy the salmon carpaccio and that French toast with honey and salted caramel which he loved. French food was unsurpassed, and he would not have an opportunity to enjoy it on assignment with the *Médecins Sans Frontières* in the over-crowded refugee camp.

Years ago, while traveling to so many countries with his parents, international cuisine became something of a hobby for him. He did feel a little guilty being able to indulge in the delicious and expensive Parisian cuisine, but he rationalized that he didn't do it that often and he was not Dr. Livingston in Africa — yet. Regardless, he felt an urgency to go and help wherever he sensed a great need. Subconsciously he believed "to whom much is given, much is required."

Alex stepped out and rang the bell at Philippe and Maya Dalle's *appartement*, but no one answered. After knocking and ringing the bell several times, Alex pushed the door open and called, "Philippe? Maya? Isabella?" But there was no answer. He walked through the corridor, searching in the living room, dining room and kitchen. He saw a plate of breakfast food half eaten on the dining room table. Opening the door to Philippe and Maya's bedroom, he saw Philippe and Isabella, the housekeeper, gagged, blind-folded and tied to bedposts.

Alex quickly removed the blindfolds and gagging rags from them and ran to the kitchen to get a knife to cut the binding twine from their feet, hands and torso.

"What has happened?" he asked.

"I've been robbed, I'm sure," said Philippe, as Alex helped him to his feet.

"These two robbers unlocked the door or was it even locked, Isabella?"

"I don't know, Mr. Philippe. I picked up the morning paper and I could have left it open. I don't know," and she started to shake and cry.

"Now, now, Isabella, we're okay. Don't worry. Sit down. I'm going to search the house and see what's missing."

"I'm not about to sit down. I'm getting coffee for everyone."

Philippe began to stomp around the house, looking on his walls and in drawers, and exclaimed, "Quite smart they are. They've stolen the Picasso and the Monet. Look, right here is where they hung." Alex and Isabella came near and confirmed the empty spots.

"Why did they take only the Holocaust paintings and leave the rest of the valuable art?" Alex asked.

Philippe shrugged his shoulders.

Isabella went to the kitchen and poured coffee for all.

"Thank you, Isabella. What and how did this happen, step by step?" asked Alex.

Philippe began, "As I recollect, Isabella had brought a delicious breakfast to the table and I had just started to eat. I was expecting you to drop by on your way to work, so when I heard a noise at the front door, I thought it was you. The next thing I saw were two masked figures, pointing guns at Isabella and me. They told us to go to the bedroom and be quiet, or they would use their guns with silencers and send us to heaven or hell. They sprayed something that made me a bit faint, but we did as we were told. They blindfolded, gagged and tied us to the bedposts."

Alex asked, "Can you add anything to that, Isabella? Did they do anything else?"

"Mr. Philippe said it just as it happened. But after they left us in the bedroom, they left the apartment. I think they knew exactly what they wanted to steal. It was over so fast, thank God and blessed Virgin Mary. Now they've stolen your two most famous and valuable paintings, the Picasso and the Monet and they have fled. It took them less than ten minutes. They certainly knew what they were doing."

"How did they get through the locked front door, get up the flights of stairs and into your *appartement*?" asked Alex. "If you are feeling well enough, we must call Lieutenant Fournier at the police station and file a report."

Philippe walked to the dining room and seated himself at the expansive mahogany table. The tall French windows and the Impressionist paintings imparted an elegance to the room, but with two paintings missing, the scenario changed. Philippe's breakfast was still sitting in front of him and he began to pick at the cold omelet as he talked. Isabella poured more hot coffee for all.

"Praise God and Holy Virgin Mary," said Isabella, as she

entered the dining room with hot croissants with ham. "Eat, Philippe and Alex. We are alive, Merciful Jesus. We could be eating with the heavenly hosts. Those men said little, but they would have used those guns if we had not obeyed them. Evil they are. They were like the cartel people I knew in Honduras. We are lucky they only took the paintings and left us alive."

"We need to call the police and file a report," said Alex.

Philippe said, "Well, yes, we must call them."

"Where is Maya?" Alex asked, as he began to call his friend Lieutenant Fournier.

"She and Claire-Lise left a few days ago for Honduras. She had to check on her tobacco plantation and the little school she started. It gives her an excuse to visit her family too. I'll notify her after the investigation gets started or maybe I'll wait till she comes home, so as not to ruin her trip. Thank God Isabella is here to help me."

Alex phoned Fournier, "There's been a robbery of very expensive art in the 16th *arrondissement*--actually, my godparents' *appartement.* Yes, less than an hour ago we'll be looking for you. I may have to leave for an appointment in the *Quartier Latin.* Great. Thanks."

Philippe asked, "What did he say? I don't think they'll do much good. There is so much art stolen in Paris they can't investigate it all. I can't bear to tell Maya, but I've got to. There's nothing she can do there in Honduras to help find this art, so I may wait a little while. It will just worry her and hinder her work there."

"Well, if anyone will try to assist, it will be my friend, Lieutenant Fournier. He and I will help find your art and return it," Alex said.

"You have an important job at the hospital. You can't be traipsing around trying to find my art. No, no, please. I'll hire a private detective."

"Philippe, investigating is a passion of mine whether it is the human body for disease or deviant acts of criminals. It's very logical work and I will help, if you will allow me to start today. By the way, don't forget, I worked several cases in the hospital in Montreal."

"We would be grateful for you to do whatever you desire, but I don't want to impose on you."

"No imposition at all."

Chapter 12

Case to Solve

The doorbell rang and Isabella answered it. Alex greeted Lieutenant Fournier, "Thanks for getting here so quickly. I was afraid I would miss you."

Alex and Philippe showed Fournier the place where the paintings had hung. Then they walked through the rooms ending in the bedroom, where Philippe explained again to Fournier exactly what had happened.

Fournier said, "There have been other art thefts in the past months in this *arrondissement* and I think they are connected."

Philippe nodded, "How so?"

"The art thefts in this sixteenth *arrondissement*, I hate to say, have been stolen from Jewish people. I'm not sure of the connection myself, but I'm beginning to think it's a personal vendetta, revenge or some other motivation, besides the profit from the sales."

Philippe spoke up, "Well, my beautiful Maya is Jewish, and during World War II, her grandparents escaped Germany to Palestine. Muslim extremists still harbor resentment against Jews. Only five years ago this Holocaust art belonging to her family was found and returned to her. I think art thieves are still seeking revenge against us in Paris."

Isabella quietly brought more coffee for Philippe and offered a cup to the Lieutenant.

"Sit down, please, Lieutenant," said Philippe.

The men sat at the dining room table.

"Tell me about the art and how it came to you," said Lieutenant Fournier.

"It was returned by the Jewish Art Restitution and Restoration only five years ago and now it's been stolen again — that's the important information."

"Okay, is there anything else you can think of that might help us?" asked Fournier.

Alex said, "Well, I had breakfast at *Café de la Lumière* down the street and was walking here, when I saw Ibrahim Soliman talking to Mrs. Pilon, the manager of this *appartement* building. He disappeared just before two men ran from the building and knocked her down as they escaped. The men were gone in minutes. I arrived and helped Mrs. Pilon to her feet and we entered the building together."

"So, who is Ibrahim?" Fournier asked.

Alex replied, "He's a Syrian man with dual citizenship. He sells his wares at a booth in the *Marché Aux Puces*, where a cartel of young refugees meet and work for him. One of his refugee workers, Houssain al-Jabar, was a patient of mine at the *Salpêtrière*. I don't feel comfortable about Ibrahim. Mrs. Pilon denied knowing him, but I saw her sharing a table with him just last week at the *Marché Aux Puces*."

"Hmm, dear Mrs. Pilon. She lives here in the small one-bedroom *appartement* we provide for the manager and we are all her family," said Philippe.

"Does she have other family?" asked Lieutenant Fournier.

"One day she told Maya her two sons and her uncle were martyrs for Iran. She said her husband was slaughtered by the SAVAK of the Shah. She probably manages to live on the small salary she is paid. Maya is very generous with her on her birthday, Christmas and Muslim holidays. We disagree with her political convictions. She was very happy when the Ayatollah Khomeini returned to Iran. I can't imagine her being involved in any robberies."

Alex said, "I'm very sorry about her history, but no one in this building is above suspicion. Things are not always as they appear, and she was talking to Ibrahim Soliman outside when the men ran out of the building. She might have let them in."

"Yes, but you said they knocked her down."

"Yes, I did, but it could have been a ploy. She wasn't hurt and it would make her appear to be a victim too. If I had not recognized Ibrahim talking to her first, maybe I would trust her more, but she is on my suspect list."

Fournier said, "So I have an assistant. The famous Dr. Alexander Winston of *Parlons Santé* television fame will be finding suspects with me?"

"You know I want to work on this case. But I've got to get to the *Quartier Latin* now.

Philippe, I will be in touch. Later, Fournier. You're the best. I'm always available to talk and I'm dedicating to this case all the extra time I can find. Philippe, you and Maya have been friends of my family for as long as I can remember. This is the least I can do."

"We don't deserve your help, but I will be forever grateful, Alex."

"We'll get right on it," said Fournier.

Isabella walked Alex to the door and stood outside with him a moment, "Thanks for coming. Philippe doesn't complain, but he misses Maya when she's gone. I think she should retire and

Philippe should sell his manufacturing business, but I'm afraid they will never stop until something stops them. I wish you Godspeed on this challenge, Alex. *À bientôt.*"

"Take care, Isabella. We will find the paintings and the thieves." As he left, he thought of his medical school, internship and residency completed in Montréal. He remembered the criminal cases he had helped solve in the Montréal hospitals. A few weeks remained before he would leave Paris for the *Médecins Sans Frontières* assignment, but within this time, he would find the art and the thieves. If he needed more time, he could delay his departure.

Philippe and Maya were more than godparents to him. They were truly family. Even with all his work at the *Salpêtrière*, he remained fascinated with the art theft business: in particular, what thieves were interested in stealing, how they did it and then how they sold and transported the art all over the world.

Chapter 13

Quartier Latin

At noon Monday after a heavy work schedule of procedures and office visits, Alex took Monday afternoon off. His parents had made only one request of him during his time in Paris and that was to contact their friends, the Hertzes. His call delighted them and they suggested meeting in the *Quartier Latin.* Alex felt it was an obligation, but little did he know he would receive an amazing tip, essential to solving the robbery.

Besides, the *Quartier Latin* was always a treat for a curious, observant man like Alex Winston. One never knew whom one might meet on those crooked, winding paths. He passed the *Musée l'Orangerie,* where for the first time he had seen the entire wall of the great Impressionist Master Claude Monet's waterlilies with Amirah. As she explained the wonderful form and light of the paintings to him, she also spoke much about Monet's struggle with depression and poverty, which gave Alex more understanding of the artist as well as the art. Then she stopped talking and did not want to share any more with him. This habit of hers frustrated and exasperated him.

He was absorbed in the robbery at the Dalles. Why had the

robbers stolen only two paintings, when the house was a treasure chest of magnificent art? Where was the art now? How did the robbers defeat the security systems of that building? His good friend, Lieutenant Fournier of the *Préfecture of Police*, had access to the city's criminal files. Alex decided after lunch he would stop by the station and talk to him again.

Alex saw his friend Fauziah, waving to him and crossing to his side of the street. "Surprise, surprise, running into you. Where are you going?" Fauziah asked.

"I'm meeting the Hertzes at a little restaurant. Where are you headed?"

"I'm going to lunch with them too. Amazing timing. How do you know them?"

"I don't know them well, but they were friends of my parents when they studied and worked in Paris years ago. My meeting them on this visit was the one request my parents made before I left."

"They know everybody, trust me. He was one of the architects for the new commercial development in the eleventh *arrondissement.* The city converted an old building into a fine art gallery. The exhibition space was massive with high digital screen walls. It resembled *Atelier des Lumières Gustav Klimt* immersive exhibition. You must go see it. He was also assistant architect for the renovation of the International Church. Mrs. Hertz designed the interiors, and if you want a *Cordon Bleu* dinner, she can prepare it. Amirah needs to meet them too. You two need to come to the International Church more to meet all these interesting people."

"Sounds like it. I don't think Amirah is very interested in cooking *á la Cordon Bleu,* but she would love eating it. I wish she could have joined us today, but she reserves her Sundays for sketching and painting."

"There they are, Alex." Fauziah motioned in the direction of the couple. Approaching Alex and Fauziah was a well-groomed, well-dressed couple in their sixties, engaged in lively conversation, when they spotted Alex and Fauziah.

"*Bonjour*, Fauziah. You look wonderful," Mr. Hertz said, giving her a hug.

"And, Dr. Alex, I'm so glad we can finally get together," Mrs. Hertz said, kissing each cheek.

"*Enchanté*," said Alex, returning the kisses. "But please, don't call me doctor."

Mrs. Hertz said, "Sorry, you deserve to be called doctor and that's what I'll call you." Alex flashed a bashful grin.

Mr. Hertz led the way down the *Rue St. Michel* to a charming little Swiss restaurant and announced, "I am a friend of the chef who makes the best cheese fondue you've ever tasted, and the *boeuf bourguignon* is irresistible. However, you're welcome to try whatever you want."

"I'm not taking any chances. I'm ordering whatever you're having." said Fauziah.

"Sounds like a plan," said Alex, as he opened the door and everybody entered the picturesque restaurant.

"*Bonjour, mesdames et messieurs. Je m'appelle Jean-Claude* and I will be your waiter today," he said. He seated them at the best table where they could see the passing street scenes and the Greek bakery across the way. "What would you like to drink?" he asked.

"Perhaps a house wine?" asked Mr. Hertz. Everyone nodded. "We'll have the *fondue au fromage* for our appetizer."

"*Excellent choix*. I will return with it soon," said Jean-Claude.

"So, Dr. Alex, how's the clinic?" asked Mr. Hertz. "I think it's great you're taking this new assignment with *Médecins Sans Frontières*. But you've seen plenty of misery right here in Paris, haven't you? I've heard you're working at *Pitie-Salpêtrière Univer-*

sité Hôspital. You must be flooded all day long with patients from the poorest *arrondissements* with viruses and illnesses."

"Yes, the clinic work is rewarding, but I'm determined to join the *Médecins Sans Frontières* in Lesbos, Greece, because the refugee situation is critical in Lesbos, and we think that's where Amirah's mother and brothers are. I don't want to bore you with my work though. I've got something on my mind I really want to share with you today that's very important to me. I've got to help my godparents, the Dalles, find their stolen art."

"Stolen art?" asked Mrs. Hertz.

"Yes, two masterpieces were stolen from their apartment in the sixteenth *arrondissement* this morning. Do you know the Dalles?" asked Alex.

"We know them," said Mr. Hertz. "We have seen them at exhibitions and art galas. Stealing anything from the sixteenth *arrondissement* would be very complicated with the high-tech security those residents normally install, but I'm sure a fortune's worth of art may be found in their homes."

"I suppose that's the way the thieves look at it," Alex said. "Sixteenth *Arrondissement* is a quiet avenue not far from *Le Trocadero* as you well know, and everyone there is extremely mindful of security. They have the most advanced high-performance components for audio visuals, monitoring, apps, lighting, guards and managers, but two masked professionals entered their *appartement* early this morning and stole two paintings."

"That's amazing. Truly unbelievable. What paintings were stolen?" asked Mrs. Hertz.

"A *Picasso* and a *Monet,* paintings once owned by Maya's grandparents," Alex said.

"Go on. Please tell us about these paintings," said Mr. Hertz.

Chapter 14

Kristallnacht

"I will give you the short version. Maya's grandmother was Jewish, but her grandfather was Christian. For many years before the war they owned an art gallery in Wiesbaden, Germany. As Hitler's henchmen infiltrated German cities, everyone was under scrutiny. Not everyone knew her grandmother was Jewish. In addition to this, she was married to a Christian, so her grandparents thought they were safe from Hitler.

"However, Maya's grandfather began to see the writing on the wall. He moved as much art as he could out of his shop to an underground group who were helping the Jews move valuables to other parts of Europe, providing safe houses as long as possible. These paintings were part of a cache put in a safe house and Hitler did not find them," said Alex.

"So, what happened to the grandfather after he got those paintings out?" asked Fauziah.

"Maya's grandparents feared for their lives and the lives of their children as the news of *Kristallnacht* spread to other countries," Alex continued. "People in certain European countries were accepting Jewish children, so they sent their three children to France with papers saying they were orphans from a Catholic Church. Maya's mother was adopted by a French Catholic family. Maya's uncle and aunt were taken to relatives of the grandfather in Sweden. This foresight amazingly saved the children's lives, but the children and their real parents never saw each other again. Think of the odds. Seventy to eighty-five million people perished, which was about 3% of the world population in 1940, but Maya is here today because of her grandparents' discernment."

Jean-Claude set cups of coffee around the table with sugar and cream. He returned immediately and said, "*Bon appetit,*" as he placed the fondue pot in the center of the table along with plates of hot, crusty baguettes.

"Dr. Alex, I want to hear every word of this fascinating story, but first, let me give thanks," said Mr. Hertz, as he bowed his head, "Our Father in heaven. We thank you for this opportunity to meet with Dr. Alex and Fauziah, who've taken time from their busy lives to share this meal with us. We thank you for their lives with purpose and meaning and we pray that you will lead, guide and direct them in all they are doing to shine light in this fractured world. We ask for protection for Alex and Fauziah wherever they go. For this meal and fellowship we are receiving, Dear Lord, we give you honor, glory and thanks. Amen." Mr. Hertz looked up, "Enjoy." He dipped his bread into the bubbling cheese fondue and took the first bite.

"Continue, Dr. Alex, with your story. We're listening," said Mrs. Hertz. "I know someone who would be very interested in this situation. Where did the art go before it was returned to Maya and Philippe?"

"Maya's grandfather kept his favorite two paintings hidden or so he thought, but the Germans had eyes in the backs of their heads and confiscated them. The two pieces were missing for almost fifty years, but about five years ago, the Jewish Restitution and Restoration League found them in the Patagonia country in Argentina in the hands of a German Nazi living there with his family. He was brought back for trial and the paintings were returned to Maya, but now, as I've said, they have been stolen again. I would like to meet someone who works for that Jewish League and find out what they know about these works of art stolen by the Nazis and sold all over the world. I must find Philippe's and Maya's art. I need to know someone who can help," Alex said.

Fauziah said, "Alex, excuse me, but I think the project's too big for you right now."

"No, I must do this." Alex shook his head.

Fauziah persisted, "But with everything else you are doing in these last weeks in Paris before your assignment with the *Médecins Sans Frontières*, it's just too much."

"I must help Philippe and Maya get their paintings back before they disappear from the country. Perhaps already they have disappeared, but I'm hoping not. I know the pain of losing something valuable myself and I see the pain of the refugees and patients every day I work at the clinic. I know I'll be taking on another task, but it will be a labor of love.

Fauziah says, "You are really interested in this art, aren't you?"

"Yes, I am, but it's not all about the art. You see, when I was eight, I stayed the summer with Maya in Honduras. One day her daughter Claire-Lise and I were playing hide and seek in the tobacco fields. I saw the reddest berries I'd ever seen across the road in the other field and had to have a taste, which I did. I raced out of the field into the road without looking. The next thing I remember is waking up and seeing the worried faces of Maya, Claire-Lise and the doctor hovering over me. I could have died from the motorcycle impact, but Maya was not going to let that happen. She took care of me 24/7 in the hospital until I finished surgery and rehabilitation. She's like my second mother. She really is much more than a godmother."

Mrs. Hertz said, "My, Alex, that is quite a story. God was looking after you and here you are today in a fine position, making a real difference in the world. Do you believe in coincidence or destiny? Either way, you're in luck today. I have a dear friend who has worked for that league for forty years although she's semi-retired now. She lives in Antony, a small suburb of Paris, south of here. Her name is Dr. Anna Israel, but most people call her Dr. Anna. She is very well-connected in this type of work."

"I told Alex you and Mr. Hertz knew everybody. Alex, this is a miracle," said Fauziah.

"Would you like to meet her?" asked Mrs. Hertz.

"Of course, I would think she will feel as sorry as I do about the thefts."

Ms. Hertz quickly responded, "Of course she will. Let me check for Dr. Anna's address and phone number. I'll give her a call and see when you can visit her. Would you want to go tomorrow?"

"Yes, I think that would be excellent. Let me check my calendar for the schedule at the clinic. Patients and procedures can be changed daily and they're not always expected." Alex glanced at his Apple Watch and then replied, "Tomorrow would be great. The sooner the better."

The waiter cleared the fondue pot and dirty dishes and returned with a sizzling fondue pot of *boeuf bourguignon* with more crusty bread. Alex enjoyed the delicious meal and was thankful for being introduced to the Hertzes.

Mrs. Hertz excused herself and stepped outside to call Dr. Anna. She re-entered and said, "I've called Dr. Anna. She says you may come to meet her tomorrow in Antony. Her grandson, his wife and son live with her, so they will all be there, I'm sure. I'll send her your contact information in a text. She said her grandson Levi will meet you at the station."

"Is there anything I should know about them?"

"They are lovely people. She is a scholar on the Holocaust and the art stolen during that time, as I've said. I know she can help you find your godparents' paintings, and if the thefts occurred in several homes, she probably already has more information about the them than any detectives in the precincts. You can learn a lot tomorrow plus enjoy a great lunch," she said.

"It seems I am constantly eating in this city. The culinary delights of France are going to be the death of me; but if it furthers our investigation, I must accept the risk," said Alex, patting his stomach. "Still I would be imposing on them to share a meal also."

Mr. Hertz said, "You must share a meal with the good family in Antony. Levi's wife, Olivia, was raised by missionary parents in Brazil and makes the best Portuguese-Brazilian *Feijoada* dinner ever. They have a dozen cheeses at all times, yogurts, home-made cookies, French *cassoulets, quiches, coq au vin, ratatouille.* Mrs. Hertz, Dr. Anna and I have enjoyed many meals there."

"Yes," Mrs. Hertz added, "and Olivia speaks several languages and has a degree in psychology. She specializes in counseling abused women."

"You've helped me a lot, but I don't plan to eat lunch with them. I really could not impose on them," said Alex."

"Impose? No, Dr. Alex, it will not be an imposition. Olivia cooks every day and would be insulted if you did not stay for lunch," said Mrs. Hertz. "I don't know how she does it, but she counsels two or three days a week, even teaches a cooking class, along with taking care of her son, and I think she's expecting another child soon. She's one of the superwomen."

"Sounds like this will be an incredible family to meet," said Alex.

Jean-Claude reappeared and began removing dishes again. "What would you like for dessert?" he asked, passing dessert menus to each of them.

Everyone studied the menu. Mr. Hertz said, "I can recommend every dessert on the menu because I've tried them all. Fauziah, why don't you order first, *s'il vous plaît.*"

"Okay, I'm not shy. I can never resist chocolate mousse."

The others followed, choosing *une creme brulée, un Tarte Tatin et une profiterole* and fresh cups of coffee for all. Alex had to pass, "Not today, just a little more coffee, thanks."

Mr. Hertz asked, "Alex, why don't you and Fauziah tell us about Amirah? Fauziah showed us photos of her art and rug designs. They are very impressive."

"Please tell us where you met her, Alex," said Mrs. Hertz.

Alex answered, "On the banks of the Seine on my way to work. She studied at the *Sorbonne* for a year and now takes classes in art and has a part-time job at the *Musée.* I think her father, Yousif, is doing quite well at a carpet shop here."

"Has she always been an artist?" Mr. Hertz asked.

"Yes, Amirah was a precocious artist, a prodigy, I believe, who could sketch images by the age of five. By the age of ten she was developing a unique style which made an original "Amirah" quickly recognizable by all the members of her father's mosque. She even invented a kind of "family quarter cubism" as she called it.

"What's that?" asked Mr. Hertz.

Alex said, "She painted interiors with a neutral floor and a complex geometric design on her father's rugs as cube shapes. Then she could draw pictures of anything inside the cube shapes. It is unique. Some families even wanted her to draw portraits of their families in the cubes. They were a successful and happy family until the Arab Spring uprising ruined everything. She and her father had tremendous difficulties getting to France as you would expect, but now they've been here almost two years." Alex sipped his coffee.

"There's a lot more to this father and daughter," said Fauziah. "I want you to meet them. Yousif, her father, owned a successful carpet business in Aleppo, but now he's relegated to working as a carpet salesman at the *Marché Aux Puces.* But before coming to France, he was a leader of the White Helmets, a rebel resistance army against the crimes and evils being committed against the free people of Syria."

"Yes, of course, it would be delightful to meet them," said Mrs. Hertz. "The refugees we meet at the International Church and at our dinners amaze us. I can't imagine escaping as a refugee, learning a new language, and maybe having no papers and no job. I doubt there would be an International Church like ours with support in most countries. We teach language and survival skills at the church. In addition, we help find housing and furniture for them, but we can't help all of them. No, I don't know how I would ever make it anywhere, especially at this age, as a refugee."

"You, Mrs. Hertz, would find a way," Fauziah exclaimed, "I have no doubt. You would be giving language and cooking classes, designing homes and a million other things, if you ever became a refugee, but thank God, I don't think that is your foreseeable future."

"I hope you're right," replied Mrs. Hertz.

"Please tell me more about the work you and Mr. Hertz have been doing here in Paris," said Alex.

"We were delighted you and Fauziah could join us today. You will have other chances to hear about us in the City of Light. We feel fortunate and thankful to be retired here in this beautiful culture. We enjoy helping and encouraging the refugees and serving in various ways. Sometimes this feels more like home than the States. Isn't that odd?" asked Mr. Hertz.

"Not at all," said Fauziah. "When I studied at the University of Memphis in Tennessee with my colleagues from Malaysia, within months I felt at home. The Americans in Memphis were generous and kind to me. What impressed me most was their hospitality and openness and their gift of talking freely about everything. They have carried the Christian traditions in their country a little further than we have in Malaysia. They say all people have equal rights and they base this on their faith in God. I found it impressive and I never felt any prejudice, but I'm saddened by what I read and hear today about discontent and racial prejudices. Enough. I am a wandering spirit, and I had always felt confined in Malaysia. I saw such freedom of expression, such joy in the States that I thought I'm never going back. I don't mean this in an unfavorable way to Malaysia because I love my country and my family is there, but I think of Paris as my home."

Alex said, "You're adaptable, Fauziah. You go right in and make friends wherever you are. It's a gift."

"*Merci, mon ami.*"

The group finished the last delectable bites of dessert and embraced each other as they said their good-byes. Mrs. Hertz said, "I want to invite you and Amirah to come to our international dinner this week. Here's my card with our address in Montmartre. It would be such a pleasure to introduce you to our guests. Fauziah comes every week and this week Reza is our guest speaker."

"It's been great," said Alex. "Thank you again for all your help. I will definitely try to come. You've been very gracious."

"See you soon," said Fauziah."

"Say hello to Reza. I'll be in touch. I'm sure I'll need your assistance soon."

They departed and went their separate ways. Mr. Hertz wondered if Amirah was the same lady he had met at the International Church one Sunday. Alex decided to walk by *Le Caveau de la Huchette*, one of the oldest jazz clubs in Paris, where his Romanian friend, Egbert, played cool jazz from time to time and where he wanted to sit in with his saxaphone again. Maybe he would bring Amirah there one night. After browsing through Shakespeare and Co., he walked along the Seine headed to the *Préfecture de Police*, until he saw lovely Amirah sitting on the green lawn of the banks.

Chapter 15

Past Fears– Lurking Dangers

"Hello, Amirah. This must be my lucky Monday afternoon, meeting you by chance," said Alex. "I just finished lunch with a very interesting couple, the Hertzes, in the *Quartier Latin* and decided to walk along the Seine on my way to see Lieutenant Fournier."

Amirah laughed and said, "I think it's my lucky day. I wasn't expecting to see you either.

Amirah spread a blanket for Alex to join her. "Please sit with me for a few moments, if you can."

"Of course, I can. I was going to talk to Lieutenant Fournier, but that meeting can wait if I can visit you; that is, if you're sure I won't distract you from painting,"

"Alex, you are never a distraction. How was your lunch?"

"Really nice. Mr. and Mrs. Hertz want to meet you. They've seen your art work and are already great admirers."

Amirah looked away. "Are you making that up just to make me feel good?"

"They really like your work and they know everybody, so they would be sure to bring lots of friends to your exhibition."

"That's good news, but I must tell you a little secret."

"Okay, don't keep me waiting. What is it?"

Amirah laughed. "Oh, Alex, it's really nothing, but I met Mr. Hertz when I visited the International Church recently."

"What? You visited the International Church and didn't tell me, and in addition, met Mr. Hertz? I'm sorry I missed out on going with you. How did you happen to meet him?"

"He was a greeter and we actually had a nice conversation about the architecture of the church and aspects of the service while we enjoyed coffee. I thought he was a very kind and gracious man."

"You are right about that. He and Mrs. Hertz will be big supporters of your art."

"I wonder if they will understand my art and what it means to me — the suffering I've endured through all this journey of darkness and destruction and the hope it's given me."

"No, they can't see all you see, but you will help bring light to them and others through your art, as it has brought light to you, dear Amirah."

"Thank you, Alex. Tell me, what else happened at lunch today?"

"I've got some big news."

"Yes, what is it?"

"Mrs. Hertz knows a lady, Dr. Anna Israel, who works with the Restitution and Restoration Holocaust Art Institute. She has arranged a meeting tomorrow for Dr. Anna and me to talk about the Dalles' stolen art.

"That's amazing. I'm so happy for you."

"I'm expecting to locate the stolen art with her help."

"Alex, I don't know about your getting involved with that art theft. It could be very dangerous. You're trained as a cardiologist. Do you really want to get involved with international thieves?

You are risking your life and you could be killed. I have heard some very frightening reports about art dealers who deal in theft and forgeries. I don't like it. Why don't you leave it to Lieutenant Fournier and the Paris police?"

"I think Fournier could use my help. We're a great team. You know, we've worked cases before. I don't want you to worry about me. Don't ever worry about me, Amirah. Let's not talk about this right now."

"Well, it's been two years since my father and I traveled from Aleppo to Greece through dangerous waters and people, but we made it to France. But now that I'm here, I don't want to see you in any danger and I will worry. I was more fortunate than many in my land. My father and I escaped and were not detained for years in a forsaken refugee camp where I think my mother and brothers are today. Sometimes I feel I was chosen. Maybe the man on the water I saw that night is still helping me. I'm sad when I think about the treasure Aleppo was and how it is now--completely destroyed. Our city was really more beautiful and famous than Damascus, but the war totally demolished it!

"I can't understand completely, as much as I want to share your feelings, but in a way my family has a similar background."

"What do you mean? You were never a refugee."

"No, but my grandparents fled Algeria during their Civil War and arrived at a poor Parisian *émigré* community, where my mother was later born. She never forgot the painful memories of being poor in the most squalid quarters of this city. Even when my dad and she married, she always remembered the struggle in that wretched place, and it gave her a heart for downtrodden people."

"Where were the poor immigrants living in Paris during that crisis? Did your mother grow up near my *arrondissement*?"

"Yes, but her parents had left a terrible situation in the streets of Algiers. The French attacked Algiers to colonize it and slaughtered so many natives in the beginning that the Arabs hated the colonizing French. It affected the psyche of my grandparents, and my mother absorbed the despair from them, although they did well in Paris."

"You are speaking of things about which I know nothing. I had no idea about the Algierian conflict or your family's sufferings."

"No, most people don't know about this history."

"Tell me more."

"The commonality of what happened to you in Syria and to my grandparents in Algiers is history repeating itself. Many Muslim villages were destroyed and whole populations were forced to accommodate the Europeans with their farms and industries. It was horrible then and again in the nineties because the terrorists were inflicting destruction in many countries. This is a painful subject for us, but we have many reasons to be grateful. My folks escaped and so did you, beautiful girl."

"Yes, we did, physically. But I still bear the wounds of separation, loss of loved ones, and unbearable memories. I hope my mother and brothers will be able to escape the filthy camp where they are. I'm encouraged that your grandparents were able to survive all the trauma and then your mother became a medical doctor. It's incredible."

"Maybe. I have always admired my mom's parents for taking such risks — first, to leave and then to make a life for themselves here. When you are comfortable, Amirah, I would like for you to share more of your experiences in Aleppo, your journey and your arrival in Paris. Will you do that?"

"I will share it with you, little by little. I have nightmares about those years. Even during the daytime, I see the look of horror on my classmates' faces as we were playing in the streets and the bombs began to fall. I knew it would be necessary to leave the country or be killed."

"You must have been terrified. Your father made a wise decision, a good plan to get you out of Syria."

"Yes, he engaged smugglers and paid them ten thousand euros to drive us part of the way in a rickety van, and then put us on a ramshackle boat to Greece. They guaranteed nothing and thought all refugees were homeless people whom they could exploit for money." A tear trickled down Amirah's cheek. "My mother was angry at my father, and my brothers were angry at me. Mother begged my father to stay there, but we all saw the writing on the wall, as your Old Testament says. We knew there was no hope in Aleppo."

"It must have been agony for your father, Amirah, worrying about you and the responsibility of such a journey, and you, how did you feel?"

"I think my father was more worried than I. He never slept. He agonized over the possibility that the authorities would pick us up and return us to Aleppo, or that the smugglers would abandon us or we would be lost at sea. He felt guilty that he left Mother under the care of my brothers. Had we all come together, it could have been worse. The plan was for them to come later."

"But they haven't arrived, have they?"

"Not here. According to Ibrahim and his cronies, they're in a refugee camp in Lesbos, Greece, and he will bring them to Paris at a big price, no doubt. Father believes them, but I'm not so sure. Terrible things are happening there and information is unreliable. Friends have drowned. Others have been thrown into prison for trying to escape." Lightening her tone, Amirah paused and reflected, "There was one note of humor on the whole trip as I look back. It wasn't funny then, but now it is. I was wearing this huge full burka that was hot and miserable. If only you had seen me, what a sight I was, but I needed to conceal myself, so there I was, looking like an elephant." She laughed a bit.

Alex laughed too. "You are such a brave girl. You grew up fast, I'm sure."

"Believe me, I certainly did and I was glad to have that burka to hide myself from those vile and lecherous men in charge along the way. I would start praying to Allah to keep my focus on our escape to freedom. Rather than thinking about the evil thugs during the journey, I thought about my home. I pictured Mother cooking and my brothers playing some mischievous tricks. But now, I don't even know for sure where my mother is and that breaks my heart."

Chapter 16

Secrets Revealed

Alex said, "You've never spoken much about your mother. How you must miss her."

"She used to be ebullient and fun. She loved to dance all the Middle Eastern dances. When we had gatherings in our home, she always had music and insisted that everyone dance, including the children. She loved to entertain and prepare feasts, and was happiest when people were around her dining table. I shudder at the thought of my brothers and her in the refugee camp, living in tents like nomads. I wonder what they are eating. We hope they'll join us soon, but we don't know who to trust. The news media lies too."

"'All things are possible to him who believes' is straight from the Bible and we'll pray that you see your mother and brothers again soon. My assignment with *Médicins Sans Frontières* is in Lesbos, Greece. I will investigate and help find them if they're there, but I'm hoping they are here even before I leave. I'm interrupting. Please continue."

"No, no, you're not interrupting. That would be amazing if they got here before you left. Alex, while I was on the refugee boat, I tried to pray to your Christian God, as well as Allah. When I was very young my father took the family to Istanbul. We Syrians used to travel, take vacations and live normal lives. Can you imagine that? Anyway, I saw the icons in the *Hagia Sophia* when I was very young, and I felt comforted by Mary, the beautiful, young mother holding her little boy Jesus in her arms. I asked Mary many times on that journey to hold me like she held her son and to keep me safe. And then I would pray to Jesus. What do you think of that? A good Muslim praying to your God? Do you think He heard me?"

"I think Jesus heard you because you are here safe. You were calling out in faith to a God who already knew and heard you. Even though you weren't certain who He was, I believe you felt the Holy Spirit of the Lord coming for you, as he has called people throughout the ages. Some ignore the call while others answer with cries for help. I think you did meet Jesus on your crossing and perhaps you are seeking to know him better."

"Would Mary and Jesus listen to my prayers since I'm a Muslim?"

"I think they listen to all sincere prayers."

She looked at Alex contemplatively and said, "I will tell my entire story to you little by little, but I must tell you one very important thing today. She turned away as tears began to fill her eyes, "It saddens me that you and I did not meet before my arranged marriage."

"What?" Alex sat up ramrod straight at this news. "What, Amirah? You are married?"

"No, no, no, I'm not married any longer. I will explain what happened."

"Yes, please do." Alex's mind was spinning.

"Following the Syrian tradition, my father and mother arranged a marriage for me to the son of a successful oil businessman. I obeyed my family's wishes and married the man, but my heart was broken. I was very young and the older man they chose for me was a playboy. I didn't love him. In fact, I barely knew him and I had rarely spoken to him. The goal of the union was to have children, but through that union, I inherited a bitter, jealous mother-in-law who tried to control the lives of her five sons and daughters-in-law."

"I'm so sorry." Alex was still having difficulty believing that Amirah had already been married and how miserable it had been. He was not prepared for this.

"I hate telling you this, but I knew I had to sometime, so I'm glad it's out, and I hope you won't be disappointed in me." She paused.

"I'm a little saddened and confused. I don't know what to think right now, except that you are an honest, beautiful woman, and I needed to know this."

"Alex, in my culture the most wonderful thing a wife can do is have children, and so it was natural for my former mother-in-law to want grandchildren." Amirah paused. She did not want to bare her soul secrets to Alex. It was painful enough for him to know she had been married. She could not reveal the rest. She cleared her throat and looked down at her hands.

"My mother-in-law cursed me and told me I was a terrible wife, because I was always drawing and not doing enough housework and cooking. She threatened to kill me one time for being such a failure to her son and family. My husband had been unfaithful to me all along. He even had another wife. It's hard to explain the families and how traditions work there, but I had to leave."

"What about your mother-in-law? You said she was threatening you." Alex reached for her hand.

"Yes. She vowed I would be sleeping one night and she would

send someone to kill me in my bed. She has relatives here in Paris, and I'm afraid she might really do something like that."

Alex realized how little he knew about this woman. Maybe she had other dark secrets. Yet, he remained intrigued by her. They sat together for half an hour and she spoke about her bizarre marriage, but there was more silence than talk from him. Alex found this relationship more complicated by the minute, although he had never been known to shy away from a challenge. He needed time to process all that Amirah had revealed.

"Alex, I will understand if you never want to see me again."

"No, Amirah. I'm thankful you're out of that awful situation, and you're here, talking openly with me." He embraced her. "I'm going to help you. I don't want you to worry about your mother-in-law. She probably cannot get to you here. I do need to leave now to get to Lieutenant Fournier's office, before he leaves. Will you be okay?"

"Yes, I'm fine. I feel better now that I've told you these things. I wanted you to know about the marriage."

He knelt down beside her and took both her hands in his and said, "Promise me you won't worry about this anymore. I'll see you soon." He gently kissed her hands.

A deep ache grew in Alex's chest as he walked to the precinct. He needed fresh air. Maybe there would be too many complications with Amirah.

Chapter 17

Préfecture de Police

After his meeting with Amirah, Alex walked along the Seine longer than he intended, watching the small boats moving along and seeing lovers lying on the grass or strolling hand in hand. It worried him that Amirah had been forced into a loveless marriage and felt threatened by her husband's domineering mother. So, Amirah had already been married. He was an idealistic guy with expectations about the woman he would marry, and as lovely as Amirah was, she might have more emotional problems than she had told him. God only knows what other things went on in those families before she arrived here. Well, did he love her? Could he love her?

It was five o'clock, and before he saw Fournier, he needed more fresh air after the sobering news of the afternoon. Passing a kiosk, he noticed a front-page picture of the Somali-born Dutch activist Ayaan Hirsi Ali, who as a Dutch politician exposed the shocking crime of "Arab Honor killings" in Amsterdam. He stopped and bought the newspaper. Alex felt a lump forming in his throat as he read about the murder of wives who had brought shame to their faith and families. He realized Amirah could become the victim of an "honor killing". Fauziah and the imam's daughter had told him these honor killings do happen here, although rarely. He grabbed a quick coffee and continued walking to the precinct.

Entering the Paris police precinct, he found Fournier at his desk, hovering over a pile of papers that could ignite the minute his cigarette missed his ashtray. Fournier looked up holding his cigarette and motioned for him to sit. His baggy eyes and sagging cheeks betrayed a man who needed sleep and healthier food. Alex knew Fournier hammered out clues and details until he completed each assignment. Until each piece of a case was in order, he never rested or found satisfaction. Fournier leaned back in his swivel chair with his hands behind his head and said, "Good to see you. What's going on?"

"Several things. I'm concerned about a Syrian refugee friend of mine. Her ex-mother-in-law has threatened to kill her. She's convinced me she has Syrian relatives here who are dangerous. She is very independent and doesn't try to protect herself. Naturally, I'm worried about her."

"Look, husbands kill their wives. Men kill women. We see it all the time."

Alex put the cover story of the newspaper on Fournier's desk. "In extremely close-knit families, any of the male relatives can get involved in an honor killing."

Lieutenant Fournier lit another cigarette and glanced at the story. "Of course, it's a concern to you, but there are lots of empty threats too. Who knows the minds of killers? A Lebanese doctor once came to see me. He had left his Lebanese wife of fifteen years and married a young French girl, and his ex-wife threatened to end his life. She said if her brother ever saw her ex-husband, he would make him disappear. I thought it was more talk than action, at least here in Paris. However, his wife did try to persuade her brother to murder her ex-husband, but it didn't happen. Anyway, I've got too many cases to be following all the threats," said Fournier.

"The more I see my friend, the less I understand her culture," Alex said.

Fournier commented, "Honor killings are disturbing, and I wouldn't doubt they are happening here, but these matters are private and the community keeps its secrets. I don't know much about that community, but when we go into any neighborhood, we're ready for anything. We just solve the crimes."

"The real reason I stopped by was to let you know I'm going to find those paintings and the thieves — with your help, of course. I heard you are trying to pass my case off to somebody else."

"Hmm. You think we can solve that case just by snapping our fingers?"

"I'm determined to solve the case, find the art and the thieves."

"Let me tell you something. Art is stolen from the ritziest neighborhoods in Paris every day. It's funny you should be so confident about this case. Captain Casseaux mentioned it today. A mafia of immigrants has organized professional art thieves to steal in the sixteenth *arrondissement.* I don't know anything concrete, but he has suspicions. A case we had several months ago involved art stolen from there. After questioning people and a long investigation, we didn't get enough evidence for a conviction."

"That was one case. This is our case. We can nail them."

"Um-hum."

"That doesn't sound too convincing."

Fournier rocked back in his swivel chair, took long drags on his cigarette and began to laugh, "Alex, you better go to the Department of Lost and Stolen Art, where you will find eight thousand records of lost art in Paris. We are the capital of forgeries, museum break-ins, and the thefts of famous paintings stolen and stored in Swiss safe deposit boxes. In addition to these, you have all the Jewish Restoration people working night and day to find Holocaust art. I really don't want to get involved in art cases. They get the art one night and send it to Marseille the next night. It's an endless search. As soon as one is found, another one is stolen. It might go to Spain, Portugal, Switzerland, the States or South America."

"That's why I need your expertise in strategy. I hope we're going to get it before it gets out of the country," said Alex.

Fournier laughed, "I knew some small-time thieves who stole petty stuff but didn't know how to get rid of it. Their wives decorated their houses with it and didn't understand when their husbands were arrested. These guys were rank amateurs and so they got caught. Most of these thieves are professional and never get caught."

"I hear you. You're not one hundred percent into this art case. You've already said it could be a mafia or criminal ring involved in other activities. If Captain Casseaux is on the case, we might beat him at his own game. Wouldn't you like that?"

"I want to do more to help you, but I've got a caseload right now. These riots in the city and the anger from the people toward the police are working us overtime. The last riot had Parisians screaming to get rid of the Jewish people. 'Go back to Israel. We don't want you,' they were yelling over and over, and then the riots erupted into violence. There's so much prejudice and racial tension everywhere. Anyway, it's keeping me busy. In fact, we believe another one will take place this next Sunday. I don't think I've got enough time to give this art case priority," said Fournier.

"What if all the stolen art is connected to drugs and smuggling for arms money? Who knows until we go after it? I want more than part-time help. We are talking about Restoration art. Remember? I've already got a great lead. I'm talking to Dr. Anna Israel, an official with the Jewish Restitution and Restoration League in the morning in Antony and I'll know more then, but I need to get the dossier about the sixteenth *arrondissement* cases. Is that possible?"

Fournier replied, "I can get you a copy, but you better return it to me after you read it. Why don't you pick it up tomorrow?"

Chapter 18

Yousif

Tuesday Morning Amirah came from her bedroom to the small kitchen and wrapping her arms around her father's neck, greeted him cheerfully, "Good morning, Father. That was a wonderful meal last night. You are a supreme chef. If you get tired of selling carpets, perhaps we could open a little *café*, and I could display my art and you could create divine meals."

"No, that's not our calling, but thank you, my precious. I hope I will get information about your mother and brothers today. When they get the right papers they can leave Lesbos, and come to us," said Yousif.

"From your mouth to God's ears."

Yousif shook his head. "I wish we still lived in Syria. Everything is different here. It will never be home. I left a big buttered croissant with *Bonne Mamam* preserves for you on the kitchen table. The tea is under the cozy. Lock the house when you leave."

"I don't know why you tell me. I never forget to lock the doors."

"Yes, yes, yes, you are a smart daughter who remembers everything, I know, I know. When you finish your classes today, let's have dinner at the *Café de la Lumière* tonight."

"Father, I would love to have dinner with you, but Maya's local synagogue and the International Church are sponsoring an art exhibit tonight as a fundraiser for a Christian, Muslim and Jewish charitable organization. I need to go. Local people will talk about how they acquired their family's art and I will show two of my paintings. It's a very good cause, and the staff at the *Musèe* will want me there too. Could we meet at *Café de la Lumière* later in the week?"

"Ok, so now you are supporting Christian and Jewish charities, but going less and less to the mosque. Do you think this would please your mother? I am confused, Amirah. When Sami, Rasheed and Mother get here, no art show will excuse you then. We will make *Kufta Kababs* and *Red Bulgur Pilaf* together. We will read books, favorite poems and show them the sights of Paris. Your mother will be proud to see your beautiful drawings and paintings. Think of these good times to come. Incidentally, I think you are spending too much time with Doctor Alex. He is not like us, Amirah."

"Yes, Father, okay," she said as she hugged him. "I miss the family too."

"Of course, you do. We must believe and have faith in Allah that we will be together soon."

Yousif walked to the door and waved goodbye to Amirah as she walked to the kitchen.

"Thank you, Father," she said, taking a bite of the warm croissant. "This is so yummy. I know we will have our family together again." With every bite, however, she doubted it.

Yousif opened the door of their small apartment in the Second *Arrondissement* and walked down the steps onto the street to the metro. Of all the twenty *arrondissements*, spiraling out from the City's center, Yousif felt lucky and proud he had found this little shoebox apartment for an inexpensive price. Some might even say cheap, but he was quite fond of the second *arrondissement.* It wasn't a hot spot for tourists; rather, it was calm and flooded with immigrants who could only afford minimal pricing compared to the rest of Paris. He passed the little ethnic restaurants and cafes and was glad that the *Louvre and Musée d'Orsay* were within walking distance for Amirah. Yes, it had been a good choice for them. And, of course, the metros were near and convenient.

At seven-thirty in the morning most of the metro commuters looked weary. A stone-faced man bumped into him in the train and barely acknowledged him. He didn't even mumble, "*Excusez-moi*". People stared at him or the floor. Most of them barely spoke or noticed anything as they waited for their stops. Sometimes the temptation to join the Syrian Mafia seemed like a good idea. He would never really be accepted here as he was in his own country. He would always be a foreigner, no matter what the news or the politicians said. He knew the truth.

Paris was a "Live and Let Live" city. In the old days before the war, Aleppo was a gorgeous city with cosmopolitan, friendly people. His relatives and friends met daily for coffee and sweets to talk about everything. The children played safely in the streets, happy with their cousins and school chums.

Grandparents and extended families often lived together there, but he noticed the young French people were losing respect for their own customs and their elders.

What did he know about this culture? Judging from the *Café de la Lumière* crowd, it was a warm and exciting, open and tolerant city to some he supposed, but not for him. The metro doors opened and people streamed past him and jumped off.

As he walked to work at the *Marché Aux Puces,* he prayed for the safety of Amirah. He missed his wife, Mehri. He had heard from her only twice since Amirah and he had escaped. He knew she would write to him every day if she could. What was going on in the refugee camp in Lesbos? He heard it was the worst refugee camp in the world and no one was safe there, including children, especially at night. What had he ever done to deserve the Syrian war? Who in this wealthy country understood what he had to endure to get here? What about his wife and two sons stuck in that filthy, crowded camp? Why was Syria tormented, ravaged and wrecked? Where is Allah in all of this? Why is the world so full of despair? He was trapped in a quagmire of uncertainty and anxiety.

Occasionally Murad, the owner of the carpet shop, brought news about the Greek camp. He told him Rasheed was in the *Médecins Sans Frontières Hôpital* near there, but didn't know anything else. Did Rasheed have a virus or a life-threatening disease? Did he really have only a broken arm? The medical risks in that camp were staggering. Nonetheless, he had another busy day ahead to concentrate on making the customers happy and selling the rugs in order to make money.

"*Bonjour*, Murad," he said, as he entered the shop.

"*Bonjour*. How is the scholar this morning?" Murad asked.

"You flatter me, Murad. I will never be a scholar."

"Okay, then, why do I see you reading on every break? Why do you speak the most literate French of all of us and why do the customers prefer to talk to you about everything? For now, get ready for some big sales. You have important appointments today."

"I hope so. I'm only a poor immigrant, but I know you are glad to have me no matter what you say. I work for lower wages and smaller commissions with a friendly personality," said Yousif. "You were smart to get out of Syria years ago, but who could have predicted what would happen?"

"It was one of my best decisions. Most people wait till it's too late in crises. It always seems impossible that something horrible could happen in one's own country." He shrugged his shoulders, and turned to greet and seat customers entering the shop.

Yousif texted Amirah to see if she was at her classes. Everything was ok.

A short, dark-skinned, bearded man about Yousif's age entered the carpet shop around nine, picked up a daily newspaper and sat down on one of the sofas. Yousif dreaded seeing his old friend, but he greeted him, "Ibrahim, how may I serve you?"

The man continued looking at his paper and answered, "Just a cup of black coffee, my friend, and a moment of your precious time."

"I will be right back with your coffee," said Yousif.

He went to the office supply room and poured a fresh cup of coffee and brought it promptly to Ibrahim. "Here you are. How else may I serve you?"

"I have some gifts for you and I will bring them to your house tonight. What time will you be there?"

"Gifts? You mean stolen goods, don't you? You know Amirah is there. Is there any other place?"

"You disappoint me most often. No, there is no other place. Don't forget the customer I sent you — Vladimir bought more rugs from you than you've sold all year, didn't he? What time will you be there, I repeat?"

"I'm working late tonight. It may be after 10:00," said Yousif.

"Very good. This is excellent coffee, Yousif. Maybe one day you will be the owner of this carpet shop if you listen and follow my advice."

Yousif saw his first appointment enter the shop. "I'm sorry, Ibrahim, but I have a customer. I must help him."

"You go right ahead. I will leave my coffee cup on this little table and see you tonight." Yousif turned away and went to greet his first appointment with a sinking feeling in his stomach. What had he ever done to deserve the situation in which he found himself?

Chapter 19

Murder

Tuesday morning at 7:00 A.M., Alex glanced at the *Eiffel Tower* from the window of his impressive *appartement*, which Philippe and Maya had loaned him for his stay in Paris. As he put on his jogging pants, he was a little distracted because he had been marking the stops on his metro map for his trip to Antony — *Denfert-Rochereau*, the Blue Line to *Cité Université* and *Gentilly*.

Before departing for Antony, he wanted to make his daily run. He hadn't gone far before he heard the sirens and saw Lieutenant Fournier at the scene of a murdered lady in a black hajib on the grounds of *Palais de Chaillot*. Alex asked, "Do you know who she is?"

Fournier replied, "There was no identification. I'm assuming she's Muslim and I will ask the imam if he knows her. Right now, the security cordon is tight. We'll move the body to the coroner soon."

"Is there anything I can do?"

"Not a thing. Too late."

"I'll be in touch."

Alex ran more than usual and then entered *Café de la Lumière.* He was greeted by Hilba, "Good morning, Doctor Alex. What would you like this morning? You look like you've seen a ghost. What's wrong?"

"I came upon a murder as I was on my run this morning near the *Trocadero.* I think the woman might have been Amirah's age."

"No wonder you are disturbed. Let me get you some water and a cup of coffee. I'll be right back. "

Hilba brought Alex *un café et un croque monsieur*, just as the morning's murder was announced on television by a prominent newscaster. The woman's identity was unknown and all details were under investigation.

Alex asked, "Do you know anything about this crime?"

Hilba leaned in near Alex, poured a little more coffee, and quietly said, "Yes, I'm afraid so. I hope I'm wrong, but rumors have been circulating that Maleeka Mansur, the daughter of Imam Mansur, was irritating certain Muslim men. She was a lawyer, and began to represent Muslim women who suffered abuse or mistreatment by their families. Recently she defended Noor Hamad, whose husband had beaten her for wearing Parisian-style clothes. The imam's daughter uncovered numerous other offenses and got a divorce for her, which did not set well in the local Muslim community. Rumor has it the men were outraged and wanted retaliation."

"Any suspects?"

"Some say it could be the imam himself. His daughter's professional practices opposed Allah's teachings and caused discord within the mosque. I don't know. My ears are listening, Doctor. I will tell you if I hear more."

Alex handed Hilba the euros for the breakfast, tipped him generously, and dashed to his *appartement* to shower and change. Heading for Lieutenant Fournier's office, he rushed down the steep stairs of the metro station and caught the next train. His mind pictured the murder scene and raced to think of suspects. From what he knew of the imam, he could not believe he would kill his own daughter. He was well-respected and a community spokesman for equal rights for wives, of whom he had two, and daughters, of whom he had five.

Alex leaped off the metro at his stop and sprinted the short distance to the precinct. Opening the Lieutenant's door, he saw him puffing his cigarettes and drinking coffee.

"Got some street gossip from my waiter at breakfast this morning," said Alex.

"You've got time for breakfast?"

"Always at *Café de la Lumière.* I hear lots of news there. You want to hear this or not?"

"Ok, shoot."

"My contact, Hilba says some suspect the victim was the imam's daughter, Maleeka Mansur. It was possibly an honor killing by one of the abusive husbands she brought into the divorce court. The murderers must have put the hajib on her, because as I understand it, Maleeka never wore one."

"You may be right, but we can't confirm the identity yet. A few days ago, an anonymous caller to the station said that a group of men at the mosque were planning a murder. The officer who took the call said it was a woman's voice, but she wouldn't identify herself. He traced it to a grocery store phone in the sixth *arrondissement,*" Fournier said.

"Did you check it out?"

"No. Casseaux said not to. He knows the Chinese owners and said they would never rat on customers. It's zero, blank, *nada.* Casseaux may talk to them, but he expects no help."

Checking his I-watch, Alex said, "I've got to get going to Antony. Did you get the dossier?"

Fournier opened his desk drawer and handed a manilla envelope to Alex.

"Thanks. I owe you one. Shall I return it tomorrow?"

"No, that's a copy. Keep it and don't let anyone touch it."

"Tell me the truth, Fournier. Is anyone doing anything about the art theft at the Dalles?"

"The case is big. It's a major assault and felony theft. There's a lead from a tip we got a few days ago. The tip confirmed information we already had. There is an *émigré* mafia stealing art here in Paris to support guerrilla fighters in the Middle East. They sell the real art to sheiks and African dictators after forging copies which they then return, so they can collect the reward. Sometimes they just sell forgeries of the art and safeguard the real art. The money is going to buy weapons. We don't know yet if this has anything to do with the art you want to find, but it fits."

"What does Casseaux think?"

"He thinks the honor killing might be the result of the Mansur woman getting too close to their operations, and they killed her before she exposed what they were up to. She spent a lot of time in Provence near the arts and worked for a guy named Rami Abadi, who owns a fine arts and antiques shop in the area."

"Fournier, I hate to admit it, but I'm impressed. How much of this can I tell the Dalles?"

"Can you trust them? I mean, they don't have any contacts with the *émigré* community who might compromise them, do they?" Fournier asked.

"I've known them since I was a boy. They are like second parents to me. You can trust them with complete confidence."

"Alright," Fournier replied. "Tell them to be discreet."

"Okay, I'm off to Antony for the meeting with Dr. Anna."

"That's a good organization and they have very powerful friends in and out of government. I've heard of several of those investigators, but I haven't met them, since I'm not usually involved in the arts recovery, except now you've gotten me into it."

Alex nodded knowingly, "You'll be a fine arts investigator, Fournier. You might even nab international mafia criminals."

Fournier glared sullenly at the stack of papers on his desk. Without looking up, he waved Alex out the door, scattering cigarette ashes all over the floor. "Good luck in Antony."

"Thanks, Fournier."

Chapter 20

Maya Returns

On Tuesday morning, Maya and her daughter Claire-Lise boarded Air France from Tegucigalpa, Honduras, to Miami to Paris. Philippe had not broken the shocking news to Maya about the art theft, so their mood was relaxed.

They settled into their comfortable first-class sleeper seats. Several times a year they made the trip to the tobacco plantation. Ten years ago, Maya took over the business from her father, and it still generated millions of dollars in tobacco sales and cigar manufacturing. The exclusive cigars were produced through a complex technique of rolling and folding the leaves like an accordion, copying the style of the Entubar method in Cuba. They exported them to twenty countries, including several in the Middle East.

In addition, she started a very successful cigar lounge in Roatan, Honduras in the 1900s, when other bars started to ban smoking indoors. She created an atmosphere of festive Latin America in her bar by featuring salsa music, tango nights, and *mucho* partying. She offered a place where aficionados could relax and enjoy a smoke, good food and drink. Soon she had established them in ten cities around the globe, her largest in Miami.

Owning the bars necessitated a hectic traveling schedule. Sleep was a luxury, and although the excitement of the work and success was tantalizing, she missed spending more time at home with her family.

Maya and Claire-Lise slept the first few hours out of Miami, then enjoyed a delicious dinner on Air France. "Claire-Lise, you were a great help. The headmistress at our school loved the changes we made."

"Mom, I know she did. Everything looked so fresh and clean. I wish I could be there at the start of the school year to help issue the uniforms and assist *Senora* Ludzmilla."

"Finish your school year and you can take your breaks down there if you'd like. You know we'll be going for the rest of our lives to check on the school and your grandparents. All your aunts and uncles would love for you to come as often as possible."

"I wonder what's been happening at home with Father," said Claire-Lise.

"I do too. He really said very little each time we talked on the phone. I'm sure he worked on his taxes while we were away, and also enjoyed Isabella's cooking."

"I missed Isabella's cooking," said Claire-Lise, taking another bite of her dinner."

"Me, too. Let's try to nap a bit before we land, so we won't be exhausted when we arrive in Paris."

"Sounds good to me," said Claire-Lise, as the flight attendant removed their dinner trays. Maya had coffee, adjusted her headsets to Debussy, and Claire-Lise adjusted hers to Adele's music for the rest of the flight.

Arriving at Charles de Gaulle, they hurried to the terminal to grab their luggage and go through customs. Leaving the arrival gate, they met Philippe. "My darling Maya, you are home," said

Philippe, embracing and kissing her.

Philippe hugged his daughter and asked, "How was your trip? How's the work at the school coming along?"

"Very rewarding as usual. I do regret I didn't get to snorkel or dive in Roatan, but next time I will."

Getting into the SUV, Claire-Lise began texting in the backseat, giving Philippe and Maya a chance to catch up. "I have a small confession to make, Love," he said.

"I hope you haven't been indiscreet or unfaithful. I doubt you've committed one of the seven deadly sins, my darling," she teased him. "You haven't been arguing with Mrs. Pilon again, have you?"

"No, nothing like that, but I confess, there's more than the taxes to worry about. I told you in our phone conversation."

"For heaven's sake, you said you needed me to check on tax issues that you thought you couldn't resolve without me, and several documents required my signature. Does the lawyer really need to see me in person or were you just missing us? So what else?"

"Well, the taxes are a big problem, but the biggest problem is that we actually had a break-in and a robbery in our apartment while you were gone."

"A break-in," Maya screamed! "When? A break-in? Are you joking?"

"No, Maya, I'm not joking. I didn't want to bother you while you were taking care of business."

"Were you home? You weren't home, were you? Were you hurt? I can't believe you didn't call me immediately."

"I was home and so was Isabella."

"Was she hurt? How did they get into that apartment with all our security? Did you not set the alarm?"

"It was in broad open daylight. I was eating breakfast and

they barged in."

"Oh, my goodness. I can't believe this. Oh, help me God. At least, you weren't hurt. Or were you hurt? Philippe, what about Isabella? Did anything happen to her?"

"No, no, we're fine, but they did steal some art."

Claire-Lise put her phone down, took out her earbuds and screamed, "What are you two yelling about? What's going on?"

Maya ignored Claire-Lise and continued questioning Philippe. "What? What? What art did they take? Paintings?"

Claire-Lise said, "Have some paintings been stolen?"

"Yes, Claire-Lise, the Monet and the Picasso were stolen from the *appartement* while you were gone," said Philippe.

"Not Mother's favorites. Oh, please. Somebody would pay a lot of money for them, but we'll get them back before they do, don't you think, Dad?"

Maya was shaking. "What? I knew getting those paintings back was too good to last. How could the robbers get into our *appartement* with all that security? Oh, no. Did you call the police?"

"Sure, I did. They're working on it and Alex is helping too."

"Alex. Why do you want to involve him in something this dangerous? He's a doctor, not a detective."

"He insisted. He did a lot of detective work in that hospital in Canada. Remember, he told us about it and he feels the loss of your art almost as deeply as we do. I had to let him. I couldn't stop him. He's working with a Lieutenant Fournier."

Maya was still in shock. "What did they do to you and Isabella? You said you were eating breakfast when they barged in."

"They broke in and tied us up, but Alex arrived and rescued us from our uncomfortable situation. A bit of good news is that a Dr. Anna of the Jewish Restitution and Restoration League is helping Alex and Lt. Fournier. Together with others, that makes a really crack team searching for the paintings. They will find them, I assure you."

Maya could not believe what she was hearing. "No, no, Philippe. What are you saying?"

As best he could, Philippe explained all that had happened on their way home and Maya calmed down a little. Arriving at home, she rushed to the *appartement*, threw open the door and ran to the wall where the pictures should be hanging, and looked at the empty space in dismay. Carrying the luggage, Philippe opened the door and Claire-Lise and he entered. Maya exclaimed, "Where have they taken them? I can't believe robbers got into our home and stole these paintings. I feel so violated."

"Alex and Lieutenant Fournier will have good news for us soon," said Philippe.

Maya sank into the sofa and shook her head.

Isabella emerged from the kitchen, "Welcome home. I have prepared a special lunch for you, but I'm sure you will want to freshen up first," sensing Maya's anguish. She knew Philippe had told her the dreadful news.

Maya embraced Isabella. "We missed you so much. You look great. We have been wanting one of your fabulous dinners and something smells wonderful. Oh, I'm so sorry about what happened to you and Philippe. Thank God you were not hurt. Both of you could have been killed. Oh, my God." She hugged Isabella again.

"Right now, I'm going to my bedroom, if you'll excuse me. I want to text some friends and make some calls," said Claire-Lise.

Maya said, "I think I'll do the same. Philippe, thank God you and Isabella are okay. I couldn't live without either one of you. Stop worrying about the paintings. We will get them back, I'm sure. Isabella, please hold my lunch till later."

Philippe asked Isabella to bring him his portion of the famous ribeye roast with mashed potatoes and *haricots verts*. He enjoyed every bite.

Chapter 21

An Important Journey

Alex left the building at 9:00 A.M. He wanted to focus on his upcoming interview with Dr. Anna, but could not stop thinking about the murder. He was very concerned since both Fauziah and Amirah were acquainted with Maleeka, and had lunched and worked with her time and again. He stepped onto the Metro again and watched the stops: *Dupleix, Sèvres, Pasteur, Edgar Quinet* and *Raspail*, waiting for the *Denfert-Rochereau*, where he would switch trains.

At the *Denfert-Rochereau* stop, he bought a scarf and compact for Dr. Anna and a gift for the baby. The young Romanian sales clerk suggested the bright shiny red fire truck. She wrapped all the gifts beautifully and asked Alex to let her know how everyone liked the selections from her kiosk. He thanked her and rushed through the open doors to the Blue Line to Antony.

The passengers looked sad and depressed in their dark, subdued and tailored clothes. Maybe it was Alex who felt sad and disappointed about the state of affairs in France this morning. The middle-class French people had had their share of heartache in the last few years, along with the hundreds of thousands of refugees in the country. How long can they remain resilient? Alex considered France and asked himself if Paris was a breeding ground for radical insurgents and future dictators. Lenin, Pol Pot, Mao, and others spent time there, returning to their own countries to seize power and assets. Paris always offered the best options for communication with the world for the messages of revolutionaries. When the metro doors opened he saw his Romanian musician friend Egbert enter with his flute. "*Bonjour*, Egbert," Alex said.

"*Bonjour*, Dr. Alex. When are you coming back to the club to play your sax with us? We're missing you."

"As soon as I can."

Egbert said, "You look deep in thought this morning. What's wrong?"

"I'm disturbed about a murder I witnessed this morning near the *Trocadera*."

"Who was it?"

"A Muslim woman about the age of Amirah. I'm afraid it's connected to a dangerous crime ring. I'm on a case to find some stolen art and the perpetrators could be involved in the murder also."

"The Roma people have a reputation for moving around and never staying in one place, but you know what? While we're moving around, we hear things and we see things, but we have quiet tongues. However, our women, the gypsy women, never miss anything. They know everything. I heard of this murder when it happened."

"What? You have heard about it already?"

"Oh, yes, we know about the iman's daughter — that she was taking risks, putting her life in danger from her own people. The Roma people have a nose for danger."

"So, you already know it was the iman's daughter, Maleeka,

who was murdered this morning?"

"That's the name I heard, but I've got to play this flute if I expect tips on this train," Egbert said.

"Here," said Alex, dropping some euros in Egbert's cup. "I'll bring my sax and play with you guys one night soon."

"*Comme ci, comme ca.* So good to see you. Come in any night."

As the train rolled on, Alex thought of the horrible dictator Egbert's family had lived under in Romania. Nicolae Ceausescu ruled the country with an iron fist for years, bringing misery and oppression to thousands of Romanians. As a faithful disciple of Jesus Christ, Alex's faith led him to help suffering individuals as much as he could. He prayed that God would help Egbert and the people of Romania. He believed in the power of prayer and was thankful for his friend. Alex collected his thoughts for today's meeting with Dr. Anna.

In twenty minutes, the train pulled into the little town of Antony, a suburb of Paris. The surrounding shops of the station needed a facelift. He spotted a man in his thirties, holding a red-headed toddler and a sign with Alex's name on it. It had to be Levi, Dr. Anna's grandson.

Alex walked over, extending his hand, and said, "*Bonjour.* You must be Levi and little Jacques. I'm Alex Winston." They shook hands.

"I use the signs when I'm meeting people at the train. Mrs. Hertz did email us an intro and a photo of you." The men began walking to the car.

Little Jacques reached for Alex, so he took him in his arms and tousled his red hair. Jacques giggled, "Do it again, do it again."

"You know, I love red-headed babies, although you hardly see them anymore. You're a rare breed, little Jacques, and look, I have a surprise for you," Alex handed him the wrapped fire truck.

Levi said, “You didn’t have to do that,” as a giggling Jacques ripped the paper off the fire truck. “I think he likes it though. Thank you, Alex. Good to have you here today. You’re from Montréal, aren’t you?”

“Yes, I did my university and medical school studies there, but I grew up in several different countries. My father was an epidemiologist and my mother an anesthesiologist, so they took assignments assisting in UN medical relief operations and mission work all over the world, and I tagged along.” Jacques tugged at Alex’s sunglasses. “This baby needs these glasses.”

“I don’t think so. Let me take him before he destroys them. Here’s the car.” Levi fastened Jacques into his car seat.”

“What’s the business around here, Levi?” asked Alex.

“We have a huge Algerian population who work primarily in education and healthcare. Most of this area was agricultural, but now the service industries have taken over. One of the main businesses is schools for nannies. We send nannies all over the world as *Au Pairs*, right out of Antony,” stated Levi.

“I had three very stern and dramatic nannies in the countries where we lived. I don’t know how my parents got them. I hope these *au pairs* are more fun.”

“They have good reputations and get placed quickly. With so many moms working full-time these days, there is a huge demand for nannies.”

Levi stopped the car in a charming neighborhood in front of a two-story brick house with a flower and vegetable garden and lovely shade trees.

“I’m really looking forward to meeting your grandmother. She must be a fascinating woman,” said Alex as they approached the house.

Chapter 22

A Serious Conversation

Tuesday, at 10:30 A.M., Levi unlocked the door and they entered the small living room of Dr. Anna, Levi, Olivia, and Jacques. No cars moved on the quiet suburban street. Alex noticed a red bird in a Japanese maple tree outside the huge bay window. Stacks of music books sat on top of an upright piano in a corner of the room. Old photographs and paintings adorned the walls. Levi set packages on the couch already filled with stacks of small boxes, stationery, candy, and notebooks. He put little Jacques on the floor in the middle of a blanket with a pile of toys and gave him a bottle of juice.

"Alex, would you like something to drink – juice, soda, coffee or tea, or something to eat?"

"Thanks, water would be great. I had breakfast and coffee at a little cafe before I left Paris this morning," said Alex.

"Do you think he has enough toys?"

"I doubt if a child can have too many toys. You're enriching his imagination. Let's hope his world will be better as an adult because of the toys. Jacques is a fun kid to watch. He's very fortunate," said Alex. "My parents didn't buy many toys that I remember. They bought me a lot of books and read to me a lot, which was good, but toys would have been my choice."

"I see. We love buying toys for him and watching him play. Since my father and grandfather were rabbis, they were intentional that everyone study, so toys were not so important in my house either. Even after my father became a Messianic Jew, we had few toys from him, but Grandmother and aunts and uncles filled the gaps."

Jacques happily drank his juice and played alternately with one toy or another, while Alex and Levi relaxed in the living room. "Did your father face a lot of opposition when he changed from rabbi to Messianic Jew?"

"Yes, he was disowned by his father, but my grandmother, Dr. Anna, worked with both of them, so they maintained communication. It wasn't easy, but it got better. Our living with Grandmother has helped everything too."

"I'm sorry," Alex said, "I didn't intend to pry."

"It's fine. I understand. Most people are perplexed, especially Jews. Call it what you will. My father was transformed by the 'Spirit of the Lord' coming upon him. He was born into a new relationship. I did not understand it until I met Olivia, my wife. Her parents were missionaries in Brazil for thirty-five years and the experiences her family had there were life-changing. I was taught from the Torah and had often read the expression 'the Spirit of the Lord came upon the prophets.' After that, they would predict a great disaster or divine news to a king. However, I did not know about the personal relationship of the 'Spirit of the Lord' coming to dwell in someone's heart."

"Your father showed courage in his convictions, but I express sympathy for the difficulty it caused in his father's relationship. I rarely talk about religious things, especially spiritual relationships, because they are personal and often make people uncomfortable." Alex cleared his throat, sipped a little water and continued, "How long has Dr. Anna worked with the Jewish Restitution and Restoration?"

"Thirty-eight years, and she's still a consultant and an occasional commander of active operations. She just refuses to retire."

"I'm honored to talk with her today, but I don't want to interfere with your plans."

"You're not interfering with anything. Relax. Make yourself at home. This morning Olivia drove Dr. Anna to the office to take care of some business and pick up some medicine. Since they've been gone more than an hour, I'm expecting them any minute," said Levi. "What kind of medicine do you practice, Alex?"

"I did an internship in internal medicine and a residency in cardiology. Here I'm preparing for an assignment with the *Médecins Sans Frontières* and practicing general family medicine and cardiology at the *Salpêtrière*, the large public assistance and teaching hospital in the thirteenth *arrondissement*. You're probably in Paris as much as Antony with your work, so you know that area."

"Yes, it's not far from my office. I swim and work out at the *piscine de la Caille.*

I'm hoping it keeps me out of the doctor's office — no offense to you."

"I go there too. It's the best metro pool in Paris. We're doing our hearts a service."

"We're big believers in physical and mental exercises. Maybe you can encourage Grandmother. She works so hard finding Holocaust art that she skips her exercises a little too much, but I'm sure you're not here to talk about health with her."

"I'm here to talk to Dr. Anna about finding stolen art. I worked on hospital criminal cases with the Montréal police while I was an intern and resident there. Detective work requires patience and logic to put the puzzle pieces together, and I find that very satisfying."

"Were your cases all in the hospitals?"

"Yes, some vicious and unusual deaths occurred there. I was able to help the police solve a few of those cases. If I weren't a cardiologist, I would be a detective. Both professions intrigue me. A cardiologist and detective are given a set of conditions to which they must find solutions. I'm absorbed in a Holocaust art investigation. But enough about me. Tell me what you do, Levi. I've heard you are a missionary-teacher."

"I'm a freelance missionary for Faith Works, an organizational umbrella that covers fifty countries. The global goal is to build bridges between Jews and Christians. Once a week I lead a Hebrew Bible study in Paris with various students — Christians, Jews, Muslims and even agnostics and atheists drop in occasionally. Fridays we produce evangelical pamphlets to distribute each week."

"What is the content?"

"The pamphlets explain sections of the Old and New Testament books relating to the Messiah. We hope to build understanding among Jews, Christians and Muslims, and help them find commonalities of faith," said Levi.

"Yes, the commonalities of faiths have contributed to the development of civilization. Unfortunately, throughout the ages, religious faiths also have brought great discontent and persecution."

"So true. France has little respect for religion and many French citizens are narrow-minded and prejudiced toward Jews and Muslims, although we have the second highest population of Jews outside Israel, following the United States. The Jews have been living here for decades, but they're migrating to Israel by the thousands every year, driven out by anti-semitism. Occasional friction used to be common, but now we have demonstrations by the French people and certain immigrants yelling, 'Death to the Jews.' Last year, anti-semitic acts rose by nearly seventy-five percent. It's also happening in other parts of Europe."

"Yet your family is Christian and Jewish. I have heard anti-semitic comments in my clinic. I'm a Christian. I believe the Word of God is as full of authenticity and life guides today as it was two thousand years ago, but this religious xenophobia in Paris you speak of is heartbreaking. I commend you for the work you do."

"I'm an ethnic Jew, but because I believe Jesus is the Messiah, I am a Messianic Jew. Dr. Anna has remained in the Jewish faith and continues to work for the Jewish Restitution and Restoration League. Tracking down art stolen from Jewish Holocaust victims and families has been her life. She attends the synagogue each week as well as our Christian services," said Levi. "My grandfather's parents were killed in Nazi Germany. Cousins, aunts and uncles were tortured and burned in Auschwitz. That war ended over seventy years ago, and yet the Jews are facing malicious discrimination all over Europe again. Even Grandmother had "JEW" written on her car parked near her office recently."

"So sorry. So sad. I don't think the Muslims bear as much discrimination here as Jews. Do you know many young Muslims in Paris?"

"Yes, I've had coffee and meetings with quite a few and I'm friends with an imam in Paris. But my main outreach and ministry is to share the good news of the gospel with all my encounters."

"Do you ever feel threatened?" asked Alex.

"Yes, but I don't focus on the danger. In the last eight months, the office windows have been defaced with graffiti. One old faithful man coming for Bible study was killed on his way home and left with a yellow star wrapped around his arm. I want to protect my family from the bigots, leftists, anti-semites, and crazed people out there. I challenge them to be brave, although I am fearful myself sometimes. The States had their 9/11. We had the bombing of those children at the rock concert in the *Bataclan, the Belle Equipe Bar, Le Carillon Bar* and others. Jewish businesses have been vandalized, but by God's grace, we will continue to bring light and hope to a disenchanted and disenfranchised world by telling our stories. We don't live in peaceful times, but neither did Christ," said Levi.

"Mrs. Hertz told me you speak French, English, Spanish and are studying Hebrew."

"I grew up here, so it's customary to speak several languages. My wife and I are studying Hebrew, but it's slow going. Wait, I think I hear them in the driveway."

Chapter 23

Holocaust Art Hunter

Car doors slammed outside and Dr. Anna Israel and Olivia entered. "*Bonjour, bonjour*, you must be Mrs. Hertz's friend," said Dr. Anna, as she put one of her bags on the sofa. "I will join you in a few minutes, but first I must go to my room and collect myself," and she walked into her room and closed the door.

"Welcome, Alex," said Olivia. "Excuse her a few minutes. She did not sleep well last night. She's been working on another art theft in Paris, and one of her contacts called her last night to say she thought she recognized one of the stolen pieces at an auction in Madrid. I'll join you as soon as I put up these groceries. I will bring you some of the *madeleines* and *macarons* I made last night. I can't keep enough for Levi." She quickly returned and passed a plate of cookies to Levi, Alex and Jacques.

"Thank you for your hospitality," Alex said. To him, Levi looked like a tough professional athlete, who was not telling his whole story. "Levi, I don't want you to bother with taking me to the train station this afternoon. I need the exercise, so let me walk and you follow your regular schedule today."

"Only if you want to. It's no trouble, but right now I'm taking Jacques up for a diaper change and putting him down for a nap," said Levi.

Olivia said, "I need to check on lunch preparations. We're expecting you to join us for lunch today, Alex. Make yourself at home. Dr. Anna will be out shortly."

"Are you the Olivia working with my friend, Amirah?" Alex inquired.

"Yes, do you know Amirah?"

"Yes, she's a good friend of mine, so have you heard anything about Maleeka?"

"No, nothing unusual. Is something wrong?"

"Yes, well, maybe. There was a murder this morning near the *Trocadera* and there are suspicions that it might have been Maleeka."

"No, no, she was so dedicated to our project and we were making great progress, although we knew it was dangerous. I haven't heard anything. I'm so sorry."

"Well, I'm not sure, but it's pointing that way from more than one source."

"How did this terrible crime happen? I don't want to believe it. She's so young, talented and smart, and now this." Shoulders shaking, Olivia sat down and wiped her tears and tried to calm herself.

Alex touched her hand and said, "I am so sorry to bring such horrible news. Forgive me, but I thought maybe you had heard."

"No, I haven't heard from Fauziah or Amirah or watched the news or anything this morning. Oh, I hope there's a mistake. Excuse me, I need to check on some things. Oh, dear me."

Alex was alone and felt very uncomfortable, so he thumbed through the magazines on the coffee table. Old brochures and coffee table art books from every country of the world were stacked in piles. The wall was covered in framed photos of a wide variety of people whom Alex assumed Dr. Anna had helped in the search for stolen art.

Dr. Anna's door opened and she entered the living room. She sat down in the Lazy Boy recliner which held several cushions. Next to it was a small table. On it was a huge extending lamp, a cellphone, laptop and a camera. Was this her home office? Dr. Anna was about 5'3" tall and wore her hair in a bun. Her skin was in great condition for her age and her eyes peered through small spectacles that sat on her nose. "So, Dr. Alex, you're from Montréal?"

"Yes, I was born in Montréal, but saying where I'm from is difficult because I've lived in so many places. My father was from Montréal, but he studied at the *Sorbonne* and did an internship at the *Salpêtrière*, where he met and married my mother. Since they took assignments with the World Health Organization, they were sent to many countries while I was growing up. I was always changing schools, friends, etc."

"How did the Dalles become your godparents?"

"They were best friends with my parents when they lived in Paris. We've always been very close as families."

"I know you're interested in locating the Dalles' stolen Holocaust paintings. What would you like to ask me?"

"Two famous paintings — a Monet and a Picasso — were stolen from Philippe and Maya Dalles' apartment a few days ago. Although they are extremely valuable, the Dalles have a very distinguished collection which includes pieces even more valuable, so my first question was why were those the only two stolen? Philippe told the police those two had belonged to Maya's grandparents, victims of the Holocaust. The police believe there's a relationship between the art stolen and Holocaust victims. I thought you might have some insight about these paintings and could offer suggestions in locating them," said Alex.

Dr. Anna Israel grimaced. "It's as difficult today to locate stolen art works, as it was when I began my work years ago. Obviously, your godparents had some originals somebody wanted. I see you have a sketchbook with you. Do you have a sketch of the paintings?"

"No, I have photographs of them," he said, handing the photos to her.

"Oh, yes, I know these paintings well. In fact, I was instrumental in locating them and returning them to the rightful owners about five years ago. They weren't easy to locate the first time. I wouldn't advise you to get involved in this operation, Alex. Mrs. Hertz told me you want to help the police find the paintings and the thieves. She said you have a friend, Lieutenant Fournier, at the police station who might help you."

"I am most fortunate to have him helping me. He's a bit reluctant to get involved, but he is accommodating. We discover data fast, but with your help, we might be able to find the art before it leaves France," said Alex. "I want to ask a question that's probably not related to the art. Do you know about the girl who was murdered near the *Trocadero*?"

Dr. Anna continued looking at the photographs of the stolen art and putting them in her lap, faced Alex squarely. "I think I know the girl. She may be Maleeka Mansur, who actually worked with me on some of my cases because of her interest in art. She was a Muslim, but she was willing to work among different religions and cultures as a crusader for women. For me, she helped locate some of the art. I don't know what happened to her, but I suspect an art thief was trying to persuade her to participate in his art sales. It could be that she found more information about the wrong people and they murdered her. We should have the proper identification by tomorrow. It could have been a random murder, but I doubt it."

"What about her family? I wouldn't think they were pleased with her art interests or her women's rights work, if it was Maleeka."

"You know, this is Olivia's line of work. She's very well-versed in the psychological and social aspects of minority and women's rights. I haven't discussed this particular case with her, but she may know more about it than I do. But in answer to your question — No, at this point, if she has been killed, I do not believe her family killed her. These art thieves are really the new Nazis. When one of my rescued art paintings disappears, I intend to do whatever it takes to retrieve it. Stealing the Holocaust art is wrong. I will continue to do all I can to punish those who profit from the art of relatives and friends who suffered and died in the concentration camps of the Nazis. On the recommendation of my dear friends, the Hertzes," Dr. Anna said, "I'm the main director of our endeavor, Alex, but we will find the Dalles' art."

"I am willing to follow your instructions, Dr. Anna. I want to solve this mystery and I need your help. I do want to mention a friend of mine, Amirah, a girl from Syria. Would you happen to know her? She's a very original artist who lives in the Second *Arrondissement.* She paints portraits and abstracts. The rugs she paints with a neutral floor complex geometric designs in cube shapes. I could talk about her art all afternoon, but my concern today is that her former mother-in-law hates her and has threatened to kill her."

"How sad for her. In my opinion, that is an idle threat, but I am not always right. I am sympathetic to the Syrians. Send me some information about Amirah and when I have the time, I will look into her case, but first, let's find the stolen art belonging to your godparents."

"I understand. I have already asked Lieutenant Fournier to

help me, Dr. Anna."

"Good. The Paris police and I are good friends and I've heard a lot of good things about Lieutenant Fournier, although he doesn't usually work on art cases. He's not your typical police detective. He really sees the big picture, I'm told."

"He can be unorthodox and unruly, but he knows how to solve cases. I should be getting back to Paris," said Alex, standing up and shaking Dr. Anna's hand. "Thank you for all your help. Here's my card with my numbers." Alex walked through the door into the living room.

"Oh, no, you're not leaving yet," said Olivia. "For a first-time guest you must eat lunch with us. I'm sautéing a few more things and lunch will be served."

"I can't impose on you like this, especially at a time like this."

"This is no imposition — you must stay. We would like your company."

Levi joined the conversation, "Jacques will sleep for another hour. Can we help you, Olivia?"

"I want you two to enjoy the fresh air and sunshine. I'm in kitchen control mode today."

"Come on, Alex, we'll take a quick walk while Olivia finishes. Should we be back in twenty minutes?"

Olivia nodded yes and waved them out of the house.

It was a beautiful warm day as Levi and Alex stepped out into the sunshine. With Dr. Anna's support, he was confident the art of Philippe and Maya would be secured.

They returned to the house in twenty minutes, washed their hands and were seated at the dining table, spread with a linen cloth and napkins, fresh flowers and a piping hot delicious stew of pork and black beans served over rice with fresh orange slices. Olivia also brought sliced guava to the feast. This is a Brazilian *fejoida.* My family always served this for special occasions and so do I, so enjoy."

"This is a first for me, Olivia. Thank you for including me in this family luncheon," Alex said.

"Grandmother Anna, would you offer thanks?" asked Olivia.

Grandmother Anna began, "Blessed are You, Lord our God, King of the Universe, Who brings forth bread from the earth. We thank you, Heavenly Father, for creating various kinds of sustenance, the fruit of the vine, the fruit of the trees, the vegetables and greens from the ground. Thank you for life and breath, and for our cherished families. Thank you for the protection, guidance and love that you abundantly shower on us daily. May we be faithful servants of yours every day. Blessed are you, O Lord our God."

Everyone enjoyed the wonderful lunch including the fabulous desserts. Alex looked at his watch and arose to leave. "This has been a special day for me. I look forward to visiting with you again. As I said this was my first Brazilian *fejoida* and it was incredible. You are *un chef magnifique. Merci beaucoup.*"

"Thank you for sharing this meal with us, and we'll certainly look for you again on a less serious occasion. You're always welcome here," said Olivia.

Dr. Anna shook hands with Alex and said, "Thank you for volunteering to help with this art theft, Dr. Alex. *À bientôt.*"

Alex walked back to the station to board the train after a very productive, gratifying day of promise, but one stained by the death of the girl on *Chaillot Hill.*

Chapter 24

Art Show

Tuesday afternoon at 3:00 P.M., Alex arrived back in Paris, went directly to the *Salpêtrière* and did rounds. He returned to his office where Hilba's wife was waiting for her appointment with him. "Dr. Alex, have you heard about the murder?"

"Yes, but has the victim been identified? What have you heard?"

"It was Maleeka, the iman's daughter. Hilba and I think an angry husband killed her. Maleeka was a fearless defender of women's rights. She counselled a Muslim woman to divorce her husband and it made this man furious. He slandered Maleeka for weeks before her murder."

"Have there been any arrests?"

"No, because there's also talk that her father, Iman Mansur, murdered her. What do you think?"

"I haven't thought about it enough. It's always possible it could have been a random act. Keep me in your loop. What is Hilba doing?"

"He's very happy. It's his birthday, and our friends are giving us a barbecue tonight. I made him a five-layer cake and we will feast and drink all night. Doctor, you are invited, of course. Please come."

"I would love to celebrate with you, but Amirah invited me to an art exhibit tonight, and I promised her I would go. Please give Hilba my best wishes. Now come with me and let's see how you're doing." Alex escorted her into the examination room and met his assistant. After all the preliminary checks, he informed Hilba's wife that she would have good news for his birthday celebration. She was much improved from the last appointment. This made her very excited. She said, "He and I may have a second honeymoon tonight on his birthday." Alex laughed with her. His assistant brought his next patient and he continued seeing patients until 6:00 P.M. when he left to rush home, shower and meet Amirah at the art show.

Tuesday by 7:30 P.M. Amirah had been setting up two of her art works earlier in the afternoon. It gave her a chance to observe the other featured paintings. She studied the valuable older works that three donors, including Maya and Philippe Dalle, had loaned to the exhibit. Later tonight they would remain to answer questions about the origins of the paintings and to offer insights into their value. She had given Alex a ticket and was looking forward to spending the evening and sharing her ideas about the art with him.

The third floor of a nineteenth century warehouse had been converted into a modern showplace, featuring an eclectic new gallery in Paris. The tall blank walls, few windows and polished concrete floors created great space for the visual arts. Amirah had concentrated on painting an illusion of an eternal presence in her country. She chose to present two abstracts, one that evoked an immortal Aleppo from Biblical days, and one from this century. She hoped they would inspire a feeling of timelessness and hope for the viewer.

She had rushed home to shower, wash her hair and dress for the evening. Weeks ago, she had found an exquisite Paris fabric shop that carried imported textiles in radiant blues, yellows and reds, embellished with gold and silver threads. The materials resembled Syria's famous damask and brocade from its earlier days. She was elated to find this fabric and to design the dress she wore tonight.

It flattered her slim figure and she needed little makeup--just a little eye shadow and lipstick that matched the coral in the brocade and damask of her dress. She had taxied back to the gallery by 6:00. As she was strolling through the gallery, speaking to artists she knew, she noticed a stylish, beautifully attired lady, staring intently at one of her Aleppo paintings. Amirah walked over to greet her, "*Bonsoir*, are you enjoying the show?"

Maya said, "*Bonsoir*, very much. It is incredibly fascinating. Let me introduce myself. I am Maya Dalle. Are you one of the artists?"

"Yes, I am Amirah Hassan from Syria. This is one of my paintings."

"How did you learn to paint like this? This is one of the most original paintings I've ever seen."

Amirah said, "I've always painted. It's been a passion of mine, but I was fortunate to be able to study at the *Sorbonne* after my father and I arrived here as refugees."

"You are incredibly talented. Do you have a contract with a gallery?'

"No, I display some of my paintings in the carpet shop where my father sells Oriental rugs — the Wide World of Carpets."

Maya was stunned. "Oh, Darling, you should be showing these in the museum. These take me to the days when my husband Philippe and I were on our honeymoon in Damascus. These paintings capture the essence of those wonderful experiences we had there. I have got to introduce you to a friend of mine. Will you be here later?"

"I'll be here till it closes."

"*Enchantée*, Amirah. We will be seeing more of you, I am sure."

"I will see you later tonight." She kept an eye on the doors for Alex. Soon she saw him and walked to meet him.

"Alex, I am so glad to see you." They lightly embraced.

Alex stepped back to take a better look at Amirah. "You look beautiful tonight. I like that dress."

"Thank you. I'm so glad. Fauziah and I searched the fabric shops of Paris until we found this fabric of perfect color and weave."

"And then you made it?"

"I designed the dress and pattern, and Nanian's wife, an excellent seamstress, made it and voilà, here it is at the art show."

"You designed a stunning dress fit for the Cannes Festival."

"Thank you, Alex." She wanted to hold him in her arms, but simply looked at him longer than usual and continued talking nervously about the fabric. "For many years, Syria produced fabrics until almost all of the textile industry was destroyed. Crusaders who passed through Damascus actually introduced these fabrics to Europe in the eleventh century, and the weaving of linen damask became established in flax-growing countries — in France, for example, by the mid-thirteenth century."

"I confess I didn't even know what damask was until now."

Amirah smiled. "At one time, enchanting fabrics like this were everywhere in Aleppo and Damascus. I'll save this dress forever."

"I certainly understand why. It is you, Amirah."

"You embarrass me. Excuse me, I think I'm nervous about the

show. I'm talking too much. I'm thrilled that you could come tonight. It's a simple show, just an opportunity for us unknowns to show a work or two of ours, mixed with a few donor paintings."

As she was talking, Alex realized again how talented Amirah was, and he was interested in the art Amirah loved and created. He was surprised by the strong chemistry he felt toward Amirah.

They took glasses of Perrier and sampled a *gougère*, a *salmon rillette* and a *panisse*, as they strolled by the paintings. Although he had been to dozens of galleries and enjoyed the art, he had never enjoyed art as he did now. He supported Amirah because he knew this event was important to her and he liked being part of her life. "You must have really developed your style at the *Sorbonne* when you studied there."

"Yes, it helped me. I was on a full scholarship there for a year."

"Was it a good year for you? Did you like it?" Alex continued, "Maugham's Philip Carey studied at the *Sorbonne*. He said they taught him shadows have colors."

Alex realized immediately he might as well have told a musician that pianos have keys or music has notes. Amirah permitted herself just a trace of an indulgent smile. "They were kind to me and the year enabled me to polish my technical skills. Masson, my senior advisor, told me I was exactly the kind of student they are always looking for."

"But you left after a year?"

"It was a difficult decision and I miss the daily contact with the people there. However, further study would have required me to master the art of one of the established schools. I enjoyed studying the techniques of the masters, but I did not want to paint like them or even in their traditions."

"I'm sure it was difficult. You are suspicious of tradition, but you come from a country steeped in traditions," Alex said.

"Yes, tradition is very important. However, an artist must have three things and only one of them can be learned in a school. The first thing is technique, which you can learn at the *Sorbonne* very well. The second thing is unique personal experiences. You don't learn these; you just have to make sense of them. The school cannot help you with this. Each person comes with his own background and personal preferences as well. Good technique lets you translate your experiences into the work of art."

"So, you have technique and personal experiences and preferences. What's the third thing?"

"For me I must have faith."

"Religious faith?"

"Yes, in a way. I say, in a way, because no imam or priest I know would understand my version of it." She laughed, "I'm at peace with this though."

"I'm sure that's all right. We all have our own ideas about faith." Still, he wondered about what her faith had to do with her art.

Maya approached with two men. "Amirah, Darling, you must meet my husband Philippe and Monsieur Farrokh Mustafa."

"*Enchantée de faire votre conaissance*, and this is my friend, Dr. Alex Winston."

Maya, Philippe and Alex were surprised and started laughing. "Amirah, Alex is our godson and I haven't seen him since my return from Honduras," Maya said.

"I didn't even know you were back," Alex said, embracing Maya and shaking hands with the men.

Maya continued, "I am captivated by Amirah's art, Alex, and wanted to share it with my husband and Farrokh before we depart this delightful evening. Amirah, Farrokh owns the *Galerie Daniel Beaulier*, one of the most prestigious galleries in Paris, featuring rising stars of the contemporary art market of which you must surely be one, in my humble opinion."

"Mademoiselle Amirah, I noticed your excellent paintings earlier this evening. Perhaps you will show me your other works in a few weeks. I would be very interested in seeing your portfolio, if you would allow," said Monsieur Mustafa.

"But of course. Thank you for your interest, sir."

Alex and Philippe stepped aside. Philippe inquired, "Any news about the paintings?"

Alex replied, "We are making progress. The art crime investigator, Dr. Anna Israel, who seeks Holocaust paintings and returns them to owners' families, has been extremely helpful. We have several leads. I will let you know our plans soon."

"Thanks, Alex. Maya took it much better than I expected. She has great confidence in you."

"Come, Philippe, we must go. We have reservations at *La Tour d'Argent.*

"*Au revoir, à bientôt,*" they all said to one another, as Philippe, Maya and Farrokh departed.

"Amirah, I think you met a man of great influence in the art world of Paris tonight and he genuinely loved your paintings."

"I don't know. It's exciting to meet a *galerie* owner, but I have no idea if he would really commend me."

"You know, I think he might. Let's stay positive. How did you like Maya?"

"She's wonderful — so sophisticated, charming, elegant, smart, and she's your godmother. I don't know what to say. So many things happened tonight. My faith has deepened that things are really going to work out here."

"You mentioned faith before in the same sentence with your painting. Amirah. What does faith have to do with your painting? You do not treat religious subjects. In fact, your work is quite modern with all the cubes and multiple points of view," he said, as he was looking at the two amazing works.

She focused her eyes on him with an expression he had never seen before. "*Monsieur le Docteur*," she said sternly, "if you must know, faith turns your talent toward others. I was blessed with what I call insight on my journey here. God saved me from my hatred and anger during the perilous voyage and increased my faith in Him. I know my talents are gifts from God and I want to offer them in his service to help others grow in faith."

"Your art can live for generations, Amirah. You have an opportunity to influence millions."

She smiled again, but then quickly shrugged her delicate shoulders and said, "I want the world to see Aleppo as I knew it, and how the Syrian and Russian leaders devastated my beautiful city. My faith was actually renewed by the vision of the Christ, who saved me that night on the Aegean Sea. I must immortalize the scenes that were burned onto my heart."

Alex wanted to talk to her all night, to look into her eyes and admire her in that incredible dress she was wearing, but other people were gathering around her and asking questions, which Amirah most pleasantly answered. Alex was proud to see such confidence in her. This show brought a different perspective on Amirah, but the show was closing soon and the people were leaving."

Amirah and Alex walked to the door and out into the street. "I would love to continue this conversation with you, Amirah. Would you like to go to the *Quartier Latin* and have coffee and hear jazz at the club where my Romanian friend's trio plays?"

Amirah looked at her watch. "I can go for a little while for coffee, but I'm tired after setting this up today. I'm meeting Fauziah for coffee in the morning before work, but yes, I would love to go with you anywhere for a little while," she said, putting her arm through Alex's, as they strolled down the walk.

Alex decided they would go to the *Café de la Paix* a nearby romantic spot across the street from the *Garnier Opéra House.* Amirah had not said anything about Maleeka, so she must not have heard. He decided not to mention that. It would cast a shadow on this special evening for Amirah.

Chapter 25

Almaealij

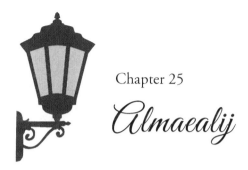

Tuesday night at 10:00 P.M., they walked along the *Boulevard des Capucines* on the cool spring evening, clinging close to each other and enjoying the evening in Paris. They passed the sumptuous late nineteenth-century *Garnier Opéra House* and decided to stop at *Café de la Paix* for their coffee. They entered around nine, and Alex felt all eyes of the guests and staff cast on Amirah and her exquisite dress. The staff at this five-star restaurant adjacent to the opera house is trained to give the guests a first-rate experience but the *garçons* were genuinely delighted to serve them. The white linen table cloth with the red roses in crystal and silver settings created an atmosphere of royal days — truly like stepping back in time.

By the most courteous of *garçons,* they were escorted to a lovely window seat where they enjoyed the glistening lights of the opera house and the surrounding buildings. "This is so delightful, Alex."

"What may I bring you this evening?" inquired *le garçon.*

"I would like a cup of oolong tea, please," said Amirah.

"One chocolate éclair for us if she consents to share it with me?" Amirah nodded assent and Alex ordered un café, *un thé et un éclair au chocolat.*

"Amirah, you know everyone was mesmerized by you when you entered this restaurant. They appear captivated still."

Amirah smiled and touched Alex's hand across the table and said, "Thank you, but I doubt they are captivated. Thank you for everything." Then she withdrew her hand.

Alex wasn't sure what she was thanking him for, so he said what he had been thinking, "I want to talk more about your faith and your art. I was fascinated by all you said tonight explaining your relation to your art. Is your faith related to Islam — any organized worship? Please tell me more."

"I love the arts associated with worship, but," she lowered her voice and Alex leaned closer to her to hear, "I have no connection to Islamism, after what my countrymen and I have suffered under the fanatics of this faith. I'm unhappy with all the "isms" — capitalism, socialism, communism as I know them and I don't understand that much. Mainly I don't like to be told what to do, *Mon Cher.* However, I am Muslim because I was born into it, and although I find the Christian's viewpoint of women a better fit for me, I dare not hurt my father. There were many good Muslims in Aleppo who were slaughtered by people claiming to be faithful followers enforcing the tenets of that faith. I'll share more at another time."

Her intimate '*Mon Cher*' had opened his heart just as gracefully as she had opened the door to a deeper understanding of art, her culture and her. Now he and this lovely woman were united in some ways. His heart was beating loudly. He wondered what he should do next. The sophisticated man of medicine and science was stymied by the graciousness and personality of this lovely woman. "You know, I stopped by your father's carpet shop in the *Marché Aux Puces* the other day and I saw some interesting paintings there."

"Oh, so you did. Yes, I have painted him some landscapes to sell with his rugs. It could make us a little extra money. I don't paint with my heart for those works because they are strictly commercial. If he can sell them and make money for us, I'm helping the family, but my abstracts are mine. When we lived in Aleppo, I designed some of his rug patterns and he always raved about them and sold them quickly, but here we cannot make those. He is selling a different kind of rug, so the art is my best gift to help him in his business."

"I saw a portrait of someone, but I didn't know who it was."

"Oh, that, yes. It is one of the few portraits I have done here. I did portraits of my relatives and friends in Syria, but they are lost, I'm sure. The portrait you saw was of Nanian's wife, but I can't let my father sell that. It will be a gift to her. She would take no money for making my dress, so I will gift Nanian and her with her portrait. In creating her features, I had to cast her in the right light. After all, she radiates a special love light from her soul. This is what prompted me to paint her."

Alex exclaimed, "It's amazing that you have such a gift to portray people's essence."

"Believe it or not, Masson, my instructor at the *Sorbonne*, said he had over the decades several students who possessed this gift. To my surprise, he saw this gift in my art. I think it's more common than you might think. I must paint my subjects in the light their life gives to me. Actually, I paint a portrait or a landscape the same way. I must choose the color that I see emanating from the person or the landscape. The color tone of the entire composition is art."

"So, then you must paint in the mornings when the Parisian lights are the best or can you paint any time in Paris because it is the City of Light?" He felt silly asking this.

"Even in Paris, I paint in the morning. The light is the clearest and most natural. It's the easiest light in which to see the truth, but you know, sometimes I continue painting all day."

"Amirah, have you ever thought about painting me? Do men make boring subjects?"

Immediately, a shiver ran down Amirah's spine. She became nervous about revealing her real feelings to Alex through her portrait and how she would portray him. She felt this handsome doctor understood her, but did he really? Did she trust him enough to be vulnerable to him? Although her past experiences made it difficult to trust any man again, it was so hard not to trust Alex, because he seemed so honest and sincere. Could he be the only man in the world who could understand her? She wondered.

She took a deep breath. The moment must not be lost. "Ah, *Mon Cher*, the morning light follows you like a beacon. You are an *Almaealij*, a healer of souls," she whispered softly. "I would love to paint you."

In that instant, sipping his coffee, Alex realized she was completely different from all the girls he'd known before, but he was afraid to let himself think more. It was getting late and Alex had work and Amirah was meeting Fauziah for coffee in the morning. "*Chérie* Amirah, I know you have a busy day tomorrow, and it's late. Let's take a taxi."

A light mist was falling as they jumped into the taxi and sped to Amirah's home. She touched Alex's hand as she slid out the door and motioned for him to go on and not worry about walking her to the door. "*Bonsoir.*"

He got out of the taxi and took her hand and slipped his arm around her waist and drew her to him. "I was so happy being with you this evening," he whispered to her, as he turned her face toward him and kissed her lightly in the falling rain."

Chapter 26

Secrets from the Grave

Wednesday Morning at 7:00 A.M., Amirah saw Fauziah seated at a corner table, alone and waiting for her. A newspaper lay flat and unopened before her. Her palms were lying flat down on the front page. Her shoulders slumped wearily over the headline. Her hair was loosely combed and as Amirah drew closer, she could see Fauziah had been crying. Fauziah was obviously lost in her own thoughts and did not see Amirah approaching.

"Fauziah," Amirah queried, softly, "Is anything wrong?"

Fauziah looked up through her tears, and exclaimed, "You don't know? You haven't heard?"

"Heard what?" Amirah was almost frightened at the sound of her own voice. She had never seen her friend so distraught.

"Ma…Ma…Maleeka has been killed!"

The news hit Amirah like a thunderbolt. Her jaw dropped and her hands went to her face, as if she were protecting herself from the bad news. The patio of the café seemed to swirl about her, as she grabbed the edge of the chair opposite Fauziah and crumbled into it.

The shock was too much to absorb at once. Amirah had already seen way too much suffering and now this new horror, right here in Paris, was upon her. She felt her sorrow turn to anger as she fought back the tears. The lessons learned from survival in Syria kicked in. There would be time to mourn. Now was the time to cope. She had to know what happened, plan for what might happen and comfort her friend.

"Oh, Amirah, we should have known. Those husbands, all those angry men. It had to be one of them. She took those cases, and put herself in danger to help those women. We should have known. Maybe we should have been more careful and not encouraged her to get involved. Maybe none of us should have been involved. One of the women we helped posted things on social media to get the information to other women. Perhaps some of the men saw it. They might come after us next."

"Fauziah, listen to me. You could not have known how things would turn out for Maleeka. We don't even know that it was the men. It could have been a random hate crime. Many women are victims of murder in France each year. There is nothing else we could have done. It's not our fault. We have to be strong now and not feel sorry for ourselves. We must honor Maleeka's life and never forget why she died. This tragedy is a flash of lightning across our lives. I thought I had left behind the terror and hatred that destroyed my country, but no one is safe from violent people anywhere. We know Maleeka's death is a message from the grave. We do not want to face it but now we must. No one is safe, even here in Paris," Amirah said.

Fauziah reached for Amirah's hand. "I must tell you some things about Maleeka you may not know. She told me a couple of months ago that she was pregnant and I advised her to talk to Reza. He confirmed they did talk, but in confidence, so I don't know all the details of their conversation. You know, the patient's privacy rights and all. She was keeping the relationship with her lover a secret from her father, but when she became pregnant, she was having difficulty figuring out what to do, where to go and what to tell her father."

"I didn't know you knew, but she came by the *Louvre* last week and told me she had met the love of her life and was planning to marry him and move to the United States. I didn't tell anyone. She truly loved him and was planning a future with him, and wanted to continue her work with the Muslim women here in Paris. However, she was very sad about leaving her family and friends, but her lover and husband-to-be was going back to join his father and brother in a very successful law practice in Atlanta and she saw it as a fresh start. She had been invited to join them in the practice while she continued to pursue her work helping women. She was facing a lot of challenges with these decisions."

"I did not know about the law practice and that their plans had gone that far," said Fauziah. "Any of the Muslim men might have found out about her relationship and maybe they wanted to kill her. Maleeka had many admirers and any of them could be guilty of her murder. Oh, I can't believe she's dead."

"Yes, she was a precious friend to us, and we will do everything we can to make sure her killer is found and punished. Now think about this. Since the man she loved was Jewish, she knew her father would disapprove and say water and oil don't mix, and make her end it, so I don't think she ever told him. If she never told him, the imam would not have been angry with her because he would not have known about it. I think that clears him of suspicion, at least as far as we're concerned. I don't even think she told her mother or any of her immediate family."

"I don't know. The imam did know about our services to help the Muslim women and I'm sure he didn't approve of that. I know the imam is against interfaith marriages. Reza and I talk about this a lot. I'm still a Muslim, although he converted to Christianity. Living together would be difficult for a couple whose religious faiths are very different. I think the imam loved her too much and was too proud of her accomplishments to hurt his own daughter. I know he thought we were too liberal in our counseling and working with Muslim women, but I think her perpetrator remains a mystery," Fauziah said. "We don't really know who is guilty. I don't know anyone who has been the victim of an honor killing here, do you?"

"Honor killings do happen here. My father would never do anything like that, but the statistics are terrifying. According to reports, five thousand women are victims worldwide each year. However, advocacy groups suspect that number is actually greater than twenty thousand. Still, I don't think the imam had anything to do with his daughter's death."

"Do you remember when she mentioned to us that she worked in *Provence* and was discovering things about the art there? She thought maybe they were involved in selling fraudulent works of art and faking the records of ownership. It was something about provenance of the paintings. She knows more about the art world and its criminal activity than I," Fauziah said.

"Of course, I remember, and that was a very dangerous situation for her. I'm sure she was contemplating what to do, but they could have suspected she was guilty of spying and reporting them to the police," said Amirah. "The faking of masterpieces is more common than people realize and it is big business for thieves."

"What will you do with all the designs you drew for the ads for the Muslim women's groups? We have to continue the work somehow, but I don't want to get Olivia in trouble. She's married with children in Antony and she could be putting herself in danger with her counseling. Maybe we should just throw the designs away, and turn our attention to other things for a while."

"No, we will continue. I made good designs. We're willing to carry on her work even though she's gone. Can you believe we were just with her and now we're talking about her death?"

Fauziah sighed, "We never know what a day holds for us. Poor, poor Maleeka. I don't think the Muslim men will like it when they learn you designed flyers and ads for her. They could cause trouble for both of us."

"I want you to stop thinking about this now," said Amirah.

"Reza has contacts with Amnesty International and deals with the cultures of Muslim families who feel shamed by what they consider sexual misconduct of female relatives. It harkens back to the Dark Ages and here we are in the twenty-first century dealing with these violent practices. I will talk it over with him tonight and get any insights he might have. Plan to come to dinner this week. In the meantime, I want you to be very careful," said Fauziah.

"What a world we live in. I've not been sleeping well. Syrian men came to the house early in the morning two days ago," Amirah continued. "They asked my father a lot of questions. I pretended to be asleep, but I listened and heard things I didn't like."

Fauziah set down her latte, "Things like what?"

"Things about paintings and storing them or moving them. I just couldn't understand everything they said, but I had a sense my father was being threatened by somebody. Maybe it was my former mother-in-law, or maybe these people could be nefarious Syrians or Middle Easterners. I don't want to complain to you."

"You're not complaining. These are serious concerns, and girlfriends listen to each other. You know that. Tell me more."

"I thought maybe they were talking about my paintings for the art exhibit, but it was something else."

"Like what?"

"I don't know, but I don't like it. Father never mentions it.

He's keeping it a secret."

"Please talk to Reza. He has influence with the refugees and connections through the university and the International Church. One of them might be able to help you," Fauziah said.

The waiter appeared and asked, "What may I get you, ladies?"

"*Peut-être un café Turc, s'il vous plaît,*" said Amirah.

"Bring us two *croque monsieurs, aussi, s'il vous plait.*"

"I've already had a little breakfast with Father this morning," said Amirah.

"You are too thin, Amirah. I want to fatten you up. You're in France. You must eat better. I'm ordering for us."

"*Merci*, I love the food and coffee here, but my nerves take away my appetite sometimes. I'll be able to handle this *croque monsieur*, even though it will add pounds on me by this afternoon."

"Nothing for you to worry about. Some of the French look anorexic to me — all bones. Not healthy. We need to eat more. How's your work at the *Louvre*?"

"The job is going well. I think my art is better. If I get only four hours sleep at night, I can't concentrate very well the next day."

"Well, it's not affecting your looks. You don't look tired. I really think Reza will be able to help you solve the mystery of the Syrians and Yousif."

"Thanks for inviting me this morning. We will push through, I'm sure."

Amirah looked around the little *café-librairie*. "I've always loved this little place. It is cozy and there are many different nationalities and languages being spoken. I often wonder what plots and schemes take place here. Anyway, tell me some good news. What are you and Reza doing these days?"

"Well, Reza and I are starting a Thursday night language class for refugees at the International Church and forty people have signed up already. One new student is a Syrian named Houssain. Do you know him?"

"No, I don't, but Alex mentioned a patient named Houssain, who turned out to be a very interesting case. Ask him if he was in the hospital a short time ago."

"I will. You try to come if you can," said Fauziah.

The waiter brought their *croque monsieurs.* "Right now, let's enjoy breakfast. Even if you don't eat all of it, I want to see a good try. I'll speak to Reza and I want you and Alex to come for dinner soon."

They sipped their coffee and ate some of the *croque monsieurs.* The restaurant was getting busier just like *Café de la Lumière* did every morning, except the customers here were mainly Middle Eastern, South American and North African men with a sprinkling of American university tourists. Bookshelves were lined with the writings of scholars, famous authors and diverse revolutionaries, as well as obscure books of poetry, cooking and travel. "I have a gift for you today — a new writer," said Fauziah. "Well, he's dead, but part of his writing concerned the plight of Middle Eastern women." She handed Amirah a book of Nizar Qabbani's poems.

Amirah received the gift like a gold treasure. Opening the book, she turned a few pages and read some lines. 'The female doesn't want a rich man or a handsome man or even a poet. She wants a man who understands her eyes if she gets sad, and points to his chest and says: Here is your home country.' Such an exquisite book by the greatest Syrian poet you have given me. Thank you, dear Fauziah."

"Though he lost his wife in a dreadful war, his deep pain brought forth meditative poetry full of strength," Fauziah said.

"Father might find the words too upsetting. Since we escaped, he tries to keep all things innocent for me. But I can never be innocent again. He used to be a prolific reader, but now literature is painful for him. Thank you so much." Amirah wrapped her hands around the warm cup of coffee and lifted it to breathe in the dark aroma before sipping another taste. "I love this pungent Turkish coffee."

"Reza and I are sorry we missed going to the fundraiser art show last night, but we needed to go to our international planning meeting at the Hertzes' *appartement* in *Montmartre.* Do you think you, Alex and Yousif can come to our next meeting? asked Fauziah. "Reza will be the speaker."

"I would love to, but I don't know Alex's schedule and I don't think Father will come. I might be able to persuade him, although he works late at the carpet shop every night."

"We're inviting Yousif anyway," said Fauziah, as she continued to sip her coffee. "Really I don't understand why Yousif would not get out and enjoy our fellowship. It isn't healthy for him to stay in his *appartement* all the time. Perhaps he is afraid." They finished their coffee and left the *café.*

"Thank you again, Fauziah, for simply being a friend. I need to confide these things in you that I would not share with anyone else." They began walking down the boulevard together until Fauziah came to the street leading her to another meeting. Amirah put her gift book in her large bag and the two friends embraced. Amirah continued walking to her metro stop. As the crowd dissipated and the sidewalk became less jam-packed, she saw two men coming toward her. That is the last thing she remembered.

Chapter 27

Kidnapped

Wednesday afternoon, her captors shoved her into the back seat of a van and slid the door shut. They taped her mouth, blindfolded her and pulled a burka over her head. One of them grabbed her shoulders and shook her, but she was numb and couldn't think or feel clearly, as she drifted in and out of consciousness. The driver sped away as she went blank again. When she awakened, she heard an awful guttural voice from the driver threaten her in Arabic: "Be quiet, Amirah. I'm warning you. If we are stopped, make no sound or you and your father will die!"

Amirah was shocked the kidnappers knew her name and referred to her father. She must protect her father. Were these the men who came to her father's house the other night? Were these the men who killed Maleeka Mansur? The questions were flying through her mind.

She wanted to rub her sore eyes, but her hands were bound. She could not speak or see, but she could worry. Amirah worried about Yousif and if her ex-mother-in-law had instigated her kidnapping. Was Ibrahim behind these kidnappers because he was jealous of her father? Some of the Muslim men hated her independent spirit. Maybe they wanted Yousif to help them in some way or maybe the Muslim men were infuriated by the ads she had designed for Maleeka's law practice. They hated all her art. They hated her dating Alex. She began plotting various escapes, as the van proceeded to an unknown destination.

The driver veered off the expressway and after a short, bumpy ride, he turned onto a rough gravel road. After a few minutes, he stopped the van and got out. She heard him walk away from the van and then heard men talking. When the driver returned to the van, he said, "Maslan, take her to the basement."

Maslan grabbed her. She did as she was told, limping on her cramped legs which had been constricted for hours. At least she knew one captor's name — Maslan. He pulled her out and led her through a yard where she heard chickens scratching and cooing along the path. Every French provincial village had an array of farmhouses, and judging from the distance they had traveled and the temperature, she assumed they were in the South of France. Entering through a heavy creaking wooden door, Amirah was led down a few steps to a basement, before she turned to her kidnapper and said, "I need to go to the bathroom." Maslan turned on the stairs and asked the driver in Arabic, "Can she use the toilet before I put her in the basement?"

"Yes," said the coarse driver, with vulgar Arabic cursing that Amirah could not fully translate. Her blindfold and burka headpiece were removed along with the tape from her hands. Her eyes had been covered so long, she squinted in the light and rubbed them hard. The bathroom might be a possible breakout route in the future, she thought, but there was no window.

"Okay, that's enough, come on out, Amirah," said Maslan, as he rattled around in what sounded like the kitchen. Maslan rebound her hands, put the blindfold on her, and taped her mouth.

She remembered Maslan's face, because he was the first one she saw coming toward her before she lost consciousness yesterday on the street. He had sprayed her with the drug, whatever it was. That drug gave her the dry mouth and thirst she felt. She must have been unconscious all night. Maslan led her to a chair and pressed her into it. Before long in the silence of the basement, he brought her tea and a soggy sandwich. As he removed the tape from her mouth, she jumped from the burn and sting her lips felt. He loosened the binding from her hands, allowing her to eat and drink at the tiny table in the basement. Then he again bound her in the chair and taped her mouth.

She sat in the darkness all afternoon hearing footsteps and voices upstairs. Amirah couldn't place where or when she had heard Maslan's voice, but she recognized his speech as the Arabic spoken in her home town of Aleppo. The drug from yesterday was confusing her. Never having taken drugs in her life, she feared she might become addicted or endangered by them.

Determined to be an ideal prisoner and cause no trouble, she wanted to make Maslan her friend. If only he would unbind her mouth and talk to her. Timing was important, and she would choose her words carefully. She was praying to both Allah and the Christian's God as best she could. Either way, her prayers were answered when Maslan walked over and took off her blindfold. "Amirah, if you keep your mouth shut and don't try anything stupid, I'll remove the tape from your mouth and this time I might do it more gently. Don't scream down here, because no one can hear you, except the guys upstairs and they might come down here and cut your throat if you make them angry."

Maslan then peeled off the tape from her mouth, untied her hands and offered her some water. "Thank you," she said. Perhaps she could learn what they were scheming to do with her father and her. She was certain Yousif would be searching to find her and praying for her safety.

Upstairs they heard the doors open and close, followed by heavy footsteps. Did they belong to the terrorists who were involved in the theft of the paintings? Did they kidnap her to get her father's cooperation? Her heart was beating wildly. Now that her blindfold was gone, could Maslan sense her fear and anxiety, as well as see it? He shuffled a deck of cards at the little table. "Let's play *Bastra*," Maslan said.

Amirah nodded yes, but said, "Is it right for us to play cards? I thought you might be forbidden to play cards."

"Nobody knows what we're doing down here." He moved the little table near her, and sat a small lantern on it. He dealt the cards and they played three or four games. The upstairs had calmed down.

"You're a good *Bastra* player," she said.

"No, you're just no challenge," he said. "I get the boring jobs like watching you."

"You were in Aleppo. I recognized your accent."

"There is no Aleppo. It died."

"I'm from Aleppo. That's my home. I thought you were from there when I first heard you speak."

"It's not my home now. These men here with me are my home. We're all refugees. Nobody in Europe cares what happens to us. I lived in Germany for a year and they used us as laborers. They didn't want to help us," Maslan said.

"I never spent any time in Germany. I traveled through Lebanon, the Aegean Sea, of course, then Greece and last Paris."

Maslan didn't seem interested. "Be quiet. I don't want the men upstairs to hear us talking."

"It sounds like they have gone. It's very quiet up there."

"No, they're just sleeping."

"What's Ibrahim's interest in my father?"

"I told you to shut up."

Silence followed forever it seemed to Amirah. Then Maslan spoke, "Ibrahim wants your father to join us. Why shouldn't he? What is his future as a carpet salesman anyway? His talents are wasted. Ibrahim figures Yousif will do anything to save you, so you're our little insurance."

Amirah had suspected all this involved Yousif, so she dropped the theory about her former mother-in-law's involvement. Forget that. It was Yousif, her father, who had been a brave rebel in the Syrian conflict. She was listening and learning. "We hope my mother and two brothers will come and join us and we can live as a family again. I hope one day to return to Aleppo."

"Dream on. Aleppo is dead and gone, unless we re-capture it."

"Why do they want my father? What can he do?" she asked.

"Your father will come around. He's a very tough guy. He led the White Helmets and the FSA." Maslan rose and started for the stairs. "There's no rest for us."

"I don't know what group you were in, Maslan, but my dad fought with the FSA until they started selling weapons to ISIL. Everyone was intoxicated on death and destruction. It makes me sick to think about it." Silence prevailed again. Maslan came back down the stairs and sat down.

Amirah remembered her days in Aleppo and felt sure Mazlan had gone to her school.

"I went to Al-Abdul Elementary School."

"So?"

"I was there the day the Syrian government bombed it for the last time. My friends and I were preparing the annual art exhibit, hanging our artwork and welcome posters. After I went home that day, the bombs hit the school. When the bombs stopped, I ran through the bloody streets — bodies of children were everywhere." Amirah fell silent for a few moments. "I fasted, cried and prayed three days, but the bombs kept coming. Why would a leader destroy schools and hospitals? Syrian soldiers were no longer humans, but monsters. Believe me, I knew hate then. Were you there, Maslan? Do you remember that time?"

"Yes," he said, as he put the cards in the box. "I went to that school too, and I was there when those bombs were dropped. I left the next day and joined the resistance. I'm going to bring the vengeance of Allah to those infidels who destroyed our families and everything good. I think I'll slice the heads off everyone who caused that pain."

"I understand your rage, because I feel it too. Can we ever rebuild our town and school?"

"Shut up, Amirah. I'm going upstairs to check on things. Don't try anything stupid, because the guys upstairs are ruthless if you cross them."

Chapter 28

Evil Intent

By Wednesday afternoon Youssif had searched everywhere for Amirah with no luck. He had not seen or heard from her in twenty-four hours. He suspected Ibrahim, his old enemy, was seeking revenge. Ibrahim summoned him and Yousif accepted.

The taxi arrived for Yousif and he jumped in. "*40 Rue Des Rosiers*," said a determined Yousif to the taxi driver. He would stop Ibrahim before he executed his malicious plans. As Syrian rebels, both Ibrahim and he had taken part in the peaceful protests against the Syrian regime. When the horrendous retaliation from the regime began its atrocious persecutions and executions, Ibrahim and he fought together against it. But Ibrahim changed. Although he hated the president's atrocities, he himself was guilty of unspeakable terror against any Syrians who opposed him. Yousif could no longer trust Ibrahim.

Yousif jumped out at the *Marché Aux Puces*. Striding through the aisles of stalls and vendors, he passed people of every nationality and creed. All the corners were filled with the aromas of smoke from the tobacco pipes of the Middle Eastern men.

French men and women sipped their coffees. Somalis congregated and displayed their wares, and the Eastern European women smiled seductively at Yousif as he passed. The international bazaar intrigued and lured everyone with arts, antiques, Persian rugs, Turkish jewels and dogs. Yousif had never seen so many dogs under one roof, but the Parisians loved their dogs. This was the fascinating and cosmopolitan Paris that reminded him of the cultural trappings of Aleppo before the Civil War stripped its bones of coverings.

Turning the corner to Ibrahim's booth, Yousif faced a dark-skinned, heavy set man with a day-old beard, sitting between two muscled men with long hair, black piercing eyes and *keffiyehs* on their heads. "*Salaam*," said Yousif to Ibrahim, ignoring the other two.

"Yousif, my friend, *Salaam, Alaikum.*" Ibrahim's mouth was easily filled with vile false flattery. "My friends and I are happy you accepted our invitation to meet here this afternoon," said Ibrahim. Yousif knew the soul and deceitful heart of this shameful scoundrel.

"Ibrahim, I am here for one reason. I'm warning you. Don't lay a hand on Amirah. Tell me your terms and keep in mind, I have terms too."

Ibrahim guffawed and said, "Well, now, listen to Yousif, the rug salesman. Since when do you make the terms of my deals? Who do you think you are, Yousif? You are a nobody now. I can make or break you, my little pawn. You do not know how to find your wife and sons and you truly have no idea about their location in the camp or if they've been moved. If it pleases me, I can arrange for their passage, but if you displease me, I can arrange for nasty things to happen to them. I hold all the chips, so now you listen to me."

"I'm listening. What about Amirah? Where is she?"

"I expect you to cooperate with us. You can meet Samir Shabab this afternoon for starters in *Aix-en-Provence.* You must find with him the fastest way to get arms to our group in Syria. We need a new attack plan for the strategic northwest areas of Aleppo. We want you back in our forces. Your countrymen need you. It's that simple," said Ibrahim. "You're wasting your time and talents."

"I don't want to be a rebel anymore. I thought I could help Aleppo. Yes, I thought we could save Syria and preserve it for our families, but now I know there is only heartache and grief for all. You're older and should be wiser too. I don't want to be part of your schemes, because your idea of helping Syria is to help yourself. I saw your soul a long time ago, Ibrahim. You should stop while it's possible. Either the authorities in Paris or the scums you work for in Syria will trap you and take you down soon enough.

"You do this and your services will not be required ever again. I no longer need you to harbor the art. I think someone may be watching your *appartement* anyway. We have Arab neighbors who can be trusted not to rat on our activities but other new neighbors have been brought to our attention as quite untrustworthy. They trust the police more than us. Can you imagine?" Ibrahim and his associates sneered. "I have all of that under control, but you can do bigger things and you will in order to protect your family. By the way, do you know Amirah has been going to the International Church?"

"No, I didn't know, but I don't think that concerns you."

"Oh, I think it concerns you, Yousif. Your daughter is defiling herself by going to that place as well as taking art classes and working in the *Louvre,* surrounded by scandalous paintings by infidel artists." Ibrahim shook his head. "But are you encouraging her to be friends with that American doctor? You're losing control, Yousif. You need to let us handle your personal problems. You saw what happened to beautiful Maleeka, the imam's daughter in the paper, didn't you? And your precious Amirah wrote the ads for that agitating Maleeka who was always stirring up women with her radical ideas. Disgusting."

Yousif retorted, "If you had anything to do with that murder, you will feel the flames of hell soon."

"You think I might be beyond redemption, but do not assume I had anything to do with her death, and I will take my chances with Allah. He might be pleased with me for killing the people and running the businesses I've built. Yousif, I'm getting us some coffee." Ibrahim motioned to Abdul who disappeared from the stall for the coffee.

"I want to know where Amirah is and what to do to get her out."

"You need to take brotherly advice from me. It is time for her to obey Sharia law and marry one of our own and have children. If she doesn't behave in a more modest way, you really should take her out yourself. Paris is no place for a free thinker like your Amirah. You spoil her too much. I tell you, Yousif, if you do not do this little task I'm giving you, she could be the victim of a very unpleasant death, but not by me," Ibrahim said.

"You are not living in Syria anymore, Ibrahim. The laws are different here. Will you ever change your ways? Why must you involve an innocent child in your plans for your own delusions of glory? You have thousands of recruits according to your websites and blogs. Why force someone who sees you for what you are to work with you?" Yousif asked.

"Excuse me, Yousif. Amirah is not the little innocent you think. She's becoming entirely too Westernized, but I have other business with you right now. You are to leave this afternoon at four o'clock. I will send a driver for you at your *appartement*. Be ready. He will take you to the *Gare du Nord*. There you will board the TGV and arrive in *Aix-en-Provence* tonight by ten. Jamal will take you to your first meeting with our operative Shabab from Syria."

Abdul returned with the coffee. Ibrahim took a cup and offered one to Yousif, who gulped the contents and set the cup down. "If you expect cooperation from me, I want Amirah released and I want assurance that my family is alive and well, on their way out of Greece and bound for Paris."

"And I want to be King," said Ibrahim, laughing with his two bodyguards. "I can give you assurance your family is alive, and your son Rasheed has been released from the *Mèdicins Sans Frontières* hospital. But until you have this meeting with our operative and satisfy him with the plans you two lay out, I cannot guarantee any family reunion. Come now, Yousif, you know you are wasting your time at the carpet shop. You were meant for more important things."

"When will my family arrive in Paris?" Yousif asked.

"Now that is a good question, but I have a man on the ground who is watching them, and he can bring them with passports in two days or he can also make it impossible for them to leave, so you don't want to mess up."

"So where are the paintings you want me to deal with?" Yousif asked.

"Ah, yes, where are the paintings we have stolen? Most have already been sold to our private buyers or museums. Frankly, a few of the paintings have made so much money that we've already bought more arms than we can possibly use in a lifetime. In fact, we have so many arms now, I'll have to dump some of them. It's quite amazing how much support we have. Get with the program and get with it fast, my friend," Ibrahim said. "Be ready."

"Yes, this afternoon, I will be waiting." Yousif then exited the booth.

Ibrahim turned to Abdul. "Poor Yousif. He should never have forsaken us, but tomorrow will be his day of reckoning. It is miraculous to hold the power of life or death over someone, Abdul. I never dreamed of this as a child, but it is my destiny now."

Abdul nodded assent and sat down to enjoy the pleasant smoke flavor of his *argile* with Ibrahim.

Chapter 29

Gypsy Prophecy

Late Wednesday afternoon, Alex arrived in Paris and telephoned Inspector Fournier to meet him at the *Musée d'Orsay* with updates on Maleeka and Ibrahim. Everyone knew now that it was the daughter of the imam who had been murdered near the *Trocadero.* Stopping briefly at the *Café des Flores* in the *Saint-Germaine Des Prés quartier,* he ordered an espresso and sandwich as he glanced through *Le Figaro* for news. On his way to the *Musée,* he stopped by the pharmacy.

"*Bonsoir, mon ami. Ca va*?" Doctor Jay the pharmacist asked, as Alex entered.

"Allergies again. A little Benedryl will clear them out."

"Sure thing." Doctor Jay handed some meds to Alex. "I'm glad you came by. I remembered that burglary case in the sixteenth *arrondissement* you were interested in. You asked if 'Devil's breath' might have been used to knock out the victims during the burglary." Dr. Jay handed Alex his receipt.

"So, you do think the 'Devil's breath' was used?"

"Burundanga or 'Devil's breath' is used by criminals in Colombia and it's brought into Paris all the time, so it makes sense.

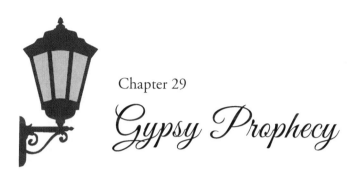

But chloroform is accessible too."

"I see," Alex remarked.

"A day or two ago a couple of men stopped in here, wanting some mace to give their girlfriends for protection and safety, but they asked a lot of questions about knock-out drugs. I didn't think much about it then, but later, it raised my suspicions."

"Did you know them?"

"No, I didn't know them or recognize their accents for that matter. But after you and I talked about the burglaries, I thought there might be some connection."

"That drug could have been used on Philippe and Isabella in the robbery of the Dalles. I'll talk to Inspector Fournier tonight."

"You take care." Dr. Jay held the door for Alex.

Alex liked walking the Paris streets in the evening. It cleared his mind and refreshed his soul.

As he approached *Musée d'Orsay*, he saw Sylvana, the Romanian gypsy prophetess with her big skirts, bustles and long-flowing black hair. A big ring rolled toward Alex and stopped at his feet. He picked it up. "Do you know who the rightful owner is?" she asked, watching him with her penetrating dark eyes.

"No, but I'm sure you do." Alex examined the eighteen-carat gold ring and the Arabic inscription inside. "Will you explain this to me?"

"You still do not understand the spiritual dimensions of your life, but you have been chosen to learn. Long before you ever heard of prophecy, your path was being formed. I know you are working on the case of Maleeka, the imam's daughter, who was my friend. I know her killer and he has the stolen art you're looking for. Do you believe me?" Sylvana asked.

"Yes, I do. What else are you going to tell me? Who is the killer and who has the art?" Alex asked, examining the ring.

"My dear child, I cannot answer more. I can only reveal and

deliver so much. You are on a special journey this time. You are touching the corners of the universe in mind, body and spirit. This is your assignment. A father is angry, but terrified for his family. You must go and help him."

"What? Who is the father? Who is the killer?"

"You will know in due time. Your spirit is still the child I saw fifteen years ago the first time you came to the French Open in Paris with your father. You're that same boy, and you have been blessed. Your questions have always been the right ones and you have always been observant. Tell me, haven't my prophecies always brought you closer to your goals?"

"I think so, Sylvana, but I'm a little confused right now."

"This gold ring will lead you where you need to go. Follow it wisely and don't be afraid for yourself or others. Wear it or carry it until you find the thieves who stole your godmother's paintings and until you bring the one you love back to Paris," as she turned to go.

"Wait. What do you mean, bring the one you love back to Paris?"

Alex looked at the glistening ring for a moment and Sylvana disappeared. He called for her, but she had vanished. Who was she talking about? What father? Did she mean Philippe or Yousif or his own father? He knew it would be wise to pay attention to her puzzling statements and predictions, because she had been right so many times before. He called Philippe, but his phone went to voicemail, so he left a message asking if everything was all right. Next, he called Yousif, but no one answered, so he left another message.

He entered the *Musée d'Orsay* and texted Inspector Fournier.

"Inspector, are you in the *Musée*?"

"Yes, in the coffee shop. I'm waiting for you," Inspector Fournier texted.

Alex always looked at this exquisite building and pictured it in another era, as the romantic train station where the Orient Express boarded passengers for exotic destinations, such as Istanbul, Zagreb, Sofia and Belgrade. *Au revoir* to that time as there is no longer an authentic Orient Express, but visitors still feel the romance upon entering the renovated railway station, transformed into an Impressionist Art Gallery. He called Amirah and left a voicemail, "I'm in the *Musée d'Orsay.* Where are you? Would you call me when you get this? I want to see you as soon as possible. How's Yousif?"

He climbed the stairs to the restaurant, where he spotted Inspector Fournier. He ordered a *café au lait* and joined the Inspector at his table.

Fournier said, "It's a masterpiece, isn't it? No station can match this for restoration. *Voici le flair et style français.* Alex, did you know I used to dabble in painting?"

"No, you're kidding me. You've been keeping a secret."

"I don't take the time to do it much anymore, but I did win an award for best amateur drawing a few years ago. Painting steadies my nerves, and makes me more observant. I need to do it more. When I take time to paint, I see with a better eye, better vision in all aspects of life. You might not believe this, but I'm a better detective when I'm painting. I might be painting a street scene and unexpectedly I'll think of a detail of a criminal case I'm working on. Not only that, but it lowers my ridiculous blood pressure, which is way out of control."

"You know what, Fournier? I think you really are a Frenchman, talking art. No, seriously, I could use better focus and steadier nerves, but I can barely draw a stick figure. My work would be abstract--very abstract. I'll leave the painting to you and Amirah. Walking the streets of Paris at night and playing tennis relax me. You and I just don't have much spare time to do what relaxes us."

"Exactly. I don't have enough time to relax anymore because of this job. By the way, how's your art case going?"

"Hey, it's your case, too. I know you're helping me. What have you heard about Maleeka?"

"A little. It was a homicide. Imam Mansur, her father, is the most likely suspect, but no one has been arrested yet. Perhaps a very zealous Muslim man who thought she was too liberal could be the guilty one. That's the word on the street from your man Hilba. The coroner hasn't finished his report yet, but we should get that later tonight. How did you do in Antony?"

"I thought it was very successful. Dr. Anna Israel works for both the Jewish Restitution and Restoration Organization and the Israeli police. She's located hundreds of art works confiscated by the Nazis and returned them to Holocaust victims' families. She's already investigating the theft of the Dalles' art. Something doesn't jibe about her grandson Levi though. He says he's a Messianic missionary, but I think he's also working with Dr. Anna on her cases."

"Good for you. They'll help you more than Casseaux."

"I have a hunch Levi is working for the Israeli police too, just like Dr. Anna."

Alex's phone rang and he answered, "Reza, what's on your mind? She's missing! What? Where is he? I'll be right there."

Alex turned to Inspector Fournier, "Amirah is missing, and Ibrahim has set up a meeting between Yousif and Samir Shabab in *Aix-en-Provence* this afternoon. Could that mother-in-law be involved in this?"

"I doubt it."

They dashed for the exit. "I told her to never go out without Fauziah or me. She's been worried about some Middle Eastern Mafia and after seeing all the cases you gave me, filled with allegations against Ibrahim, I think it could be Ibrahim and his lackeys at the *Marché Aux Puces.* Put out a missing person alert at the station for Amirah."

"That's not a good idea. That might alert the wrong people."

Alex called Reza again. "When did Fauziah see her last? Okay, thanks."

"Fauziah had breakfast with her yesterday and has not been able to reach her all day. Yousif is furious."

"Shabab is on our terrorist list and we can't let Yousif meet him," said Inspector Fournier.

Alex said, "Reza is stalling Yousif at his office. He asked to borrow Reza's car for a few days. I think you need to visit Imam Mansur. Find out what's happening around the mosque. I'll take a taxi to Reza's office and make plans with Yousif. Get back with me as soon as you check out Mansur. Are you sure you should not call the police department about a missing person?"

"Oh, no, not missing persons. This is dealing with the dark side of Paris, if Ibrahim is involved. I'll check with Casseaux, as much as I hate to."

"I'll check with Dr. Anna and get back to you within the hour. We've got to get out of the city and find Amirah."

Chapter 30

Rescue Plan

Wednesday Night, the taxi careened to a stop at the university. Alex jumped out and dashed up the steps to the open door of Reza's office, where he and Yousif were talking.

Alex said, "We are going to find Amirah, Yousif, but you've got to tell us what you said to Ibrahim today."

"I don't have time to explain the whole situation. Ibrahim wants me to meet Samir Shabab tonight in *Aix-en-Provence.* He was sending a car with a bodyguard to drive me to the *Gare du Nord,* where I was to board the TGV for *Aix.* He said Jamal, a rebel in my White Helmets squadron back in Syria, would meet me there, but I doubted that," Yousif said, "After considering everything, I decided I had to take matters into my own hands. Ibrahim simply cannot be trusted."

"Who's Jamal and the White Helmets squadron?" asked Reza.

"A rebel group I commanded in Syria against Hamoud. Jamal was one of my best fighters. I haven't seen or heard from him since our days in Syria. I don't believe he's in France, or that he's involved with Samir Shabab, but if I don't do what Ibrahim says, he might kill Amirah."

"None of us trusts Ibrahim," Alex said. "He's been on the terrorist list for years, but someone else is involved in this kidnapping, I think. I put in a call for Dr. Anna. She'll have information for us."

Yousif said, "If Ibrahim lays a hand on Amirah, I'll kill him. He claimed to be helping the rebels against Hamoud, who continues to kill thousands of innocent civilians, but Ibrahim is delusional. He wants power and wealth only for himself, just like Hamoud. He has turned on the people he wanted to liberate in the beginning."

"Inspector Fournier told me the police have never arrested, charged or convicted him for anything, although they claim to be watching him," said Alex.

"It's a joke, Dr. Alex. They're watching hundreds of illegal refugees, some of whom are criminals, but most are hard-working like me. We don't need people like Ibrahim. He stays under the radar of the police and dreams of restoring Syria. He's primarily out for Ibrahim."

"Whatever he said about meeting Shabab his friend tonight, I'm against it. It's a set-up. Your comrade Jamal won't be there either." Alex said.

Yousif paced the floor. "Ibrahim made it clear he doesn't like Amirah being your friend or the way she dresses or her art. He wants to choose a good Syrian man for her to marry. Where would they take her? Is there anyone we can talk to?"

"Hold on," Alex said. "Amirah told me men came to your *appartement* last week late at night and you talked about paintings with them. She heard your talk, but couldn't understand it, so what was going on? Think, where would Ibrahim take Amirah, and who is helping him? Would he take her where he has the cache of paintings?"

"Oh, he's involved, but I don't know where they go."

Alex added, "I have a contact in Antony who is a veteran pro at locating stolen paintings and the thugs who deal in them. Maybe Ibrahim is working for someone else, like her ex-mother-in-law or those guys who came to your *appartement* and left some art with you. And maybe one of them kidnapped Amirah. Oh, and there was an art raid yesterday of the Russian Mikhail Horowitz in the sixteenth *arrondissement.*"

"Keep me out of anything else," said Yousif. "I know Mikhail. I believe Russian thieves joined Hamoud in committing war crimes. They're still operating with some Syrians in a combined Mafia. I can't get involved with the law, because I know what could happen to me, a Syrian refugee. The French have always been good at expelling people they don't want. One slip and Amirah and I could be gone. France would not hesitate to rid itself of two members of its teeming refugee population. I may be killed tonight, but I don't want to risk getting sent back."

Reza spoke, "Yousif, we're not going to let them deport you. I have connections and I can vouch for you, but you need to give us any information you can about Ibrahim and his gang. Forget about what could happen with the law. Think what can happen to Amirah if we don't find her."

Yousif said, "You guys know that Russian Mafia are all over Europe. They're into arms and drug trafficking, extortion and kidnapping. You name it and they're there, including smuggling guns and people. One of the guys who helped get the arms into Syria was living in a one billion euro estate with stolen paintings all over the walls. I think he was sent back to Russia. Nobody is as mean as they are."

Alex said, "Yousif, you might never arrive in *Aix* if you try to meet Ibrahim's contacts tonight. A train collision, an execution — anything's possible. We will get Amirah. Just tell us about your involvement with Ibrahim and these guys. I'll call Dr. Anna again. She suspects the Syrian Mafia and may have missing puzzle pieces that could pull together a case against Ibrahim and the Mafia. We want to know why they're so interested in Holocaust Art."

Reza said, "The short story is that criminal elements of the Muslims believe the Holocaust cost their brothers their land. When the Jewish people returned to Israel after World War II, as you know, they were hardly welcomed by the Arabs; rather, they were attacked by them. All these old Biblical rivalries-Abraham and Ishmael and thousands of years of wars live in their hearts and are taught to their children. Stealing from the Jewish descendants is historical and natural for the Islamic extremists, who often work with Russian bad guys."

"Reza is right," said Yousif. "Even though Syrians have suffered horribly in this never-ending war, they have persecuted Israelis. And now anti-semites are trying to write the Holocaust out of history. Ibrahim not only hates the Jews, he also hates me because I don't want to participate in his schemes to take over Syria again. I think he would work as an agent for the Syrian government in Damascus only for more power."

"Can you think of any names you've heard Ibrahim mention?" asked Alex.

"Yes, now I remember. A man works with him — yes, someone he mentioned once — Rami, a guy who owns an *Arts and Antiquities Shop* in *Aix.* I think he steals a lot of art and sells it through that shop, and then buys weapons and explosives from the Russians. It would make sense to take Amirah where they work in the South."

"*Aix*, you think?"

"Somewhere in the South of France, maybe *Aix.* One time, I heard them mention *St. Emilion* for some operation, but Ibrahim is connected all over Europe. He recruits vulnerable Muslim refugees who don't have jobs. The money the art makes is used to fund Ibrahim and his operations," said Yousif. "I think that guy Rami hired the imam's daughter for advice on some of their art, and maybe she found out too much about what they were doing."

Alex's phone rang. "Yes, I see. No, we're not on our way anywhere yet. We're still in Reza's office, but we've got information. So, keep checking around. Okay, I'll get back with you soon."

"Who was it?" asked Reza.

"Inspector Fournier. He has received the coroner's report on the imam's daughter. She was three months pregnant and the killer wanted to be sure he killed the baby too," he said.

Reza added, "I should have notified someone or done something sooner. I'm partially to blame for this situation."

Alex asked, "What do you mean?"

Reza answered, "She came to me for counseling and told me she was pregnant. She was very much in love with the baby's father, but did not want her father or the community to know. I should have been more proactive. I advised her to go to a doctor and take a trip, leave the country until the baby was born and she would have time to think. I even suggested that she and the young man get married secretly, and then no one would need to know anything about the situation."

Alex asked, "Who was the man?"

Reza said, "She never would say. I was sure her father would not give his blessing to the couple. Having a baby out of wedlock is immoral behavior in most religions, but for the Muslim women, it could be a death sentence. She had not told her mother or anyone except me, as far as I know. I never saw her again, but Fauziah saw her once at a women's conference and she was actively speaking on behalf of all persecuted women. I feel so bad. What are we going to do, Alex?"

"Why don't you call Dr. Anna, Alex? She still hasn't called back," Yousif said.

"Hilba sent a text message that someone threatened to report him to the authorities if he didn't tell them where I was. The guy told Hilba that he was going to *Aix* to see Yousif."

Reza asked, "What can I do to help? What do we need to do?"

Alex said, "You take care of everything here. We'll stay in touch with you. Fauziah might hear from Amirah. You could call Mr. Hertz and find out if he's seen or heard anything. We're heading to *Aix*. We hope to hear from Dr. Anna soon."

Chapter 31

Golden Ring

Wednesday night, Alex called Dr. Anna again and this time he succeeded in reaching her. "Where is Amirah?" he asked.

"South of France. Use the gray Renault outside Reza's office. The keys are in it, and it's fitted with a satellite beacon. Fournier and Levi will join you in *St. Emilion.* We think that's where Amirah is being held."

"Let's go, Yousif. We're going to *St. Emilion*, instead of *Aix*."

Yousif said, "What about the men in *Aix* that I'm supposed to meet? How does Dr. Anna know that Amirah is in *St. Emilion*?"

Alex said, "We've got to trust her. She's been finding people for years, and she's got contacts all over the world. She probably knows more than the Paris police about these things."

"Well, okay then. I wanted to go alone to *Aix* to meet Ibrahim's men. I know their techniques and how to negotiate with them. Instead you want me to go with you to *St. Emilion* to find Amirah?"

"Obviously, Dr. Anna already knows something more than we do about Amirah's kidnapping."

"But will Dr. Anna want to help me, a Syrian refugee? Does she believe I am guilty of cooperating with them?"

"No, not at all. Besides, you may help her find missing links to the Paris art puzzle we're piecing together. Her knowledge of these criminals and their tactics is more comprehensive than you and I can imagine, Yousif. She knew about Ibrahim, although she didn't call him by name. Also we are supported by Inspector Fournier."

"If you're sure," said Yousif. "At least no one can identify and sabotage the car with Dr. Anna and the Mossad tracking us."

Good, Alex thought, as he texted Fauziah to go visit Mrs. Pilon and learn more about Ibrahim.

With Yousif in the passenger seat, Alex got behind the wheel, started the engine and left Paris with the GPS set for *St. Emilion.*

"Alex's cell phone rang. "Hello, Fauziah. What is it? Did Reza tell you what's going on?"

"Yes, he did. I'm with one of the curators at the Louvre. Are you wearing that ring the gypsy lady gave you?" Fauziah asked.

"Yes, I'm embarrassed to say."

"Don't be. I know Sylvana, the gypsy prophetess. Sometimes she comes to the International Church to talk to Reza and me. One Sunday she showed us the famous gold ring you're wearing. It's a warrior's ring that belonged to Yusuf al-Azma," said Fauziah.

"Yusuf who?" Alex asked.

"He was the leader of the Syrian forces who fought against France in the Battle of Maysalun in 1920 after World War One. Get your history book out later, but his followers strongly opposed French rule in the newly established Arab Kingdom of Syria."

"Fauziah, I'm with Yousif. I can't talk unless this is very important. Where's this conversation going? Does the ring tell us any information we can use?" asked Alex.

Fauziah said, "Just hold on and listen. The French and Americans have claimed to support human rights, but have not always followed through when it affected their interests. The French wanted Syria for themselves and had a very sophisticated army to back up their power. Young Arabs formed groups to oppose any rule by the French and advocated complete Arab independence, but this leader, Yusuf al-Azma, owner of this ring, led his troops against the French army."

"Okay, Fauziah, I'm still not sure where all this is going."

"Just give me a few more minutes. He led a small band of ill-equipped soldiers and civilians against the French army. Although he knew he could never defeat them, he did it for history to show the French government that they had no legitimacy with the Arabs. He was killed in battle, but his sword and ring have come to symbolize the constant desire of Syrians to maintain their independence and to fight against those who persecute and kill them for their own selfish interests."

"Okay, Fauziah, thank you for this information about the ring, so do you think possessing the ring can help us in our mission ?" asked Alex.

"According to Sylvana, the ring says, 'You have a heart for Syria'. Rescuing Amirah and capturing these criminals are part of a larger struggle to restore peace and security to Syria. You have the blessings of generations behind you."

Alex said, "That sounds too noble for me. I don't know what it means for us, but I hope it means God is with us today. Now listen, go by the *Préfecture de Police* and ask for Captain Casseaux. Tell him you are the sister of the deceased imam's daughter, and get any new information and text me immediately. Go by *Café de la Lumière* and see if Hilba has information for us. If you don't find him there, go to the *Trocadero* and asked his buddies if they know anything. Don't let anything slip and don't stop until you find him. We may need Hilba tonight."

Fauziah said, "Listen to me, Alex. Sylvana, the prophetess, obviously believes that you have the power with you to accomplish what you are trying to do. You must not doubt. Go, with the grace of the God who saved the children of Jacob and Ishmael in times just as dangerous as these."

"Thank you, Fauziah. Your brave words give me confidence. Here is the plan. Get out of the Louvre. When you find Hilba, ask him to go with you to Maya and Philippe's *appartement* building. If Mrs. Pilon is there, ask her if she's seen Ibrahim and tell her the police are looking for him. If she isn't there, Hilba can pick the lock and get into her office and bug it. I want you to look for anything that can help us — phone numbers, contacts, pictures, appointments, you know. Since I saw her talking to Ibrahim at the *Marché Aux Puces*, and despite the fact that she denied knowing him, I know a connection exists between them," Alex ended the call.

Fauziah headed for the police station.

Alex's phone was ringing. "Hello, Dr. Anna. I'm here with Yousif. Have you heard anything about Amirah or her location?"

"Yes, Alex, we know Amirah has been kidnapped, and we have an idea where she's been taken. We have infiltrated the art thieves and have a mole within, who is in a very precarious situation. I see you have not followed my advice to distance yourself from this, so I sent you the car, in order for us to keep up with you. We are expecting big arrests tonight by the Paris police and the Mossad in this joint operation."

"Ibrahim is still threatening Yousif and his family, unless he joins the Syrian Mafia. Ibrahim was sending two men to pick up Yousif this afternoon to take him to the *Gare du Nord* to meet a man who would accompany him to *Aix*. After the arrival in *Aix*, he was to meet Samir Shabab to talk business about a proposed organization. We thought the threat level was too high for Yousif; however, based on the intelligence you have provided, we're on our way to *St. Emilion.*"

On the cellphone Dr. Anna continued, "Alex, the men want to kill Yousif and pin the blame on him for the thefts. They will create a dossier about Yousif and his involvement, take credit with the police for finding a criminal and continue their crimes. The Mossad are near *Aix-en-Provence.* We are watching Ibrahim and his movements in Paris as well as his men in *Aix.* When you get to *St. Emilion,* you need to go to the *Château Grand Barrail* and wait for Fournier. Levi will arrive there and give you further instructions. Do not go on your own anywhere except where Levi tells you. We have Levi wired, so any conversations he has, we hear and record. Stay close to him.

Alex asked, "Dr. Anna, is this a job for Levi? He's just a missionary, isn't he?"

"Don't worry about Levi. He lived in a kibbutz and trained with the Israeli commandos. He can take care of all of you."

"Among the many old farmhouses is one owned by Mrs. Pilon and her brother, Rami, the owner of the *Arts and Antiquities Shop.*"

"I knew it. I knew she was deeply involved. Philippe is too trusting. I wouldn't be surprised if she's a crucial member of the organization," Alex said.

Dr. Anna said, "Just a word of warning, Alex. All may not be what it seems. Don't be too hasty in accusations." The call ended.

Yousif looked anxious, waiting for Alex to fill him in on the details of the conversation.

Alex said, "We're supposed to go to *St. Emilion* and meet Levi at the *Château Grand Barrail.* The Israeli police are going to move in on a farmhouse in *Aix-en-Provence.* It's a good thing you never met the men Ibrahim was sending to meet you this afternoon."

Yousif put his head in his hands and exclaimed, "Is she sure Amirah is in *St. Emilion*?"

"Calm down, Yousif. She didn't say. She has members of the Mossad at farmhouses on the look-out, but we must get to *St. Emilion*."

"This is looking bad to me. If I don't meet those men, Ibrahim will kill Amirah, wherever she is. I should contact him and tell him I'll meet with Shabab and Jamal, but I've just been delayed. I've got to do it my way," said Yousif.

"Yousif, Dr. Anna just told me those guys were planning to kill you. She knew Amirah had been kidnapped before we knew. She is watching from afar what happens to you and Amirah. Believe me," Alex said, she has the Mossad, the Israeli secret police, cooperating with the French police working on this case. Ibrahim knows where Amirah is as well as the paintings I'm looking for. We're going to follow the leads of Dr. Anna, the Mossad and the Paris Police."

Yousif said, "Where does she think Amirah is?"

"In a farmhouse. They've been watching Ibrahim, and they have videoed his frequent visits to this particular farmhouse, but there have also been other people who meet him there."

"Where is it?"

"Dr. Anna is texting the address to me, but she does not want us to go there without the protection of the Paris police and Israeli special forces," Alex said, handing the text message to Yousif.

Chapter 32

Winning Over

Wednesday night, Maslan was bored with his duties and removed the tape from Amirah's mouth and untied her hands. After serving her soup and water, he ate some himself.

Amirah spoke, "You and I know what it's like to be in school one day and see its ashes the next. All of our families know what bombing raids are in real time. It's hard to believe we survived."

"I saw more in Aleppo than you can ever imagine. No one cared."

"You and I care. Were your parents able to escape?"

"My father and uncle went to our relatives farther north and said they would send for us. I joined the rebels as soon as they were gone. My mother and sisters stayed in Aleppo, and I haven't heard from any of them. I'll probably never see them again."

"I don't know if my mother and brothers are in the Lesbos camp or not, and I don't know if they're safe. I hate this bloody war."

"At first, I believed the rebel resistance would make a difference and we could restore Syria, but the government treated us like anarchists, stripping us of our citizenship. When the filthy Russians got involved, they bombed everything. This world is gone for us. When my girlfriend left Aleppo to escape the war and came to Paris to study, I left the rebels. I came here and searched everywhere to find her, but I had no luck."

"So, you weren't a jihadist? You were truly fighting for the people of Syria."

"Yes, I believed the US, England or some government would help us. But instead Russia and Iran helped the despicable dictator destroy the country."

"Does your girlfriend know you're here?"

"No, she probably married someone and moved to another country. She was not like the typical religious girls. She liked dancing and pop music and hated wearing all those scarves. She wanted to dress like the Europeans. Crazy girl!"

Amirah said, "If she loved you, I don't think she would do that. I don't think she'd like what you're doing now either, do you?"

Maslan looked at Amirah for the first time, shook his head and said, "She wouldn't care what I'm doing. What's it all about? Money, power and connections win every time. We're the pawns in the wars. Women usually get a better deal in wars in this rotten world. I might as well be a martyr too. You know my girlfriend just wanted to go to school, be a teacher and get married. I hope she's getting to do those things."

"I'm sorry. First, you're mistaken. Women do not do well in any war. I believe that your girlfriend may still get to realize her dreams. She wants justice, freedom and peace in Syria against all odds, just as we do. She could have found it with you in Syria, but our government caused suffering and death. If leaders acted like godly men, not raging madmen like Ceausescu and Hitler, we could live in peace. Power and money can make evil rulers.

The world has lost its way, just as Mohammad and Jesus told us."

"Watch your mouth, Amirah. Even the walls may shake if you start using Allah and Jesus in the same breath. Dictators are adept at bulldozing peacemakers from any country. These guys I work with think they know everything. I don't even like them, but I've got no choice. That's the way a lot of Syrian men feel. What have you got to gain if you go against them? You're like a dead tree with no live branches, no connection to the earth and merely a speck without their group. This is my group."

"It's only your group because you haven't met the right kind of people yet. These people you are running with aren't interested in saving Syria. They're kidnappers and they hate my father. He truly loves Syria and I believe you do too. You should be true to yourself. You want to change Syria, and so do I. Paris is not our home. You and I are Syrians, first and foremost. My father and I would prefer to live in our homeland, but we don't expect to ever return."

"Your father should have stayed in Syria and fought. If he had died there, he would have died courageously, fighting for what he believed."

"How can you say that? My father was trying to save his family. I want to live where my family and generations of Syrians have always lived. We fought the Turks, the British and the French for independence. Somebody always wants what someone else has. We've had six Syrian Wars over territories and kings since 248 B.C. We have constantly been in a war against our Arab neighbors or Israel. Where is the hope? I see nothing but despair in Syria and its leadership. The government has aligned itself with despots." said Amirah. "The true Syrians need hope and eventually, they may triumph over their enemies, although it won't be in our lifetimes."

"You sound like a history book, Amirah."

"I know because my father read to me and taught me about heritage and family life as well as our history. But, I will tell you, Maslan, I learned two different lessons from different teachers. My history teachers taught me politics, but my father taught me faith and his religion. Sometimes these concepts are mixed together, but really they are different."

Maslan laughed. "You are a woman. You speak in riddles like a child. Our faith, religion and politics are the same. We must defend Islam against the invaders. You don't understand the duty of a man in the real world. You live in the world of art, fairy tales and raising children."

"My father did not teach me as a woman. He taught me as a child of Allah. We are all children of the great Allah, who saved Isaac and Ismael. You would be wise to pray and ask Allah to help you see the difference between what you call a fairy tale and what wise men have called a pillar of wisdom."

"I know the pillars of wisdom. They are prayer, obedience, charity and the Haj. I pray and do my duty. I do not need a second-hand lesson from a rug rat's daughter to teach me my duty to Allah."

"So, is it Allah who teaches you to insult my father? Are you cruel in Allah's name? Where did you get the idea that Allah wants you to ridicule others? The Koran forbids it. The Christian Bible forbids it. The essence of the third pillar is charity even for your enemies, and my father is very far from being your enemy. He is devoted to our culture, religion and way of life."

"You and your father are enemies of Islam, and you are helping the godless harm the faithful, so the prophet says that we must defend Muslims from harm. You've worshipped in other houses of worship. You even make pictures for heathens to decorate their houses, and you did those signs advertising that Muslim lawyer's business to help other women act like you."

"Your mind is confused, Maslan. You've been deceived by evil men."

"No, Amirah, our duty is to defend the faith. Our faith is under attack everywhere. No one cares what happens to us."

"Maslan, think. You have been deceived. We are not under attack by the French government or anyone else in Christian Europe. France has shown us charity and so has Europe. The United States has created a land of equality for all faiths. The Christians have their failures, God knows, but they still try. People in the United States have given more humanitarian aid to us than any country in the world."

"I don't believe that. The charity and aid of America and all other countries come with a big price, Amirah. They want our resources."

"You know so much about charity. Do you believe it is charitable under any condition to kidnap women, steal property, blackmail and intimidate the faithful? I just don't understand why you stay with these guys. You're smart enough to leave and make a life for yourself."

"You're getting on my nerves. We only do what our enemies have done to us. They make money and accumulate power, wealth and pleasure, but we do what we do to honor Allah. Think about this, Amirah. I'm a refugee from Syria with no degree, no home, and no family. How many people are interested in hiring me for work? How many schools will accept me as a student? No, I'm lucky to have these guys as comrades, as bad as they are. We speak the same language; they feed me and give me work. They've become my family — my only family. It's more like an adventure, a purposeful adventure for me. I'm not always sitting around, watching some captive like you," he said.

"I suppose this is the most boring part of your work?"

Maslan answered, "It would be, because I can't normally sit

still this long, but you're decent company. I have to admit you understand some things that I have never thought about. Some of the guys in this group have grown up in bourgeois families, but they rejected that lifestyle after they saw how ridiculous it was. Nothing matters to them except to prepare for the Caliphate. This other stuff is worthless."

Amirah thought about what he said. She could not have hoped for a better captor. She had heard horrible stories about the imprisonments, the beatings, manacles and tortures of relatives and friends who became captives of groups like Maslan's. Her uncle was held for months, and when he was released his arms had turned black from the torture. He was in constant pain when she left Syria. Maslan and she had similar backgrounds and he actually liked her. She wondered how many refugees were being held captive in camps, caves, villages, and jails, or had already been executed. She could be in one if she had not escaped Syria. She was lucky and blessed. Maslan lay back in his chair as if he were about to sleep.

She thought she had a chance to escape. She knew she was strong enough and capable. One thing was sure. Alex and her father would be searching for her. Right now, she was focused on getting out of this place. Maslan opened his eyes and Amirah was looking at him. "Thank you, Maslan, for removing the tape from my mouth and talking to me," she said.

"You know, they don't want me to talk to you at all. I am a Muslim man. I have faith in my duty."

"No, Maslan, you are a Muslim man sitting on a two-legged stool. You lack the third leg. The Christians are right in this one thing for sure. You may speak with the tongues of angels, but unless you show love and charity and kindness to others without exception, then your fine words come to nothing."

Maslan was silent. His face was sullen and confused. Amirah's words had hit home.

"You are missing so much, spending your life like this. You and I are both victims of this war. Don't continue working for those liars and deceivers. You know Ibrahim is a crook. Think about this. You might find your old girlfriend if you break away from these thugs. There are other people who can be your comrades."

Maslan asked, "Where do you get these ideas? You are not like the girls I know. I think you enjoy life too much."

"Yes, I am different. I always have been, even now as a captive. However, I think about what we would have missed if we hadn't had the chance to have this conversation and learn about all the things we have in common. We got to play the card games and talk about Aleppo. I really like you, Maslan, even though you're with them. You're a better man than all of them. You're more like my father, who helped hundreds of Syrians escape. You would do much better working with him."

Maslan nodded. "I would, but your father doesn't want to be involved with me. He knows that I'm with the rebels and dealing with all kinds of criminal acts — art-for-arms, art smuggling, and now kidnapping."

"The art thefts?" Amirah had not heard anything about the art since she and Maslan had been talking. "What's going on? Are you involved with those thefts?"

"Yes, of course, I am," he said. He got up and stretched his legs.

"Do you like the art you're stealing, Maslan?"

"Art is not the least bit interesting to me. I think it's a waste of time. I'm more mechanical. I like to build and tinker with things. Put me in a locked room and I can be out within six minutes. I have the skills of a professional criminal, as well as chemical and guerilla warfare training."

Amirah continued, "With your skills and talents, you don't need to be a criminal. I think you need to strike out on your own and forget these guys. Why don't we pray to help you get away from these guys?"

"I cannot pray with you. You are a woman. It is forbidden."

"Oh, my friend, you are speaking of superficial differences in the eyes of God. A woman, an American, a Jew, a Catholic, a Buddhist or anyone can pray with you."

Amirah fell to her knees and ask Maslan, "Will you pray with me?" Maslan disdainfully looked the other way. She began to pray, knowing she was praying to the man who had rescued her that night on the water. That scene had become a frequent theme in her paintings. "Father of all creation, God of all, author of mercy and light, healer of broken fragments of our lives and Savior of our souls in most desperate needs. Please mend our shattered spirits so that we may once again be living vessels of grace. Our hearts have been broken by the lies and deceits of spiteful souls. Heal our hearts so that we may receive the blessings of peace and love which only your grace can bestow on us. Bless this good man whose spirit wrestles here with the false prophets of the world. Please let my life or death here in this place be a guiding light for this good man. Thank you for this cherished time Maslan and I shared. Bless his life and guide him in all his decisions. Keep us safe. Amen."

When Amirah looked up, she saw Maslan on his knees in an upright position. His lips were clinched. He stood up quickly and mumbled, "I don't want to talk anymore. I must go upstairs."

"What if they decide to do something bad to me?" asked Amirah.

"What if they do?"

"I mean would you let that happen? I don't believe you would. I think you're better than that. You could help me like my father helped you on the water crossing. I remember you that night, Maslan. You've grown that beard and lost a little weight, but I think you were on that boat with us, helping my father. I'm sure it was you. You have a good heart. My father will help you. You don't have to do this."

"I told you to shut up, or I'll put the tape back on your mouth and blindfold you." He listened for footsteps on the stairs.

"Maslan, get up here," a voice said.

Maslan whispered in Amirah's ear, "Don't do anything stupid. Sit quietly. I'll be right back."

Maslan went up the stairs and opened the door.

Amirah heard them talking but couldn't make out anything. In a few minutes, Maslan came down and Amirah heard him turning the cylinder of a revolver, clicking it as he rocked in the straight back chair. She heard talking and moving around upstairs.

"Okay, Amirah, your wonderful father did not keep his word."

"What are you talking about?"

"Ibrahim asked your father to wait at his *appartement* this afternoon for the driver he was sending. He was to bring Yousif to *Aix-en-Provence* this afternoon. When the driver arrived, Yousif was nowhere to be found. Ibrahim is furious at him."

"What else did they tell you?"

"Yousif thinks Ibrahim kidnapped you, but Ibrahim is not responsible for your kidnapping. We're waiting for directives to deal with you."

Amirah straightened herself and looked straight at Maslan, "I'm not afraid, but you should be. Since my father wasn't waiting for Ibrahim's men, he has a plan to rescue me, and he will. Look, Maslan, help me get out. Don't wait around to get caught. There's more going on than you know. If you do the right thing and help me, the police will show you leniency."

Maslan looked startled. "Let me think. They have one more load of paintings to deliver before the sun sets. They're leaving now. You can hear the engines. You're going to do everything I tell you to do before they return. I don't want to hear a word from you. This time you just listen."

Chapter 33

Solitude

At four-thirty Wednesday afternoon, Mrs. Pilon's phone rang. "Hello, where are you?" she asked.

"I am in a black Mercedes heading to the *sud de la France*," Ibrahim said, "but we have had a little setback. Yousif did not follow my instructions. I don't know where he is. I sent one of my men to his *appartement* at 4:00. From there he was to go to *Aix* and meet with Shabab. He thinks I have kidnapped Amirah. I would like to get rid of both of them. It would be easy to make Amirah another Paris statistic like the imam's daughter."

"Don't even think about killing Amirah or Yousif. You have a personal vendetta with Yousif. If you kill him, you'll be the first one they'll suspect. Come to my *appartement* now. I have fresh coffee. Calm down and talk with me, I insist, before you leave the city."

"I will come by to pick up the list. Do you have it ready?" asked Ibrahim.

"Yes, I have it. *Á bientôt.*"

Opening the bottom drawer of the black filing cabinet in her office, Mrs. Pilon lifted a small *khatan* inlaid jewelry box, hand-made in Iran. She rubbed her hands over the smooth, beautiful surface. It was the gift her husband had given her many years ago, before she left Iran to move to France. She held it close to her heart and wept.

Today marked the twentieth anniversary of her sons' slayings. She felt weary of the fighting and questioned why Allah had allowed her to live so long. Why hadn't she died with her husband and sons? The creamer and sugar bowls sat on the small round silver tray which she placed on the little table flanked by two upholstered French chairs in her office. From this vantage point she could see the passers-by through her lace curtains on the front window.

She saw Ibrahim approaching and heard the doorbell ring for the large doors to the *appartement* building. She pressed the enter button. Then she set the box down, walked to her office door and opened it. Ibrahim entered and said, "I'll kill Yousif and his entire family, I will. He is a trouble maker and the girl is an infidel."

Mrs. Pilon said, "I hear you. I see. Let's sit down a minute. I want to talk to you." She brought the coffee pot to the table and poured steaming hot coffee for Ibrahim and herself. She offered cream and sugar. "You hold such hate in your heart. At times I appreciate the infidels and see some goodness in them. Once a happy wife and mother, I have withered through the years. When I arrived here, I found the lifestyles of the wealthy detestable, with all their extravagant dining, drinking and partying. They were irreverent and disgusting to me, and never considered an afterlife, like we do in the Muslim faith, but some of them have shown kindness and mercy to me."

"Have you forgotten the horrors inflicted upon us for years by the white men of France, Britain and Russia? I seek revenge because I must," said Ibrahim. "And the Arabs must save Syria."

"Do you really think Allah is with us? My sons are martyrs,

but Allah took my husband and my sons and left me to work here among infidels, who scorn my faith. For me the world is a sad place to live."

Ibrahim said, "Yes, and it will not end until we have a Caliphate. Your sons are feasting at heavenly tables with lovely, pure maidens and receiving rewards for their bravery. They are at peace, waiting for the great Judgment Day, when Allah will balance the good and bad deeds a person has done in his life. Thank God, you Iranians got rid of the dissipated sycophants of the Shah."

"Forgive me, Ibrahim, for doubting," said Mrs. Pilon, "but the blood of all Iranians and Syrians runs red. There must be a better way than wars year after year. You still carry a grudge against Yousif because he married Mehri."

"Absolutely not. I don't carry personal grudges. Mehri was destined to be my wife, but she chose Yousif and her family let her do it. He is a turncoat, a traitor to the cause. He fought with us as a comrade in arms, but now all he thinks about is his personal happiness. How can I respect him? He is no help with the struggle against the infidels." He raised his voice. "I must do all I can to help the Muslim Brotherhood."

"Yes, I hear the noble plans, but the strategies are wearing me down. You have enough power and control. Leave Yousif alone. I'm sick of these scenes. We have a terrorist attack and then an attack comes back at us, and our fine, brave young men are murdered by the thousands in these conflicts, but for what justifiable reason? Americans, British and Arabs are all victims of war. Their mothers must suffer their sons' deaths, as I suffered for mine. This earthly life is important too — not just the heavenly afterlife."

"The memory of your family should strengthen you for the continuing battle we wage. You sound weak tonight. You are here for our particular task, and you must never doubt it. How the tables have turned on our enemies. If we are not one hundred percent committed to the cause, we will lose. The theft of a few masterpieces is meaningless compared to our great mission. We must defeat the infidels, no matter the cost."

Mrs. Pilon said, "Leave Yousif and his family alone. Rami can deal with it."

Ibrahim walked to the cathedral window and looked at the drizzling rain. "I will take care of everything. You are getting weak in your old age. Do you have the memory stick for me? I have helped you in every way, but you plead for Yousif's life. Yet, I have expanded the thefts of the art tenfold for Rami's export business."

Mrs. Pilon opened the box and took out the device that held the names and locations of future victims of art thefts and attacks. It was passed to her earlier in the week by a university student, about the age her sons were at their deaths. "Ibrahim, I don't think you show enough respect for my brother. He knows you are stealing art on your own and not handing it over to him. He pays you well. You should be very satisfied."

Ibrahim said, "I don't want to talk about that now. Did you look at the information on the memory stick on your computer?"

"No, of course not. I don't want to know anything more about the art thefts."

"You are wise. Your brother has already received this week's extraordinary paintings in *Aix-en-Provence* and they have been placed in safe keeping for our first buyer. You won't believe it, but the buyer is an American with oil connections in Saudi Arabia. He doesn't know or care where or from whom we got the paintings. He simply wants the art. The poor American fools. They don't know we are plotting their destruction from these sales and they greedily help us." He sipped the last drop of the divine coffee and took the last bite of the sugary cookie.

"If you will forgive my boldness again, I think indeed they may know, but they see all the fighting as just political. They are not religious at all."

"They are indifferent to the higher truths of our religion. They may go to churches, but look at the way they abandoned my people in the Syrian War and as far as that goes, they didn't do you any favors in Iran either. Everything they do is about money and power."

"These Americans who buy art from us know it's illegal and probably know how we're spending the money. They couldn't care less."

"No doubt, they are not American patriots, but rather they are committed to greed, my dear Ibrahim. I am with you in disgust and disillusionment with the infidels and their greedy lifestyles."

"Yes, and praise Allah, for that's what keeps our business thriving. They're very stupid. Consider our group in Florida years ago, when they were emboldening themselves to bring down the Twin Towers in the 9/11 attacks. The stupid Americans, even those Christians, thought our men went to those filthy burlesque bars to entertain themselves before they carried out their mission the next day. If they had any real discernment they would know our followers went there to remind themselves how deplorable the Americans are to allow filthy bars exposing naked women with such lewdness and tawdry appearances. They went to reinforce the justification for the acts they were eager to perform against the immoral American infidels."

Mrs. Pilon said, "Yes, the appalling Western societies must be altered. The immodesty of their young girls with their tight-fitting clothing, piercings, tattoos, foul language, and sexual immorality is shameful. I remind you here that Yousif is not allowing his daughter Amirah to become like them. She is a modest young lady who studies art. I knew her when I attended meetings at the mosque. She is a good girl."

Ibrahim was no longer listening to Mrs. Pilon. In his mind he was already moving toward the *Sud de la France.* "May Allah reveal the wickedness of their ways to them before it is too late. Thank you for the contents of this memory stick. Whatever happens, your life has made a great difference. You are a true disciple."

"Ibrahim," she said, as she reached into the box and pulled out a small envelope. "Here, take this. Inside are four keys from *appartements* two Metro stops away. I have a very good, old friend there who will help us. She will never compromise us, I assure you."

Ibrahim said, "*Salam Alaikum,*"

"*Salam Alaikum,*" said Mrs. Pilon, closing and locking the door. When he left, she picked up her mobile phone and called Rami.

Chapter 34

St. Emilion

Early Wednesday night a full moon rose in the starry sky, so darkness did not completely cover the men who were seeking to find Amirah tonight. Alex and Yousif didn't know what they would find in the farmhouse where they were headed, but they knew from the dossiers created on Madame Pilon that it was owned by her brother Rami and her.

As Yousif and Alex left Paris, Alex called Fournier. "We think Amirah is in *St. Emilion.* Are you still meeting us there?"

"Yes, I can leave right away. What's happened?"

"Yousif was supposed to meet one of Ibrahim's men at the *Gare du Nord* and ride the train with him to *Aix-en-Provence,* so who knows what Ibrahim's planning since that didn't happen?"

"Fauziah, your girl Friday, brought the flash drive back to my office with a recorded conversation between Mrs. Pilon and Ibrahim. I would have arrested both of them, but they are nowhere to be found. I made a copy and put it in my desk and left the original drive in Fauziah's care. We presume Ibrahim's on his way to *Aix* because of the appointment book Fauziah and Hilba took from Mrs. Pilon's office."

"They did it," Alex exclaimed. "That's really great. What about the appointment book?"

"Fauziah rummaged through the drawers and found those important calendars. She discovered that art is being transferred tonight from a warehouse in *Aix* to some clients in *Marseille* or in *Aix*," Fournier said.

"Let Captain Casseaux handle the *Aix* raid. Get down here to *St. Emilion* and help us rescue Amirah."

"Where's the meeting point?" asked Inspector Fournier.

"The *Château Grand Barrail* around six in the evening."

"On my way."

The drive was long and no one was interested in talking. Alex and Yousif arrived by six at the *Château Grand Barrail.* Alex could not believe Fournier had beaten them there. He flashed the car lights at Fournier's car and saw him smoking his Camels.

They waited in their parked cars. At 6:10 Levi called Alex, "I'm here. Leave your car and walk to the road nearest the vineyard. I'll pick you up in less than fifteen minutes. Your friend in the Volvo can follow us."

Alex updated Fournier on the phone, as Yousif and he walked to the vineyard.

"Yousif, this is it. We're in this together. I know we'll get Amirah and the art. We must cooperate with Levi and Inspector Fournier."

Soon, a small Audi stopped and the door opened. Alex and Yousif got in. Alex said, "Yousif, this is Levi, Dr. Anna's grandson." Yousif and Levi nodded respectfully to each other, and the journey began. Inspector Fournier in his trusty Volvo followed the Audi closely.

Levi was concerned about the operation.

Yousif said, "Levi, what do you know about Amirah? She's all I care about right now."

Levi said, "Yousif, we're doing all we can to get Amirah to safety. Ibrahim's on the terrorist list and we know he's involved in this too. Amirah could be our eye witness to his organization, and with your testimony about the stolen art, we might finally be able to put him away."

Alex added, "We know he runs operations in a few villages, and we think Amirah might be captive in a farmhouse here in *St. Emilion*, near this vineyard."

In his Audi at Grand Prix speeds, Levi accelerated around the twisting curves as Alex was receiving a text message. "Listen to this--Fauziah texted that she has damaging evidence about Ibrahim and his gang, after listening to the office recording of Mrs. Pilon and Ibrahim and re-examining Mrs. Pilon's papers and diaries."

Levi said, "Excellent work. I'm thinking Ibrahim is losing his magic with age, or he's not the main operator. Someone else may be giving the orders. We know his allegiance is not to the Syrian government, but to himself. When the art was stolen from Jewish owners, I interviewed the victims and created a dossier on the crimes. As I compiled this information, I discovered who Ibrahim really is. Dr. Anna and I probably know more about Ibrahim than he knows about himself. We're sure he's involved in the art thefts and connections with Syria, but he's not the chief running this operation."

"Levi, I don't care how much Dr. Anna and you guys know about Ibrahim." Yousif's mind flashed back to a moment when he was sitting with his family on the rooftop of their home in Aleppo. Mehri and he were a happy couple in the days before the war. Now in this car he felt like he was in hell, speeding down the hillsides of France to save Amirah. His life had come to this: escaping, hiding, trespassing, and seeking freedom. Now his beautiful Amirah had been kidnapped. He wished he could assure her he would be there soon. She had to know he was coming. That thought gave him courage.

Levi said, "We think she's in a farmhouse in *St. Emilion* or in *Aix-en-Provence.* A few months ago, we started surveillance on Mrs. Pilon. Ibrahim and she have a lot of business at her brother's vineyard in *St. Emilion.* Agents of ours received tips about an Iranian rug dealer, Rami, in *Aix* who is in the import-export business. We searched and rummaged for a connection until one day we met an Iranian rug dealer in *Aix* who fit this profile. It all began to come together."

Yousif was growing impatient. "Levi, are you saying it wasn't Ibrahim who kidnapped Amirah?" Yousif was shaking his head.

Levi said, "We're good at staying under the radar, and getting the job done, whatever it is, but Ibrahim may not have kidnapped Amirah on his own."

"Well, then, who?" asked Yousif. "And how do you know so much? I thought you worked in the church, not espionage. Who took her and where is she?"

"Maybe his boss ordered him to do it."

Alex said, "Yousif, Dr. Anna works with the Mossad, the Israeli secret police, as well as the Jewish Restitution and Restoration. Levi's main job is with Faith Works, but I've realized unofficially he's with Mossad. Am I right, Levi?"

"Yes."

Yousif shook his head again. "Just get me to Amirah." Yousif was expressing Alex's concerns too.

Alex continued, "The Mossad are experts in every area of their work, and they won't make a move unless they know everything is optimal for the rescue. There are many Arab networks operating in the *Sud de la France,* especially in *Marseille.* They can help us there or in *St. Emilion.*

"Don't worry, Yousif." Levi's phone rang and he answered,

"Yes, Dr. Anna, we're here. No, we have not received communication from the Israeli agents yet. I understand." He shut off his cell.

Yousif asked, "What is it?"

"The agents arrived at Madame Pilon's brother's house, but it was empty. They searched the property and saw evidence that people were there recently, but no one was found anywhere on the property."

"Is that all? What else did she say? Did they find evidence Amirah had been there?" asked Yousif.

Levi hesitated. "It looks like she was held in the basement, but she's not there now. That's all I know." Levi sympathized with Yousif. He had his little Jacques at home and could imagine the agony of a missing child, but he had to stay on task.

"Take me there. I want to see for myself."

Levi said, "We can't go there without orders."

"Come on, Levi, Yousif needs to see for himself and frankly, I do too. We want to investigate where Amirah was supposedly held captive," said Alex.

Levi said, "We can't go there. They have searched it and cleared out. We have to move on. We can't stay here."

Yousif gripped Levi's arm. "No, I want to be sure. Take me there. It'll only take a few minutes, and I want to know if she was there, not just that it looks like she was."

Levi knew it was against orders, but he decided to grant Yousif this request. Levi was a father like Yousif. He drove directly to the farmhouse without calling headquarters, which was a clear violation of regulations. "Okay, we'll go there, but make it quick. She could already be in *Marseille* or," Levi stopped. He didn't want to state the possibilities.

"Where will your men search now?" asked Alex. "She's not in the farmhouse, so let's formulate our plans. I know Ibrahim's group asked Yousif to go to *Aix* for a special assignment this afternoon. She could be there or in *Marseille*. You remember the terrorists who killed the children in the school near *Marseille* a few years ago? A lot of evil people are in *Marseille* who could be working with them or hiding Amirah."

Yousif said, "Rami, the Iranian rug dealer you mentioned, has lots of contacts. He is an enemy, spying on us Syrians and reporting to his Iranian cabal. He was in illegal business long before Ibrahim started his. Neither of these men is interested in helping Syrians unless there's a payback. I don't know this Mrs. Pilon at all or if there is a relationship between them, but Ibrahim was well-connected with Syrian rebels who were working against the Syrian government at one time. He's worked with large, powerful, well-heeled groups, as well as new immigrants like me. However, Rami has another much more successful business than his arts and arms involvement. He charges exorbitant fees for bringing in refugees escaping Syria."

Levi said, "We followed the trail to Rami's *Arts and Antiquities Boutique* in the *sud de la France*, and soon we realized he is the brother of Mrs. Pilon. They must have discussed business when she visited. His warehouses nearby could be holding more than art. Amirah could be in any one of them. We suspect he's operating another business — hiding illegal immigrants in the warehouses and torturing enemies of Iran who escaped to Paris. He is a suspect in Maleeka's murder also."

Yousif said, "I believe you, but why would he want to kidnap Amirah? It's more logical that Ibrahim would be the major suspect. He hates Amirah and her behavior and has never liked me, so he would kidnap Amirah to teach me a lesson. I must come clean. I cannot tell you the whole story today, but Ibrahim helped me get out of Syria. I paid him dearly, but Rami wrote the papers, as he's had lots of experience with the refugee smuggling business. I know Ibrahim will expect lots of money to deliver the rest of my family from the Lesbos camp, if he ever does."

Alex said, "You have not been in contact with Rami personally and want nothing to do with him, unless all else fails. You're just anxious and think you must resort to his help to get your wife and sons out of Greece. Frankly, I think I have a better chance of getting your family out of Greece than Rami will have. He's going to be locked up. Justice takes time, but eventually the truth prevails. It's disappointing that it takes so long, but I am confident it wins in the end."

Levi texted Dr. Anna, but got no answer. She was monitoring events as they unfolded. She was aware of the raid scheduled for tonight.

Levi turned off the highway onto a gravel road, drove a short distance, and stopped in front of the farmhouse. He opened the glove compartment, took out three guns and handed Alex and Yousif 357 Magnums. "Here, you probably won't need these, but just in case."

"I have a lot of experience with guns," Yousif said. "I've never used this particular model, but I anticipate no problem handling the gun." Inspector Fournier got out of the Volvo and walked to the car to join the men. Levi led the armed men to the porch.

Alex hated the thought of killing anybody, even evil men. If he encountered a young immigrant criminal face to face pointing a gun at him, would he shoot him? Yes. He knew he could, if he had to, but he would try to avoid it except to save Amirah's life.

Levi knocked and when no answer came, he pushed open the unlocked door. The French police had already been there and left signs of their entry. No other sign of life was anywhere, but Yousif investigated the house, opening each door, slamming doors shut, flinging closet doors open and searching the basement. He emerged from the stairs with a small round artist brush. He recognized the bristles. He knew it was Amirah's and she had been smart enough to leave a clue, so he would know she had been here.

As they were about to leave, Yousif took one more look and spotted a USB flash drive behind a heavy center leg of the kitchen table. Quickly he picked up a very important piece of evidence. "Here, look at this. Where can we play it? Maybe it's important. Also look at this little airplane jigger bottle. I assure you Ibrahim has been here."

"How do you know?" asked Levi.

"Ibrahim hides one of his little habits. He drinks booze in spite of the Islamic prohibition. He carries these little bottles with him and takes nips when he thinks no one is looking. I am sure it belongs to Ibrahim," said Yousif.

"Let's go," said Levi. "We can play that flash drive on my laptop in the car."

Chapter 35

Black Apparitions

Early Thursday morning, as the men are leaving the farmhouse, Levi recognizes something on the ground. "Alex, take a look at these tread marks. They're from a panel van. Who uses panel vans in his legitimate business?"

"Of course, Ibrahim has a fleet of white and unmarked Ford Econolines, but there are hundreds of white vans in France. They've probably moved Amirah to an underground network and ditched whatever they were driving," said Yousif.

Alex caught his breath and exclaimed, "Levi, my father was a fraternity brother of the American Ambassador. I'm betting he can arrange electrophotography of *St. Emilion* for us."

"Dr. Anna is aware of that technology, but we don't have the capability right now," Levi said.

"My father divulged this to me in strictest confidence. It's a kind of satellite reconnaissance with an electron camera that can locate objects hundreds of miles away from anywhere. I'm sure he can get a scan for us if I can reach him," said Alex.

"You think he can get the operators to locate the white Econoline using one of their security satellites."

"Yes, I'm sure of it."

"Use my phone. No, get Fournier's, because it's encrypted. I need to call in those satellites," said Levi.

Alex took Fournier's phone and texted his father's private number. His father called back in two minutes. They talked briefly.

Alex clicked off the phone. "It's done. The Paris police already had the Ambassador up to speed on Ibrahim and his gang. This new development fits right in with an operation already underway. He asked me if we needed extra security detail. I told him we had enough with the Israelis. Fournier will be sent the coordinates for the van."

"An Israeli team will meet us on the road," said Levi.

"Let's listen to that flash drive," Alex said, as he put it into Levi's laptop. They read all the names of the artwork, owners, addresses and dates of the next thefts. Good work, Yousif. You have sealed and delivered the case against these criminals with that flash drive you found in the farmhouse."

Yousif said, "I hoped it might tell us about Amirah."

They proceeded along the serpentine road back to *St. Emilion* city center. Every farmhouse had twinkling lights and glittering lanterns on the porches. The residents were unaware of the developing chaos in their peaceful village. They did not suspect international terrorists were sneaking into *le beau village* tonight.

At a junction where the road turned into the expressway, they veered onto the ramp and were suddenly followed by two motorcycles that fell in tandem. Alex was disturbed by their abrupt pursuit. He looked closely at the reaction of Fournier and Levi. Fournier's face in the rearview mirror was impassive, but Levi's showed professional satisfaction. The extra security had arrived. Alex studied the two black apparitions tailing their vehicle. The riders appeared immobile on the bikes because their bikes followed at precisely the exact speed and distance, with a perfect imitation of their Audi's every curve, swerve and change in direction. The men's timing, intensity and appearance were nothing less than lethal. If Amirah's rescue required the spilling of blood, Alex had no doubt that these men would not hesitate to do it.

Fournier's phone bleeped. "We've got the picture of the Ford Econoline. It's parked near a small vacation cottage on the outskirts of *St. Emilion.*" The GPS coordinates were the only caption below the picture. Fournier highlighted them and punched them in. "We're only twenty minutes away. Amazing technology."

The scent of honeysuckle hung in the evening air, and wild flowers and ivy spread all around in the moonlight, as the car came to a stop on a small cobblestoned street one block from the kidnappers' cottage. Alex thought of mysterious Sylvana, the Romanian prophetess, as he looked at the ring she had given him and rubbed the gold band. He knew everything mattered and was confident that her prophecies like those of old Biblical seers would be fulfilled in their mission tonight. Amirah would be saved and the paintings found. "Let's go," he said.

Behind the cottage was the Ford Econoline.

The motorcycle team peeled off their leather gear and helmets and put them in a compartment behind the seats. Standing on the sidewalk, they looked like tourists. They approached Fournier and Levi.

"I am Ishtak. He is David." Pointing across the street, Ishtak said, "We can use that playground over there for the drone."

David got the tiny, toy-like drone helicopter from the back of the motorcycle along with other items he needed for the operation. As they all crossed the street to the playground, Levi explained, "This drone will use ultrasound to map the interior of the house. We'll know walls, doors, furniture and people. After a few passes with the drone, we'll know how many terrorists are in the house and where they are. We'll also know Amirah's location."

Yousif asked, "Will it be safe for Amirah?"

David said, "Yes," as he put on goggles and launched the drone toward the cottage. "I can see what the drone sees. A recording is being sent to all our secure phones."

Yousif was visibly anxious as he scrutinized his phone. "Okay, there's a man in a lawn chair outside, two figures at a table in the front room and two more figures in a smaller backroom with a door opening to the larger room. Wait, one of the figures in the back room is decidedly smaller than the other men. That must be Amirah. May Allah's will be done," said Yousif.

Alex exclaimed, "She's alive. We must be careful. Do you agree she's in the back room?"

Levi asked, "Is our plan to burst through the front door?"

Everyone agreed.

The desperation and danger of the situation was sinking into Alex. "I think I know the man at the door," Alex stammered. "He is Houssain al-Jabar, a young patient of mine who suffered a severe heart attack. I did a conference with two colleagues over it."

Fournier looked impatiently at his friend. You cannot save him again. He has made his choice and a very bad one at that. There is nothing more you can do for him."

"No! No! I can't just let him die. We've got to give him a chance. He is a young man. He has his whole life ahead of him. I cannot let him be killed."

"There is nothing you can do. He is a terrorist. He will kill you if he sees you. The bullet he puts in you will warn his friends. They will kill Amirah before they run out the back door and get away," said Levi.

"I know. I know. I am terrified for Amirah, but she would want me to try to save him. We must convince the Israelis to give me a chance."

Fournier said, "Talk to them if you must. They will tell you the same thing."

Alex knew no sentimental moral appeal would move these dedicated commandos. He thought quickly as he approached Ishtak, the more talkative agent. "I know the watchman who is guarding the front door. I believe he has useful information which could help us with an ongoing case in Paris."

Ishtak glanced at Levi, who nodded his head up and down. "Well," Ishtak said, "we can capture your potential informant for you, but it will seriously endanger the hostage."

"Give me a chance to talk to him, please."

Ishtak was incredulous. "These are dangerous men. They will kill you as soon as they see you."

"I am prepared to take that risk. I have saved his life once already. I believe he will listen to me. I will stand back far enough for you to kill him if he makes a sudden move."

"You believe in his potential as an informant?"

"Yes."

Ishtak looked coldly at Alex. "Your way might be better. A kill shot will make less noise."

David had been listening to the conversation. He knew the plan and concurred, "I'll park the drone on the roof."

Ishtak said, "Yes, and be ready to take position one at the door when the doctor is finished. Levi, monitor the drone. If a male figure comes to the window, signal me and I will kill him, as we all charge into the cottage. David will take care of the other males. Fournier, you must kill the doctor's informant if he makes a threatening move against the doctor. Are we all set?"

Everyone took his position. Alex circled the house and approached it from the wide side most visible to Houssain. Before stepping into the open, he said a quiet prayer. "Please help me to save this poor child of God who has lost his way. Give me strength."

As soon as Alex came into view, Houssain recognized him and stood up. Alex held his breath for an instant, hoping there would be no gunshot. "Dr. Alex, Dr. Alex?" Houssain's bewilderment probably saved his life.

"Houssain," Alex replied in a calm, quiet voice, "Trust me, please. Drop your weapon. I've begged these men to save your life. They have their guns pointed at you, but they will not shoot if you obey us. You must lie down motionless on the ground and stretch your arms out over your head. If you resist or run, you will be killed instantly. I'm begging you. I saved your life once and I'm going to save you again, if you do as you're told. You do not want to die here. We only want to rescue Amirah."

Houssain's body trembled. Falling on his stomach, he dropped his gun and began sobbing like a lost child. Fournier rushed over with handcuffs. David jumped to the door. Ishtak sprinted from behind the garden wall holding up two fingers to David, who shifted his pistol to his left hand and knelt down in front of the door. Ishtak reached the stone step and David opened the door. Two muffled shots sounded simultaneously. Each shot was instantly fatal and no louder than a champagne cork. David and Ishtak charged toward the bedroom door.

Maslan called out, "What's happening?"

Before he could get his gun, Ishtak opened the door. He saw Amirah directly behind Maslan. In the wink of an eye, he kneecapped Maslan. Then Ishtak raised his gun and was ready to fire at Maslan.

Amirah leaped in front of Maslan, "No, no, Maslan is not like these other men. He has helped me and I know he would have helped me escape. He's young. You don't need to kill him. You've already terribly wounded him. He cannot possibly hurt me now."

David, Levi, Yousif and Alex entered the room. Alex and Yousif rushed toward Amirah. Alex pulled her away from Maslan. "It's okay. No more worries."

Yousif hugged Amirah, as he never had before. Then the three of them embraced and wept together for joy.

But Amirah shook herself loose and screamed to the others, "Do not kill Maslan. We can use him. He is not a danger."

Ishtak looked at Levi who nodded his head and said, "We'll take him in." Ishtak shrugged his shoulders, holstered his pistol, picked up Maslan's pistol and walked out. Amirah breathed a sigh of relief and Yousif put his arm around her.

Chapter 36

Light and Darkness

Alex knelt down to assess Maslan's wound. "Levi, please get my bag from the car. I'll do all I can for him until the ambulance arrives." As Levi left the room Alex realized he, Yousif and Amirah were alone with the wounded man on the floor. Ishtak and David had evaporated like the wind. They could not risk recognition of any kind, working for the Mossad. "I wanted to thank those two, but they've gone."

Maslan, lying flat on the floor, groaned as Alex applied a tourniquet to his leg, wrapping it tightly around the thigh above the wound. He was concerned that the popliteal artery was injured.

Amirah knelt down beside Alex. "Try to keep him perfectly still," he said, "because we don't want him to move any way that will worsen the bleeding and secondary injuries." He gave Maslan an IM shot of morphine while they waited for the ambulances. "You know I felt the healing hand of God guiding me tonight."

"Alex, you are the *Almaealij*. We both have been given powers through our hands. You feel the touch of God healing through you as I feel the Infinite creating art through me." She lowered her head and kept a careful eye on Maslan.

Soon they heard the ambulances arriving. Levi came back in with the attendants and said, "That's the man over there. We'll provide protection at the hospital in *St. Emilion.*"

Alex asked, "What about Houssain? Where is he?"

Levi replied, "We're taking him to the *Emilion* jail for now. You saved his life, but he will still have his day in court. I let you do what you wanted to do, but risking your life like that was a pretty stupid thing to do."

Amirah closed her eyes and breathed deeply. "What did you do for Houssain, Alex?"

"The Mossad men were going to kill him. I took a risk after arguing with them a lot, but it worked out. I talked Houssain into giving up and dropping his gun."

"What else did you do? You could have been killed."

"I was in shock. I wasn't expecting to see a patient of mine sitting there guarding these terrorists. You remember Houssain, who was my heart attack patient who worked for Ibrahim. I couldn't let him die."

"I can't believe you did that. You're a doctor. Where was Fournier?"

Levi said, "I tried to talk him out of it, but he wouldn't listen. He had to do it his way."

Amirah embraced Alex. "You saved my life. All of you could have been killed. I can't bear the thought of that."

"You don't need to," said Levi. "Dr. Anna has arranged for you to go to one of our special safe houses tonight for rest after all you've been through. You and Alex have a few minutes to talk, while I give some instructions to the attendants about the bodies, and then we've got to head to *Aix* to rescue art at a warehouse."

The attendants were putting Maslan on a stretcher, as Amirah watched. "You were the best captor I could have had, Maslan."

She turned toward Yousif. "Father, I know you will help Maslan when he gets out of the hospital. He does not want to stay in this Middle Eastern Mafia business he's gotten into."

Maslan was in pain, but he looked at Amirah and spoke, "Thank you for saving my life. I know I've got a lot to think about. I was not going to let those men hurt you. I was trying to figure some way we could escape, but I'm thankful that you're safe now."

"And thank you, Doctor," he said. The attendants carried him to the ambulance for transport to the hospital.

Levi spoke, "Yousif, come with me for a moment."

Yousif left Amirah's side and spoke, "Dr. Alex, we are indebted to you for our lives. You have reunited us." Yousif and Levi walked out, leaving Amirah with Alex. They embraced again in silence.

"Only a split second separated you from death, Alex. I admire you, but in an instant, you could have been attacked and killed by these evil criminals."

"I know how to protect myself. Don't ever worry about me, Amirah."

"But I will worry about you because you take risks. I'm proud of you, but I'm afraid you could be hurt or killed. You're a doctor. Leave the criminals to the police."

"You were in more danger than I was. I don't know how you ever stayed alive with those men and even made Maslan your friend."

"When I prayed for him this morning, I looked up from prayer and saw the light of God in his eyes. What risk I took was for that special light in his eyes."

"You see the light in people's eyes as well as in your painting. You see the light everywhere, but here you risked your life for a man who might have killed you. You must be more careful."

"Listen to me, Alex. The imam at our mosque in Aleppo was a well-educated man. He told me your Messiah said he was 'the light of the world.' I have thought about that many times since my vision on the boat. The men who deceived Maslan think of the light as a searchlight, or light at the end of a tunnel."

"Tunnel, Amirah?"

"Yes, I have realized that Jesus did not mean a light you follow blindly without knowing where you are going or what your destiny is. He meant THE LIGHT that illuminates everything. When you see the world in THE LIGHT, as I see it, as a painter in a complete way, I see clearly my vision of that night on the Adriatic Sea. Nothing is as beautiful as a sunlit morning and nothing is as ugly as a deep dark pit. I would not have risked my life for Ibrahim, because he does not have The Light of the World in him. Maslan was different. I saw the goodness in Maslan. I have had many moments of darkness in my life, but I am coming out little by little through my art, my spiritual seeking and you, my *Almaealij*.

Levi entered and said, "Dr. Anna has informed the Mossad that Amirah and Yousif need to go to safe houses tonight. She's sending a contact to get them. Her contacts said Ibrahim and his gang took a private plane from *Bordeaux* and will arrive in *Aix* in less than an hour. Dr. Anna is sending a Nachshon jet to *St. Emilion* waiting to fly us to *Aix* after we handle business here. Tonight could be the finale on the stolen art cache, when we stop the transfer and capture paintings from the warehouses."

Fournier said, "I'm concerned that Ibrahim will suspect something when his thugs we shot here don't show up at his warehouse operation. I spoke to Captain Casseaux and he has updated the local *Emilion* station chief, who will keep Houssain here in jail. As soon as Maslan can leave the hospital, we'll move them to Paris."

Levi looked at his watch. "We need to go. We'll put Yousif and Amirah in the hands of the Mossad contacts for delivery to their safe houses. We must get to *Aix* and capture the paintings."

Yousif was thankful for the bravery of Alex and Levi and the concern they had shown Amirah and him. He was also impressed with the efficacy of Dr. Anna and the police in this investigation. Hugging his precious Amirah, he said, "Alex, you would not give up. You knew we would find Amirah, and I now believe we'll find the paintings."

Alex looked at Amirah. "I think I see the light in you." They hugged each other as Alex added, "Yousif, I'm sorry, but you can't go with us on the raid tonight. You need to go to your safe house and Amirah to hers."

"Certainly not, I am indebted to you men. I would never leave you at this point. I want to go with you to *Aix*. I must be part of the raid. I fully expect we will find Maya's paintings tonight. Amirah can go to the safe house with the Israelis."

"Yes, Father, you must go with Alex and the rescuers. I will be fine now. I am so grateful to all of you."

Alex said, "No, someone bigger than all of us was taking care of you, Amirah. We were only instruments. Yousif, I'm sorry, but I don't want you to go on the raid with us. Please accept this."

Fournier joined in, "Yousif, I know you have experience in combat, but I can't allow you to go with us. Not only is it against all rules since you are not a policeman or detective, but you would be causing us to break the law. You must listen to Alex and me on this one. You must go to the safe house."

"Well, I guess I don't have a choice."

The Israeli policemen escorted Yousif to their car. Amirah got into a separate car to go to her safe house. Alex was torn. He wanted to forget the paintings and instead run after Amirah. He envisioned a simple life with her along with his medical practice;

nonetheless, he joined Inspector Fournier and Levi for the trip to the airport. In his heart he knew he would see her again and again. He watched Amirah and Yousif get into their unmarked cars, and he saw her turn her head and look at him.

Alex said, "We've done all we need to do in *St. Emilion.* Let's head to the *Art and Antiquities Boutique* in *Aix.*"

Levi said, "If all goes well, this job should be completed by six in the morning in *Aix.* We've got to get to the airport in *Bordeaux* and board the private jet. Are the Paris police already in route to *Aix*?"

Inspector Fournier said, "Yes, they should arrive in half an hour. They'll begin checking the warehouses. I will be in constant contact with them to see what they are finding."

Fournier spotted Captain Casseaux running toward them, shouting, "Well, it's about time I found you. You were supposed to be looking for me, Lieutenant Fournier."

"I'm sorry, Captain. Everything was happening so fast that we had to move. I wasn't sure you were coming to *St. Emilion.* I thought you would go straight to *Aix.* I will not be forgetful again."

"Thank you, Lieutenant. Alright, now bring me up to date on the evening plans, so I can contact the Paris officers bound for *Aix.*"

Levi spoke, "The *Art and Antiquities Shop* in *Aix,* owned by Mrs. Pilon's brother, was locked and closed earlier. We have not been able to locate anyone who has seen him."

Captain Casseaux said, "We think someone got to the Iranian rug dealer, Rami, Mrs. Pilon's brother, and informed him of trouble. Let's roll. We have no time to waste."

The four men got into a BMW provided for them by the Israeli security services, and headed to the airport. Alex asked, "What happened to the rental car you were driving this afternoon?"

Levi responded, "That car, my friend, has already been disposed of in *Marseille.* Someone else will be using it there. Sit back and relax for the thirty-minute ride to the airport. We have a big night ahead of us." Levi started the engine.

Alex leaned back and allowed himself a minute to think about Amirah and the wise decision he had made moving to Paris. He looked forward to life there, but he wanted to go with the *Médicins Sans Frontières* to Lesbos, Greece. Perhaps Amirah would go with him and they could locate her mother and brothers, if they were not already in Paris. Why couldn't he continue as a part-time detective and a full-time doctor? He had two callings and he was good at both of them. He wondered for whom Maslan was working, and if Ibrahim was not in charge of Amirah's kidnapping, who had been?

Chapter 37

Road Trip/ Air Flight

Early that Thursday morning, the men got out of the BMW and walked to the small private terminal in *Bordeaux*. It resembled a third world building. A drip coffee maker with a cup of old coffee sat on a corner shelf next to a small dormitory refrigerator holding Cokes and bottled water. A couple of attendants and two security guards stood around switching television channels. Levi showed some papers for Alex, Inspector Fournier, Captain Casseaux and himself to one of the attendants. Within minutes everyone walked onto the small airfield and boarded the small private Cirrus Vision SF50 waiting for them. As soon as they were belted, Levi nodded to the pilot to take off.

Captain Casseaux asked, "Did you know Maslan was part of a Syrian rebel force at one time, and now he's a wanted criminal in Paris?"

Levi said, "Yes, I knew he was a member of that army."

Casseaux began, "We've got these bad Syrians running us ragged, making the good ones difficult to recognize. It would help us if you would identify any bad Syrians you locate, so we can get information faster. How do you know Maslan's really changed and will talk? I tell you I don't trust anybody these days. People don't change. That silly painter thinks she convinced Maslan to change. I've been dealing with thugs all my life. They don't change overnight."

Alex, Levi and Lieutenant Fournier were embarrassed at Casseaux's rant, but it was best not to argue with him.

Casseaux said, "We could do a lot better handling these thugs if you'd give us more information."

Levi said, "I know that, but you tend to forget that there's a difference between honest refugees and criminals. The reason we don't share any more information with you is that you don't always deal with it properly."

"That's crazy. We deal with thugs all the time."

"These people come from all different backgrounds. We think the Paris police deal well with local criminals, but we think you could do a better job with refugees."

Captain Casseaux scratched his head. "It's such a massive job. We're doing the best we can. You know what I think? I think the Jews and Muslims should stay in the Middle East. I don't mean that in a bad way, but it's your promised land, isn't it? So why wouldn't you work out your problems there?"

Alex and Lieutenant Fournier were again embarrassed for Levi, who was their staunch ally. They knew prejudice among the French police was the major reason Israeli Intelligence sometimes has trouble working with local law enforcement. There was anti-semitism right up the chain of command and you never knew when you would run into it. In fairness to Casseaux, Fournier had heard remarks like this often from other superior officers. He knew none of them realized how insulting these remarks could be.

Alex took charge of the conversation. "It would be nice to keep all the racial turmoil bottled up somewhere else. The thing is, it's here. We must deal with it here. When I see someone like Yousif trying to live a good life and somebody like Ibrahim trying to destroy him, I'm required to do something. But the prejudice is the tip of the iceberg. It can actually breed dictators. All the dictators of the world thrive on hate and prejudice. Who knows which country will produce the next dictator?"

"You're right, Alex. Dictators can get themselves elected to offices or just take over a country in a coup by killing whoever stands in their way," said Levi.

Alex added, "The same story played out in Hong Kong, Myanmar, Ukraine, and Crimea. Ibrahim is the kind of guy who wants to be a dictator, but Syria still has one. Replacing him with somebody like Ibrahim doesn't help the people. Every revolution starts with one goal, 'Follow me and we'll be victorious', and the followers go into a brain freeze."

Inspector Casseaux said, "I have my police precinct and I keep order the best I can, but my problems are coming from these men from the Middle East. I've seen it all. It's impossible to know who the enemies are. It's like the French in Vietnam. Were the little Vietnamese kids going to throw a hand grenade or just hang out with them? Frankly, like I said, I don't know who to trust anymore. Oh, well, enough of that crap. We've got a job to do."

Levi's cellphone rang, "Hello, yes, Dr. Anna. The plane is landing in *Aix* now and we'll head to the *Arts and Antiquities Boutique*. No, what happened? Okay, we'll keep together."

Inspector Fournier asked, "What is it?"

Levi said, "Ibrahim may be heading to the warehouse, but she's not sure. It's possible he has scheduled a showing of some of the paintings to an international dealer tonight. Ibrahim plans to deal with Yousif later, but right now he's focused on getting as much money as possible from this dealer to fund his art-for-arms operations."

Casseaux said, "This could be a bigger cache than we've ever dreamed of seizing in one night."

The plane landed on a strip in a field lit only by the moon and stars. The four got out and walked to an Audi Q7 waiting for them with keys in the ignition. Levi checked under the hood and car. The inspector checked the trunk. Casseaux and Alex checked inside. They got in and headed into *Aix-en-Provence* city center.

Captain Casseaux called the police assistant in *Aix*. "What's going on?" he asked. "Yes so who's at the bar? Are you sure?" He clicked off the phone and turned to the others. "Two of Ibrahim's henchmen took a detour and stopped at the Clarinet Bar in *Aix*. They are with the bar owner now. Your boy Yousif was bosom buddies with Ibrahim at one time."

Ignoring the Captain's implication about Yousif, Levi asked, "Do you know the owner?"

Proud of his knowledge, Casseaux responded, "Yeah, I know him. He's co-owner with Rami of the *Arts and Antiquities Boutique*. They are in on this art theft business in a big way. Even Rami's sister Mrs. Pilon is working in it. Nice little family."

Levi said, "We know, Captain Casseaux. It's in our dossier. It doesn't tie Yousif to any of the thefts."

"On the contrary, it does in my mind. Why wouldn't a poor refugee working as a rug salesman want to cut a deal that's worth millions? Think about it. His countrymen in the Middle East Mafia are stealing antiquities in Aleppo and Raqqa and then pretending on the videos to destroy them. They're not destroying the real art. They're selling it. These thieves make my skin crawl."

Levi said, "Let me correct one of your assumptions. Most of the Syrians are not destroying their heritage. ISIS and most radical Islamists are the destroyers. Are you sure Rami's partner is in the bar?"

"What did I just tell you? My men are going there now to take care of those miscreants."

Everyone was quiet as Levi put the Clarinet Bar into the GPS. It's only five miles from the main drag. We'll enter through the alley behind the bar."

After a few turns, Levi found the alley and parked the car.

Casseaux said, "I see my men in the white van under that canopy. They're waiting for instructions from me. I'll tell them to follow us."

"We don't want Rami or Ibrahim to know the Israelis had anything to do with these raids and captures tonight," Levi said.

Casseaux said, "Come on. Do you think they don't know?"

Levi said, "They think it was all a Parisian security team, and that's what we want them to think. My face will be covered, so they won't recognize me, and they don't know Alex. You are lead man tonight, you know."

Casseaux said, "Well, I'm appointing Lieutenant Fournier the lead man tonight."

"We're going in," Alex said, opening his car door."

Casseaux followed the men to the door, but went to the van to get a couple of his officers.

Levi and Alex entered through a side door. Inspector Fournier checked the rest of the building to make sure no one else was there. They heard people talking, more like mumbling, in a room at the back of the bar. Inspector Fournier signaled them into their positions and then smashed the door with a ram, "You're all under arrest. Put your arms in the air. You, step out here," he said, signaling to one of Ibrahim's henchman he recognized from former arrests. As Fournier was putting the handcuffs on one of the men, the owner pulled a gun from his jacket and started to fire, but Levi shot the gun out of his hand. In two seconds the second man lunged at Levi, but Alex hit him in the head with his gun and the man fell across the desk. That left the man the inspector was handcuffing.

Captain Casseaux entered with two more officers and instructed them, "Take these two men straight to the jail here in *Aix*. The local captain will allow you to guard them as long as I want them guarded. Don't leave them until I call you."

The third man, the owner of the bar and the co-owner of the *Arts and Antiquities Boutique*, held his bleeding hand and spoke, "What is the meaning of this? I am outraged. I do not deserve such treatment. You will be sorry--very sorry. I have been running a respectable business for years. I demand you take me to the hospital. My lawyers will be speaking with you."

"Put him in a separate car and take him to our farmhouse," said Inspector Fournier. "We have some questions for you, and we intend to get the answers."

Rami's partner said, "You need to mind your business. What are you talking about? What's all this about? I'll remember all of you for this disgrace. You'll be very sorry," and he moaned in pain again, holding his bleeding hand.

Fournier spoke, "I'm already sorry about a lot of things. Go with the officer. We have other business tonight. A doctor will meet you at the farmhouse--our farmhouse."

Captain Casseaux checked on his officers, giving instructions again and then joined Levi, Alex and Fournier. "Okay, good work, men. Is this where you leave it up to the Paris police, Levi?"

Levi replied, "Almost. We can follow you to the warehouses, but I'll be heading back to a safe house tonight. You've got Alex, Fournier and plenty of good men for the raid. But I have one special request I expect you to honor."

"Okay, what's that?"

Levi said, "I want you to give Maya's paintings to Alex, so he can personally deliver them to the Dalles. If we get them tonight in the raid, I think he deserves that privilege. After all, he's provided us with most of our information. Plus, his timeliness saved our lives tonight, so you can show respect by honoring Alex."

Captain Casseaux said, "I don't think two paintings missing from the confiscation will be too much of a problem, assuming we find them. Usually, we allow the Israeli Restoration Group to deliver the goods of Holocaust findings. They need to go back to Paris first."

"That's not what I asked, Captain Casseaux. I insist you honor this simple request. And by the way, I'm sure the Israeli Secret Security could always use Detective-Doctor Alex Winston and Inspector Fournier and their skills in our operations. We expect to continue working with you and them. If you're not careful, we might steal them away from you," said Levi.

"You can't steal them away from us, but okay, okay, Alex can take them back, but you know the value. We cannot lose these artworks. I'm heading to the warehouse with the men from the Paris precinct. We'll see you there."

Alex said, "We're on our way."

Chapter 38

Raid

Early Thursday morning, Inspector Fournier and Alex arrived at the warehouses. Fournier parked the car on a lot near where men were transferring boxes and loading them into semi-trucks. Dr. Anna had said this would be the mother-load of the paintings and artifacts Ibrahim and his Middle Eastern Mafia had stolen. She now was almost certain that the owner of the Arts and Antiquities Boutique was also involved. Rami had met too many times with Ibrahim and Mrs. Pilon at their farmhouse.

Alex asked, "Where is Ibrahim? I don't think he's with them, do you?"

Inspector Fournier replied, "I don't see him or the two thugs who are usually with him. We may not get to nail him tonight."

Captain Casseaux arrived in the distance at an area that could be locked down. His officers were sealing off that entrance and moving toward the warehouses.

Alex's phone rang. "Yes, we see you, Captain Casseaux."

Captain Casseaux said, "We're ready to move in."

Alex replied, "Ibrahim is not with them. We've been watching everything and we don't see a trace of him or his bodyguards."

Captain Casseaux said, "I've got my brigade ready to launch the attack. We can't wait for Ibrahim. I'll give you ten minutes to see if he shows up and then we're moving in. We'll take whomever we can."

"Wait," said Fournier, "here comes a silver Audi. Who's getting out? He's talking to one of the guys who must be chief of this operation on the ground. He's going into the building with the assistant. Should we make our move, since you intend to storm this warehouse tonight one way or another? Are you willing to settle for the middle men if you can't get Ibrahim?"

Casseaux said, "I'm pretty sure he's there and they have no idea we have the warehouse surrounded. I don't want to fire a shot unless it's absolutely necessary." He clicked off his phone.

"Is everyone set?" asked Alex.

Fournier said, "Maybe we should send some officers down to the *Arts and Antiquities Boutique.*"

Alex said, "Yes, I think something could happen there, despite the fact we found no one earlier. Alex's cell phone rang. "Hello, Dr. Anna. Yes, what's up? Are you sure? Right."

Fournier asked, "What is it?"

"Dr. Anna thinks Ibrahim has been in an accident. One of Casseaux's officers reported a car bomb caused the accident, and they found Ibrahim's ID in a wallet near the scene. What do you make of that, Fournier?"

"I wouldn't put money on my hunch, but my guess is it's a staged bombing. Ibrahim has his cars checked by his Syrian security guys. Unless someone has outsmarted them, it's simply a ploy to throw us off track."

Captain Casseaux called Alex as his men drew closer to the warehouse. "I don't see Ibrahim. What's going on? What do you think?"

"Fournier overheard Casseaux and took the phone from Alex and said, "Sir, I apologize for any blunders my team made by not arresting Ibrahim, but he disappeared before we got to Mrs. Pilon. He was gone when we got there. I told you that." He handed Alex the phone.

"Captain Casseaux, we've received a call from Dr. Anna that Ibrahim was in a car bombing on his way here. We don't know if we should believe it or not."

"Right now, forget about Ibrahim. What's done is done. We're forging ahead. Get ready." All the men under Casseaux were waiting for his command. Turning to them he said, "This is it. We're arresting these thieves tonight. We've got the chance to deliver one of the largest caches of fine art in the department's history, and we will succeed. It's time to get moving. I want every one of Ibrahim's men at this warehouse arrested and thrown in jail. We'll forget about Ibrahim tonight. There will be another day of reckoning for him. Go, do your jobs."

Captain Casseaux, Inspector Fournier and Alex along with a few Paris police officers worked with precision and stealth. The Captain had worked with his men so long that they understood him. Although he never showed much gratitude to them for their dedication and professionalism, they performed well nonetheless. They were all good men. Within minutes Casseaux and his fully armed team approached and closed in on the warehouse. Alex spotted a colossal man of about thirty standing guard at the front of the building.

"He's mine, Alex," whispered Fournier. He dashed toward his unsuspecting opponent. Once he stood directly behind the huge man, Fournier whistled, and as the man turned, Alex struck his head with his gun. The guy fell unconscious.

Now that Alex and his colleagues stood in front of the door to the warehouse, they nodded at each other before putting on their masks.

"One, two, go." Alex commanded. The tear gas they had placed at the door immediately exploded.

"Go, go, go!" he commanded again and the men rushed into the room.

Alex threw another tear gas bomb into the warehouse before they charged in farther.

"Paris Police! Drop your weapons, and put down all the goods in front of you," Alex shouted.

Knowing they couldn't run away, the thieves immediately froze, coughing violently from the tear gas.

"Get down on your knees," Fournier said.

The thieves complied. Casseaux commanded his officers to round up the men and take them to the jail in *Aix* to join the others already there. The Paris policemen handcuffed the thieves and led them to the police cars.

Alex looked around and saw a man dashing from the side of the building to the silver Audi. "Halt or I'll shoot." The man ignored him and made it out of the building before anyone stopped him. Fournier ran outside and shot the two front tires. The man started running, but was overtaken by other officers, who proceeded to handcuff him. Alex looked at him and took his identification. "You're Rami, owner of the *Arts and Antiquities.* What are you doing here tonight? You can tell me now, or we'll know after we raid your shop tonight and your partner tells us what is going on."

"Where is my partner and what has he told you?"

"He's at one of our farmhouses after suffering a gunshot wound at the Clarinet Bar. I'm sure he will tell interesting stories about your art-for-arms business." Fournier said.

"We've done nothing wrong," Rami said.

"Take him to the *Aix* jail under armed guard. We'll talk to him later," said Casseaux.

Alex immediately began looking through the paintings, searching for the Picasso and the Monet. Casseaux ordered the officers to open the paintings and get a count.

"Where in Hades are those two paintings?" Casseaux shouted, after forty-five minutes had elapsed.

The men, too scared to say a word, simply stared at him. Alex walked around inside the warehouse. "Where would I hide the two most valuable paintings?" Walking outside, he noticed the silver Audi.

The answer immediately came to his mind. He opened the trunk and found it empty but didn't give up. He took a small pocket knife and tore at the covering of the trunk. Hidden there were the two paintings he had seen the first time he had visited his godparents. He looked with wonder and thankfulness at the Picasso and Monet.

"Fournier, here they are," Alex shouted. He showed him the paintings. The night had been a big success for them.

The thieves hired by Ibrahim had now been handcuffed and taken to jail. Eventually they would be transferred to Paris, where they would await trial. Rami was declaring his innocence as he was led away. The investigators had finished their job with the greatest skill, but there was no Ibrahim.

The paintings were carefully checked and would be taken to Paris, where the representatives of Jewish Art Restitution and Restoration would identify and classify the rest of the art. They would work with the police to return them to the rightful owners. Alex was holding the Picasso and the Monet. "I'm taking these with me tonight to Dr. Anna's safe house and then to Maya and Philippe tomorrow," said Alex.

"I want to let you do that, Alex, but if I let two of the most valuable paintings go with you and something happens to them, the consequences for me would be huge. We must take them back to Paris first with the entire cache," said Casseaux.

Alex said, "You heard Levi and you agreed. You're going back on your word. There must be a way."

Fournier said, "I'll go with him. We'll get them verified with Dr. Anna tonight. She's on your team anyway, and I've been wanting to meet her. We'll check with you tomorrow morning at the station on our way to Maya and Philippe's. This is the right way. We're leaving. Don't try to stop us. It will take days to sort and classify all the art. We will explain that these two paintings have already been returned to the rightful owners."

Casseaux nodded reluctantly.

Alex and Fournier got into the unmarked car with the paintings and headed to Dr. Anna's safe house. Captain Casseaux turned his attention to dealing with the art work.

Chapter 39

Dr. Anna's Safe House

Tuesday night, Alex and Fournier drove to Dr. Anna's safe house. As Captain Casseaux was transporting the artworks, the other officers were moving the thieves from *Aix* to the jail in Paris. The night had been a great success. Alex was exhilarated to have Maya and Philippe's two paintings in his possession. He could hardly control himself. "Fournier, we've got them — the Monet and the Picasso. Can you believe it?"

Fournier said, "*Mais oui.* The stars aligned for us. Do you think the Romanian gypsy and the gold ring really had something to do with it? I've seen some amazing gypsy fortune tellers who have helped the police in ways our forensic department can't explain. I mean most of the time they are charlatans, out for a dime, but this Sylvana seemed to foresee our success and her prophecies were accurate. I've seen predictions like this before. It makes me wonder."

"We had help from above, Fournier. That's the truth of it."

"Well, the Paris police will take any help they can get. Where do you think Ibrahim and Yousif are?" Fournier asked.

Alex's phone rang, "Hello, yes. Where? We're on our way.

Strange, isn't it?" He clicked the phone off.

"What was that about?"

"Dr. Anna has an update on that car bombing. It was reported to Casseaux's officers before our raid by Bordeaux police. The report said no other vehicle had been in the accident. It appeared the car's driver lost control and the car veered off the autoroute and caught fire. No one was found in the car and no 911 call was made until the car was completely burned up." Alex looked at Fournier. "She has some other news too. Yousif has escaped from the car on the way to the safe house."

"Why would he do that?"

"Yousif wants to take matters into his own hands. I think he'll go after Ibrahim, but he doesn't know where he is and he's getting himself into a lot of trouble."

Fournier said, "It's possible Yousif could get to Ibrahim if someone tipped him off to his location. The Syrians are fed up with Ibrahim's outrageous war games, thefts and killings. They could have contacted Yousif. Moreover, Imam Mansur and his wife are claiming that Ibrahim is responsible for their daughter's death, so they might know where he is and might have alerted Yousif."

Alex said, "But how could they get that information to him, when he was in the police car? He must have known something himself about where Ibrahim might go. I can't let anything happen to Yousif. I promised Amirah."

"We can't do anything until we safely deliver these paintings to Dr. Anna. Maybe she'll have more information by the time we get there."

"If something happens to Yousif, Amirah will be devastated."

"Nothing's going to happen to him. How much farther is it to the safe house?"

"Only forty-five minutes." While maintaining control, Alex

broke the speed limit the rest of the way.

They arrived at Dr. Anna's safe house in thirty minutes and she greeted them, "Come in. I have breakfast and coffee for you. Sit down. I'll get it and we'll talk."

They were famished after the night's operations and ate voraciously the eggs, bacon and coffee cake, and drank an entire pot of fresh hot coffee. Feeling a bit refreshed after a grueling night, Fournier said, "You're a celebrity, Dr. Anna. I've heard a lot about you."

"Most of the praise is not deserved, Lieutenant Fournier, but thank you for the compliment. We've got a great cache of paintings I know, but we're missing Yousif and Ibrahim. Any ideas where they could be?"

Alex said, "No, but we were hoping you would have an update. I know Yousif is furious with Ibrahim and he may seek revenge. Have you heard anything from Amirah?"

"Yes, she is being driven to my safe house just outside Paris and I have two special Israeli agents there to take care of her."

"Would it be possible for me to call her tonight?"

"It would, but I prefer you wait until tomorrow. Too much is unsettled tonight."

Alex said, "We learned that Rami, Mrs. Pilon's brother, is very involved in the art thefts. In fact, he's in charge of the operations and is in a little competition with Ibrahim."

Dr. Anna said, "Yes, we've suspected him for some time because of his frequent meetings with Ibrahim and Mrs. Pilon at Rami's farmhouse. Right now, let me update you on what we know about Ibrahim. He hasn't left the country by airplane at any of the major airports. He can't, because he's on the suspected terrorist list, but he can escape the country in a car or on rail. Lots of Syrians would be happy if Yousif took care of Ibrahim, so he would never threaten them again."

Fournier said, "Yousif has intentionally put himself in danger by escaping. He knows Amirah is safe. He should have left it to the rest of us."

Alex looked concerned. "I'm sure he is hunting for Ibrahim, but in his quest, the poor guy may end up getting himself killed."

Dr. Anna looked at the two men and the wrapped paintings on the nearby table. "Are these our paintings?"

Alex immediately got up. He unwrapped the paintings at the table and showed them to her. The two men looked at her reaction, as she held the paintings with reverence and awe.

"I can't believe I'm seeing these wonderful paintings. Many people risked their lives to acquire them, and others died trying to save them."

Fournier said, "I can't believe they cost so much."

"They are perfect works of art," said Dr. Anna.

Alex knew they couldn't spend any more time with her. The safe house felt warm and cozy and they were exhausted, but they had to find Yousif as soon as possible and save him from himself. "We can't delay the search for Yousif. We'll leave these paintings with you, Dr. Anna, and come back to retrieve them as soon as we can."

"I'll guard them with my life. Have no fear for these paintings."

Alex spoke, "We know when and where Yousif escaped from custody. He told the police he needed a bathroom break and when they stopped, he went in and never returned. So, Fournier and I have got to take off tonight and find him."

Dr. Anna replied, "We know he would search for Ibrahim, so the question is, where is Ibrahim? We know some of the houses in that area are drug houses and we suspect there are refugee and immigrant safe houses that Ibrahim runs. I think he would go to one of them." She gave them addresses and maps.

Fournier asked, "How would Yousif know those places?"

Dr. Anna said, "Ibrahim and Yousif have a long history. They both wanted to save Syria in the beginning, but their paths diverged. I suspect Yousif knows about the houses."

The two men listened carefully to Dr. Anna. Alex said, "We owe you our gratitude. Are you okay here by yourself?"

"Oh, I'm not by myself. Please."

Alex didn't see any bodyguards, but he knew Dr. Anna had a deep relationship with the Mossad. No need to worry about her.

Fournier said, "*Enchanté*, Dr. Anna. We'll stay in touch. *Merci beaucoup.*"

Dr. Anna walked them to the door. "I promise to have the paintings waiting for you just as you see them now when you return. You will see Maya and Philippe as happy as newlyweds when they see their paintings returned."

She accepted Fournier's hands in hers, as they touched cheeks. Then she turned to Alex and took his hands likewise.

"Take care of yourselves."

The two men waved at her and walked to their car.

Chapter 40

Amirah's Ride

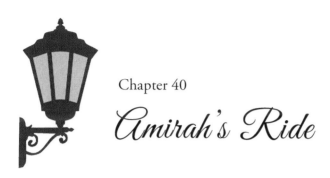

Early Wednesday morning, sleep-deprived and exhausted from her recent captivity, Amirah was thankful to be on her way to a safe house. She hoped for a comfortable night of sleep. Yet, Amirah was overcome by fears for her father's and Maslan's situation. She spent much of the ride ruminating about Alex's bravery and the incredible capture of her kidnappers, but then her thoughts turned to the traumatic memories of Aleppo. It was a nightmare she could never escape. She had seen the massacres of innocent civilians, the carnage of bodies exposed to chemical weapons, and her friends and family members being dragged from their beds in the darkness of night by the butchers of ISIS.

She relived the days and nights her family and she had huddled together as the walls of their apartment collapsed from another bombing raid. She lost count of the raids as bombs and missiles hailed down during her last two years in Aleppo. After living in France for two years, she had read that the Parisians had listened for the Nazis' bombing of Paris in the 1940s, much as she had done in Aleppo in 2012. The dreaded planes came quickly. She could be studying, washing dishes, or laughing with friends, when the Satanic enemies dropped the bombs destroying schools, hospitals and homes, leaving only piles of rubble and dust everywhere. She had heard men and women pleading to put them to death, so they could be put out of their misery. Sometimes they heard the sirens, but mainly they knew the missile sounds.

She continued to remember scenes in the midnight car ride. Houses in her neighborhood had underground tunnels and rooms to be used as bomb shelters or triages, but everyone knew it was only a matter of time until the families who resided there would be bombed by rebels, terrorists or government soldiers. She saw Sami and Rasheed pointing their fingers at her and saying, "Papa should have taken us first and come back for you and Mama. You may never see us again, Amirah." Everyone had to leave or be killed. Even if you locked yourself in your house, someone was coming — ISIS, rebels, looters or the government army, and they would drag out the men first and maybe kill or torture them in front of the family.

Torn between the guilt of leaving her brothers and mother behind and the desire to go with her father to a safer place, she would never forgive herself if they were not rescued from the refugee camp and brought to Paris. She believed they had at least made it to the camp. She knew she was a brave woman as her mother had told her many times, and she would make sure they joined Yousif and her. Or was she really brave? Was she kidding herself? She wondered.

As Amirah rode to the safe house, she thought her mother's prediction that things would go bad was coming true. The journey out of Syria was ghastly and now she was sick and tired of all the struggle.

"Oh, my head; it's numb. I don't want these memories anymore," she told herself. "Things will get better. I will overcome. Alex will protect Father tonight. I'm praying for them. 'Father of all beings, please shine Your grace on Alex and my father. Give them the wisdom to understand your will and the courage to obey it. Let them feel my love for them now in mind and spirit and let them know that if we should be parted forever in this life, our spirits will be together again when these trials are over. Guide us to forgive all and have faith in You.'"

She drifted into sleep, but awakened with memories of stepping into the war-ravaged streets of Aleppo outside her Uncle Daniyal's home. She watched him, alone and frightened. Was anyone taking him bread and bits of sweets or meats anymore? Then a terrible thought seized her. He was probably dead and his precious papers and books were likely burned to ashes. His tiny courtyard garden must be barren. There were eyes surrounding her from his spirit coming to her, but they were not comforting. They were terrifying and she cried out, as if from a nightmare.

"Are you okay?" asked the driver.

She shook herself. "May I have a bottle of water, please?"

"Yes, of course." He passed one back to her. "Would you like to hear some music or news on the radio?"

"No, no thank you."

"You've been through quite an ordeal this week. You know, I visited Syria with my wife in the sixties."

Amirah was thankful for someone to talk to, but she was surprised that someone driving her to a safe house had visited Syria. "Where did you go?"

"Oh, the oldest city in Syria, Damascus, of course. It has the most gorgeous mosque and my wife loved to shop in the souk for cooking pots and pans, and fabrics for her wardrobe. We loved to eat there too."

"Are you with the Paris police now?"

"No, Amirah, I work for a man who helps people like you."

"Who?"

"Monsieur Mustafa, whom you will be meeting soon."

"But I'm going to a safe house, aren't I?"

"You may call it that, if you like. We call it Mr. Farrokh Mustafa's *château*."

Amirah was caught totally off guard. She could not take any more confusion.

"What is this about?"

"You will be safer with us than the original safe house. Just relax. We're almost there."

Amirah dozed off until the car stopped in front of a lovely *château* surrounded by gardens you could see by the moonlight and stars. She was helped out of the car by the driver and escorted to the front door.

Chapter 41

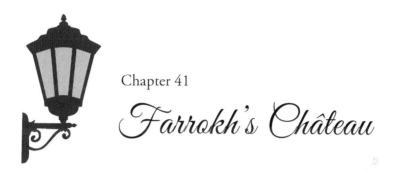

Farrokh's Château

Amirah stepped out of the car and saw a *château.* She had gone to the Louvre many times and that was really a former *château,* but now it was an art gallery, and it didn't look or function like a real *château.* Even though it was too dark to see the *château*'s beautiful surroundings, she saw that it was a magnificent edifice.

Suddenly she was overcome with feelings of her family's home in Syria and the suffering they had endured from both the National Army and ISIS, and how everything had been destroyed. How could some of the world be so cozy, comfortable and stable, while her country was full of death and destruction?

Her driver took her arm gently and led her to the door. A lovely lady answered. "Bonsoir, Monsieur and Mademoiselle Amirah. Please come into the dining room. We have a hot bowl of soup for you after your long ordeal. Mr. Farrokh, your host will be down soon." Amirah was totally confused. Who is Mr. Farrokh, she wondered. She sat down at the elaborate table and slowly sipped her soup. She had not realized how hungry she was. How divine real food tastes, she thought. She was alone in the dining room with huge Medieval windows, heavy wood furniture, Chinese hand-painted silk wallpaper, a sparkling crystal chandelier, and damask draperies. She had been transported into an eighteenth-century setting. Certainly, this was not her idea of a safe house.

Into the dining room came the lady again, accompanied this time by a man of medium height and dark complexion. Amirah guessed he might be about sixty years old, and something about his gait, gestures and body posture was familiar to her. He introduced himself. "Dear Amirah, I am Mr. Farrokh, and I have the privilege of being your host here while Fournier and his assistants arrest the miscreant mob who abducted you. This home is at your disposal. Do you remember we met at the art show with Maya and Philippe?"

Amirah, speechless and physically exhausted, began to sob quietly. Her secured safety and the kindness of her elegant host momentarily overwhelmed her."

"Oh, my dear, I have distressed you. Please forgive me."

"No, no, not at all. It is just all so strange. One minute I am the captive of terrorists. I fall asleep and wake up in a *château*. I don't know what to say. I apologize. I'm not like this, usually. This is all just so much."

"My dear, it is completely understandable. You have been under much duress. If there is anything you need this evening, please ask Antoinette," he said, pointing to the petite lady standing at his side, "and she will get it for you. She will be near your bedroom, across the hall all night." Antoinette smiled and exited the room. "You are in my headquarters, my dear, and Dr. Anna warned us to make sure every request of yours was met immediately and with the utmost concern for your safety and happiness. Did you enjoy the soup?"

"It was divine. Thank you."

"Please let me provide you with something else. *Thé, café, chocolat*?

"I love *chocolat — un chocolat chaud*, if that is possible."

"Yes, of course." Mr. Farrokh grasped the right lapel of his dinner jacket and spoke into the air as if someone else were standing beside him in the room." Please prepare un *chocolat chaud turc* for the lady and an espresso for me."

"You are most kind."

"First, you have every reason to be disoriented. May I tell you a story about the hospitality I'm offering you and my connection with helping the police?"

"But of course."

"I will tell you only a bit of my story tonight."

"Oh, please do."

"First, I am the grandson of a Lebanese quarry worker. He taught me faith in God and duty to others. My grandfather carried a fifty-pound pry bar a mile to and from home six days a week for the first five years of his adult life. The Lebanese didn't have dynamite, so the workers pried the marble loose with a wedge. In order to work you had to carry the wedge. At the very end of his long and eventful life, he told me those less fortunate than us are the wedge we still carry. Our wealth is only possible because of their hard work. I have tried never to forget that lesson. I honor him by supporting numerous charitable organizations. I cooperate with the police. We have extensive shipping enterprises now and the docks are a superb source of undercover police work. Sidon Shipping has an international police force of several dozen officers in its employment right now."

"You own Sidon Shipping?"

"Yes, it is our family enterprise. I am gratified you have heard of us."

Mr. Farrokh's old-world manners were new to Amirah. Her

father had talked of such men but she had never met one quite like this. Sidon ships were in every harbor in the Mediterranean. They dominated the cruise line industry.

"Madamn Brodeur of the Noumena Gallery informed me about your abduction."

"She has exhibited two of my paintings at her gallery. It's amazing she knew about my abduction and contacted you."

"I contacted Fournier to offer him my accommodation here as a safe house. I had already spoken with Dr. Anna. I wanted to meet you. I saw your work at the gallery and discussed it with Madam Brodeur later. She's as fascinated by your work as I am, and she likes the spiritual quality of your work that sets it apart. I am most interested in people whose faith has survived the nightmare of modern racial and religious politics and conflicts now engulfing us."

Antoinette entered the room with the espresso and *un chocolat chaud turc* and a bowl of whipped cream on a silver platter. "Thank you, Antoinette. I think you can prepare Amirah's bed. I'm sure she is weary and needs her rest soon."

"Yes sir."

"Now, Amirah, I have a lovely surprise for you in the morning, but I have enjoyed sharing part of my story with you tonight," he said, as he swallowed his last sip of espresso and exited the room.

Immediately Antoinette re-appeared. "Are you ready to see your room, Mademoiselle?"

"Yes, yes, thank you, Antoinette. How amazing all this is. Antoinette, could I ask a question?"

"Yes, of course," Antoinette answered as they walked to Amirah's room.

"I thought it was interesting that my driver spoke my own language. Who was he?"

Antoinette said, "Your driver has a very good ear for languages and he speaks seven, one of which is Arabic as you would speak in Aleppo. The friends of Mr. Farrokh have many team members who speak many languages. They hoped it would make you more comfortable and not cause you distress. I suppose hearing your native dialect, after your experience with Ibrahim and his gang made you anxious."

Anna asked, "Just a little for a moment. Do you have any idea who is being questioned about my kidnapping?"

"We think Rami is being questioned in the farmhouse in *Aix* right now, and he is talking. Ibrahim wanted to seek revenge on Yousif, and Rami wanted to use you to make duplicates of the stolen masterpieces to double his sales, so they were able to work together to carry out their purposes. We think Rami had the imam's daughter killed when she learned too much about his business."

"How do you know so much?"

"I am Mr. Farrokh's personal assistant at this *château* and hence, I am connected with the Mossad. In the morning, you may possibly meet Mr. Farrokh's wife, who is a very busy, social lady. Enter, my dear. This is your room. You are safe and I am in a room across the hall."

"*Merci*," said Amirah, "*Bonne nuit, Antoinette.*"

"*Bonne nuit*, brave Amirah."

After a marvelous hot bath with a most fragrant soap, Amirah put on the clean Egyptian cotton pajamas. She could have chosen any of the silk nightgowns, but she preferred the simple cotton. As she climbed into the high bed with firm mattresses, she felt comfortable and relieved, but her mind drifted to thoughts of where her mother and brothers might be sleeping tonight. She had hope. She was in France, where things were civilized and where life had value, where humans could be free people. Where were the monsters of the world who had destroyed Syria? As she drifted to sleep, she knew she would find peace and be able to help others to a better life. "Oh, God, thank you for saving me on the boat and rescuing me from evil tonight. Use me, Lord, for your service. Give me good, strong dreams and visions. Bless my father and Alex, and keep them safe wherever they are and bring them back to me. She let herself sink into the cool sheets and her body totally relaxed as she fell asleep."

Chapter 42

Morning at the Château

Amirah had slept soundly and awakened early. She tried to open the floor-to-ceiling French windows, but they were locked. She then cracked open her bedroom door and there was Antoinette. "What is it you need, my dear Amirah?"

"I would like to open the windows in my room, if I may?"

"Let me unlock them for you." As Antoinette unlocked the windows, she said, "Amirah, Mr. Farrokh would like you to join him for breakfast at nine on the terrace."

"I only have my clothes from last night. I'm embarrassed."

"No need to worry. I will bring something for you. Give me a few minutes." Antoinette left and returned in less than ten minutes.

"We knew you would be our guest, so we prepared a bit." She held up a dress cut in a flowing fabric in a floral print enhanced with shiny threads, as well as a pair of casual, comfortable sandals. "Would you like these?"

"Oh, I can't believe this. They're perfect. Thank you so much. Shall I go down with you before nine?"

"I will knock when it's time to leave. It's 7:30, so just take your time dressing. There are some books on the table, and I will be happy to walk with you on the grounds should you decide you would prefer a bit of walking before breakfast."

"No, I think I will enjoy the sunlight coming onto the balcony until closer to nine."

"Enjoy. *À tout à l'heure*," said Antoinette as she closed the door.

Amirah hurried to the window and drew in deep breaths of the morning air. She was alive and free. She actually pinched herself. She stretched a bit as her thoughts strayed to Alex and her father. Where were they now? Did they have the paintings to return to Maya? She wanted to talk to them, but she didn't know what had happened to her cell phone. No one took it. She didn't lose it. She could ask about everything at breakfast.

Then, as she looked over the grounds, she wanted to paint what she saw. Three deer were standing in a wooded area — papa, mama and baby — but close by was a magnificent garden laid out in the French manner, based on symmetry and the principle of imposing order on nature. All those geometric shapes were very similar to the style she used to create the rug designs for her father in Syria, and incorporated them into her paintings. These designs restored a sense of order and balance to the chaos she had endured. "Thank you, God, for the light of this day after nights of mourning. I am renewed. Thank you for kind men like Mr. Farrokh."

She enjoyed a shower and donned the lovely dress and shoes. She then joined Antoinette for the walk to the terrace, where they were greeted by the kind, gentle Mr. Farrokh and a lady she recognized.

Mr. Farrokh invited all to sit down. "Amirah, I believe you know Madam Brodeur from the Noumena Gallery."

"Yes, of course. She exhibited two of my paintings at the art show where I met you. *Bonjour*, Madam Brodeur."

"*Bonjour*, Amirah. So good to see you again. What a horrible ordeal those terrorists put you through. We are so thankful that you are here with us today. It's amazing how well you look."

"It will take some time to pull myself together, but with my faith and good friends like you and Monsieur Farrokh, I will get well and soon be back to normal," said Amirah.

"Madam Brodeur has provided you with a modest range of canvases and paints, if your stay here should become tedious. The light in the conservatory is by most accounts excellent. The grounds of the estate cover fifty acres, and your balcony provides an exceptional view," said Farrokh.

"I just thought this morning that I would love to paint that view. Thank you for your thoughtfulness and generosity."

Coffee was served, followed by fresh fruit, scrambled eggs and French pastries. "Amirah," Farrokh began, "I want to hear about the spiritual journey which Madam Brodeur sees in your paintings. I assure you my concern is not idle curiosity. As I mentioned last night, I have my grandfather's faith. I help many charitable organizations, but I also use my money to help individuals attain their goals, especially when their faith in life has been challenged by severe difficulties."

"I will share with you part of my story as you shared part of yours with me last night, but first, may I ask a question?"

"Of course, my dear. What is it?"

"Do Lieutenant Fournier, Alex and my father know about all this? Do they know where I am?"

"Oh, yes, it was a bit of a last minute arrangement, but my home offers a second layer of security and an even more obscure hideaway. From time to time at the request of Dr. Anna or Lieutenant Fournier, I volunteer to keep people like you here."

"I'm glad to hear it. My father needed to know I was safe.

Poor Alex has been through so much because of me. Thank you for letting them know."

Madam Brodeur said, "We were glad to help you. Amirah, Mr. Farrokh is one of the patrons of my gallery and one of the first to see my opening exhibitions. I am forever indebted to him, not only for the financial support he provides, but also for his phenomenal eye for art. He can look at works of new artists and tell me within minutes how important they are or will become. He has an unusual gift and because of it, an extraordinary art collection. I honestly don't know how he does it. Amirah, please share with him anything you care to about your painting."

"Well, I have been drawing and painting since I was three years old. I have always drawn geometrical cubes, blocks, and squares with all kinds of edges, but I have also, as you know, Madam Brodeur, done portraits and landscapes. My style is evolving but my faith has led me to show my beautiful homeland before all the death and destruction occurred. Aleppo was one of the most gorgeous cities in Syria – actually, the most beautiful. As an ancient city, it had weathered all the storms of life until the Arab Spring. Its people were warm, friendly, and loving."

"Many Muslim men think of art, music and dance as a waste of time. I imagine this was a big problem for you in your culture," said Mr. Farrokh.

"Yes, exactly. My father admired my work, but still there were rules of expectation for girls — not all bad, but choices had to align with family and community. You were to wear certain clothes, study a little, but not too much, and marry. My family was more liberal, but by the time the whole country was caught up in the civil wars, women had to follow the rules and traditions of extremists. When I was seventeen my family chose a husband for me. He was ten years older and very handsome, but the only reason I was chosen was to please the families and to have children. He cared nothing about my art. It was an inconvenience for him actually, and his mother especially hated it. She preferred that I cook and clean."

"Women have had much to overcome for so long, haven't we, and regrettably, your plight is still common in many parts of the world. Think of all the talent that never comes to fruition," said Madam Brodeur.

"Yes, here in Paris I've been free to explore and develop my art. I've even dabbled in impressionism. My father knows some Muslim men in Paris who don't like my independent and creative spirit."

"I'm sorry, but not surprised, to hear that, Amirah, but we know this was one of the reasons for your kidnapping. You were helping the imam's daughter in Paris advertise her legal services for Muslim women who were in abusive situations or having serious marital issues. Certain Muslim men did not want their wives and daughters to see the ads, lest they be encouraged to report the beatings or torment they faced from them. The men knew the laws of Paris would not be as lenient on them as Sharia law had been. We have some of the same problems in Paris that you had in Syria, but we do have better laws to protect women here. Please excuse my digression," said Mr. Farrokh.

"I agree with everything you've been saying. Before I left Syria, I sought the help of Allah. I live and breathe my art now. Every minute that I can create something to share with others, I am in my element. I think the Spirit of the Lord is guiding me in new directions, especially after my experience on the boat from Syria."

"What did you experience?"

"I had seen pictures of Jesus in Istanbul and I recognized His image on the sea the night we were escaping. I prayed to Him and I believe he saved us from the storm that night. I feel called to capture the truth and beauty of that miracle. I want my art to speak for me."

"My dear, you speak quite well, and the quality of your art is stellar. Madam Brodeur and I have a surprise for you. We would like to have a small exhibition of your works in the Noumena Gallery when you are ready. Would you like that?"

"I am deeply honored and really at a loss for words. Your kindness is a gift beyond measure."

"Consider yourself a member of my family. We will talk of good things when the time is better. Madam Brodeur and I have appointments in Paris, so we must leave. Canvases and paints are in your room, and please let Antoinette know if you need anything else while you are our guest." Madam Brodeur and Monsieur Farrokh exited and Antoinette re-appeared. She and Amirah then enjoyed another cup of coffee.

Chapter 43

The Search for Yousif and Ibrahim

Alex spoke to Maslan on the cell phone, "Tell me any place you think Ibrahim might be hiding, or do you think he's already left the country? If you cooperate with us, the judges might reduce your sentence. I promise you. I'm working on a lenient sentence for you. I understand. I've got it. Call me if you think of anything else."

Fournier asked, "What did he say?"

"Maslan gave me the addresses of three primary hide-outs that Ibrahim frequents. He thinks Yousif is headed toward one that's a good two hours' drive from here. That address was also one that Dr. Anna gave us."

"A lot can happen before we get there."

"Let's go." Fournier stepped on the gas.

Alex said, "What a relief that Amirah is safe. Nobody is going to find her at Monsieur Farrokh's. How did a guy like you get to know a guy like that?"

"You Americans think all cops are just flatfoots on the beat. In France, we have this thing we call 'culture'. We share a history of fine art, cuisine and sophistication."

"Fournier, you are so full of it. You know bloody well what I mean. He's a billionaire international businessman. He's not hanging around the same places you do, or the clinic for that matter."

Fournier chuckled. "Mr. Farrokh is a devout Muslim who hates the jihadists. I have actually never met him. He has several executive assistants who help train and place underground operatives on the docks of Sidon Shipping to give us inside info on gun running and illegal immigration."

"What did Yousif say when you told him Amirah was going to stay with one of the richest philanthropists in Europe?"

There was an awkward silence. "I messed up. I didn't tell him."

"You what?"

"I know, I know. There was so much to do. The ambulance, the forensic team, the coroner. He left for his safe house before I could tell him."

Alex shrugged. "We've got to get to him as fast as we can. He can get us all in big trouble. Let's hope we don't get there too late."

Speeding towards the hide-out, Fournier arrived in the vicinity two hours later. Everything was quiet and they saw no guards.

Fournier motioned and said, "Look, over there at that jeep behind those trees."

Alex and Fournier grabbed their guns, got out of the car and walked toward the house. Nearing the porch, they heard Yousif's angry voice from inside, "You are a disgrace to Islam. I thought you were my friend when you helped Amirah and me get out of Syria. But you have revealed yourself to be an enemy. You charged me so much money and still you have not delivered Mehri and the boys, but I've got you now."

Fournier said, "I think we should arrest them."

Alex motioned for Fournier to listen, "Not yet. Let's hear

some more."

Ibrahim said, "You don't know what I've done for you here, my countryman. I have kept the men from harming Amirah. I've tried to warn you that they don't like her independent spirit, but you've ignored me. The men I train here have not lived the life you and I lived in Syria. They hope we can take the country back. Some restoration is taking place in Aleppo as we speak. I need money to help the rebels fight. Yes, I stole some art but the people I stole from have so much money, what is it to them if I take a few pieces to help build our country?"

"You've been using that money for yourself, Ibrahim. You have given a bad reputation to all of your honest Syrian brothers trying to make a go of it in Paris."

"You should be thanking me for helping you escape and knowing that I am going to help your family. All you needed to do was to follow my instructions. You were to meet my man at the station, go to *Aix*, meet the most important man in this operation, and then work out the details to help Syria, but you failed. You always think you know best. Yousif, you've always thought you are smarter and better than anyone."

"Not at all. Ibrahim, you have changed through the years. You've lost your soul and I feel sorry for you."

"Don't feel sorry for me. You have lost your way. Your wife was right. You should have stayed in Syria and fought. That would have been the noble thing to do--not run away."

"I did stay and fight, until it was too dangerous for all my family. You know I wanted to take Mehri and my boys with me."

"Well then, why didn't you bring them all?"

"You told me we could not come together. You are the one who said we had to come this way. I trusted you. Now I think you hoped the separation from Mehri would open the door for you to become some kind of hero to her. And if you did not kidnap Amirah, who did?"

"Another man, an Iranian. Look, Rami wanted Amirah to paint copies of the masterpieces he had stolen and he planned to sell them as originals."

"You are a disgrace to Islam. I don't believe you. You kidnapped Amirah because you have always been jealous of me. You wanted my wife. I've known your scheming soul for a long time. Now I can get rid of you. I should finish you off right now."

"Come try, if you can. I told my men to stand down and let me talk to you. There was a time when I would have taken great pleasure in slitting the throats of you and your daughter, but not now. Life has treated both of us unfairly."

"I don't trust you or believe you."

"We've got to move now," Fournier said, as he sprinted to the door. "We don't know how many men Ibrahim has out here guarding the house. Just then a shot whizzed by Fournier's head. That shot changed their plan.

Fournier spotted two men on the other side of the house and another behind the trees.

"There are at least three men out here, but now Ibrahim and Yousif have heard the shot. We've got to get in there to prevent Yousif from doing something stupid," said Fournier.

The two men nodded. The man behind the tree moved and Alex quickly aimed and shot him. He fell to the ground.

"Cover me," Alex told Fournier. He re-loaded his gun and headed for the front door.

Fournier saw another man aiming at Alex. In an instant Fournier shot him in the leg. "Take care of things out here, Fournier. I'm going in," Alex shouted.

Fournier said, "I'm calling for back-up." He checked the two men who were shot.

"Make the call," said Alex. Holding his gun firmly, he kicked the door open and rushed in.

He saw what he had feared. Yousif and Ibrahim were slugging it out. Ibrahim's shirt was covered with blood. He had been shot. Yousif's nose was broken and blood was running from his mouth. "Freeze, police," Alex shouted.

Yousif and Ibrahim, ignoring Alex's command, continued fighting. Ibrahim punched Yousif in the stomach, causing him to gasp in pain. Alex raised his gun to stop the fight but then heard footsteps behind him. He turned and saw one of Ibrahim's men, about to fire at him, but Alex shot him first. The man dropped to his knees. Ibrahim was yelling for help from across the room, but no help was coming.

Yousif exclaimed, "Why shouldn't I shoot you, Ibrahim? You are a bully and a disgrace to Islam. You killed innocent Syrian people trying to start a new life. You are a traitor to all good men. I know you had Imam Mansur's daughter killed, and you kidnapped my Amirah and want to kill her too."

"No, no, you are wrong about me, Yousif. I'm telling you the truth. Rami arranged to kidnap Amirah and I happen to know he killed the Imam's daughter."

"Why? What did she have to do with Rami?"

"He asked her to help him with legal issues and they became friends, but she began to snoop and asked too many questions, and Rami feared she was going to report him. She also saw that he was copying masterpieces and selling them as originals. He could not afford to lose his profitable counterfeit art business. Put the gun away."

Alex said, "Yes, Yousif, put your gun away. If you kill him, you'll go to jail for the rest of your life. Is that what you want? Do you want to be separated from Amirah and the rest of your family and live behind bars? No, you don't want to be a murderer. You don't want to kill Ibrahim in cold blood. He may yet find redemption for his sins. Let us handle it."

"Wait," Yousif said, ignoring Alex, "you were involved in the art thefts, weren't you?"

Ibrahim admitted, "Yes, I was, but I work for Rami and do my own jobs on the side. I am a partner as well as a competitor. He pays me fairly well for the jobs I do for him. My men and I want to help Syria — something you used to want to do. Rami isn't interested in that. He is a thief for the money alone. It's sad. I never planned to do this; you must believe me, Yousif. Who will help us? Where is the UN? Where is the United States? We're on our own in Syria with nothing and nobody. I don't know why I did the things I did, but I swear to you, I'm not the evil man you think. Life just happens. You should understand."

Yousif says, "I liked you in Syria when we were fighting together, but you became a brutal leader. I always suspected what you were doing in Paris, and now you're only sorry because you know you're caught."

"Maybe you could help me escape, Yousif. Turn the gun on Dr. Alex and his police friend."

"No, Ibrahim. I won't do that. Maybe your contacts with money can help you plead your case and defend you in the courts."

Fournier burst in, "Drop the gun, Yousif. Freeze, all of you." Yousif dropped the gun and Alex picked it up.

Suddenly Hilba entered the back door holding one of Ibrahim's men whom he had found in the yard, guarding the house. "What should I do with him?" After Alex got over his initial shock at seeing Hilba, he realized that he must have spoken with Dr. Anna and found out where they were and drove there to help.

Fournier tossed Hilba a pair of handcuffs and two pairs to Alex. "Put these on Ibrahim and his accomplice and Yousif too. I'm expecting backups any time."

Yousif resisted the handcuffs, but unsuccessfully.

"Why shouldn't you shoot him, Alex?" pleaded Yousif.

"Fournier and I heard you and Ibrahim talking. We are witnesses to what you said. We can provide testimony in a court of law."

"I want him punished for all he did and I know that if Ibrahim goes free, he'll seek revenge on me and victimize Amirah. You've seen and heard what he's capable of. He is ruthless and violent."

Yousif held his head, weeping from the strain of what was happening to him. "I really am sorry for your bad choices, Ibrahim. I came here to kill you for all you've done, but now I feel pain for what all of us have suffered. We were fighting in a living hell in Syria. Our old lives will never be restored."

Alex said, "Yousif, he won't threaten you again. And Rami will never come after Amirah. Ibrahim will be locked away for life with the evidence we have on him. You know, you could have destroyed yourself today."

Sirens sounded and lights flashed as police cars pulled in front of the hide-out. Heavily armed officers jumped out and ran to the crime scene.

Alex said, "I think we have this under control, as the police officers entered the house.

Fournier said, "Ibrahim, you're under arrest for art thefts, and possibly murder. You have the right to remain silent as anything you say can be used against you in court."

Ibrahim let out a cruel laugh. "I shall not rest until I prove how I was used by Rami in this dirty business. My motives were pure as the driven snow, but something went wrong. I will prove my innocence, so help me, Allah."

Fournier said, "See you in jail, Ibrahim." A police officer led a protesting Ibrahim to the police car, while the wounded gang members were put into an ambulance under police security.

As Yousif was being put into a police car with another officer, he asked, "Does Amirah know I escaped and went after Ibrahim?"

Alex said, "No, she doesn't. She is in a safe house. We'll get her to you as soon as possible, but you'll be under guard until you get checked by a doctor. You will have to answer charges for escaping while under police protection, but I will help you. Don't try to get away again."

Yousif thanked Alex. "I have no reason to escape from the police now that I know Amirah is safe and Ibrahim is arrested. This has been another nightmare. My heart is growing weary with all the trials I have faced in my life."

The hide-out was cleared, and soon Alex and Fournier drove away, thankful that Ibrahim had finally been captured. They sped to Dr. Anna's safe house to pick up the art and return it to Maya and Philippe.

Chapter 44

Return to Dr. Anna

It was a long tiring drive back to Dr. Anna's safe house. Alex and Fournier were exhausted after the harrowing night's experiences. The mental and physical stress was taking its toll. They called Dr. Anna and were surprised to hear Levi answer the phone. "Dr. Anna returned to Antony so I'm protecting the paintings," he said. "When will you arrive here?"

"In a few hours."

They arrived early in the morning, and saw in the sunlight the charming little stone cottage with its hedges and tall trees. Darkness had covered the area the night before, as there were no outside lights to draw attention to the safe house. Now they could see the bright *Provençal* fabric curtains covering the windows with the chalk colored shutters. No one would suspect this charming, benign-looking cottage to be a safe house used by Israeli intelligence officers.

Levi opened the door and said, "Welcome, come in. Follow me." He and the men walked into the cozy kitchen. Levi continued preparing biscuits, eggs, sausages and fresh blackberries. A big pot of coffee was brewing. Soon the men poured big mugs of coffee and sat down at the rough-hewn wooden table and began to fill their plates. They hadn't realized how hungry they were, after all the night's tension with Ibrahim and Yousif.

Levi said, "I know you guys are exhausted. Dr. Anna made the beds with fresh linens and placed bath towels on the beds for you, so you can sleep here as long as you want and then we'll deliver the paintings."

Alex asked, "Did you get any sleep last night?"

"About four hours, my usual."

Fournier asked, "What can you tell me about Ibrahim?"

Levi said, "We've been trailing Ibrahim for several years because we know his history. He has contacts in Argentina with Nazi war criminals who escaped after World War II. He's kept friendships with children of those Nazis. His partner, Rami, also has contacts all over the world with terrorists and Neo-Nazis. Rami's prosperous and upscale *Arts and Antiquities shop* in *Aix* has been under our watch for several months. At first, we did not have our radars set on him. Now we believe he hired someone to kill Maleeka Mansur. We will be expanding our investigation in Paris."

Alex said, "Ibrahim told us that Rami was the murderer. If we can believe him, we were witnesses to information to seal your case against both Ibrahim and Rami. It always amazes me that the Nazi butchers escaped to countries all over the world, and many of them were never tracked down. Take a country like Argentina. Many of the citizens still hold deep anti-semitic prejudices. Only a few years ago the only Jewish Synagogue in Buenos Aires was bombed."

Levi agreed. "You're right. Olivia's parents were missionaries to Argentina. They witnessed the prejudice and hate toward Jews even after all these years. Still, the haters are a small minority taking advantage of the hospitality and good nature of the Argentinian people. Do you remember when Dr. Anna met you that she did not tell you about all the art that was stolen from Jewish people throughout Europe and South America after the war? She cracked some of the most famous Holocaust art thefts in history, but there are still countless works of art to recover from that period."

Alex said, "People like Dr. Anna, who invest their lives in this tedious, painstaking detective work, should receive Nobel peace prizes. It's a big challenging puzzle that pulls one into a web of intrigue and danger. Dr. Anna had to have lots of pieces for each puzzling case. She worked painting by painting, case by case, examining the stolen Holocaust paintings, jewelry and money that the Nazi butchers brought with them when they fled Germany."

Levi said, "She's the most persistent investigator I've ever known. She and her colleagues worked endlessly, at times putting their lives at great risk. She knew the Germans would help each other hide wherever they moved, so her team faced danger around every corner. Dr. Anna is revered by the Holocaust victims' families."

"I know that the Allies found plundered artwork in more than one thousand repositories across Germany and Austria. Now with nearly seven hundred thousand pieces identified and restituted to the countries from which they were taken, presumably they have been returned to the rightful owners," said Alex.

Fournier added, "Alex, our police department has an entire unit dealing with only Holocaust stolen art. Most of the pieces they deal with were confiscated from Jews by the Nazis, but our inventory lists were not released until 1985."

Levi said, "True, although Dr. Anna was already working on cases when the locations of the paintings weren't as well documented in books and media. Now, Hollywood is making money on this history and making people aware of these cruelties. The databases in our computers have certainly helped with the process of returning the art, but in our case with the Dalles, the returned art was stolen again, this time by the Middle Eastern Mafia."

"I think they wanted to torment the Jewish people for today's issues in the Middle East, and so the cycle continues. I believe the majority of people of every race and religion are good people who love their families and want peace. However, they have a hard time forgiving the centuries of wars and violence, as well as overcoming prejudices taught them by their parents," said Alex.

"You're right," Levi said. "Children inherit the prejudices of their parents. In the Book of Jeremiah in the Old Testament it says, 'Just as I watched over them to uproot and tear down, to demolish, destroy and bring disaster, so I will watch over them to build and plant, declares the Lord. In those days, it will no longer be said that the fathers have eaten sour grapes and the children's teeth have been set on edge.' This gives hope that one day the children will no longer commit the sins of racial prejudice and fanaticism, because in part, the fathers will not teach them prejudice."

"These are extraordinary problems deep in the culture and the human spirit, far beyond the reach of medical science. They are diseases of the soul, not the body," said Alex. "These animosities and prejudices are older than the Bible, but the Bible records them. People need to forgive each other and start over, as Yousif did tonight, when he actually felt sorry for Ibrahim and forgave him."

Fournier chimed in, "I think part of the motive for Ibrahim's art thefts is definitely revenge and retaliation against all the dictators who've wrecked his country, as well as other nations who've disappointed him, but I doubt someone like Ibrahim is in it only for revenge. It's also for money and power. He says he wants to see Syria restored and he doesn't have the money to make it happen. He knows Syria's government steals billions from the people, but he won't be able to put his hands on that, so what means were open to him? He went into the art theft business. He is the victim of desperate times."

"It's disgusting and disheartening for the law-abiding refugees to see the likes of Ibrahim. What does your group say about helping the refugees, Levi?" asked Alex. I know the Old Testament is full of prophets telling the people to take care of the refugees, but then in the next chapter they are telling them to go to war and not marry the foreign women."

"We are to welcome them, because again we do not know when we might be serving an angel unaware. The verse about refugees continues, 'I was hungry and you gave me food, I was thirsty and you gave me drink,' and I would say, 'I was lost and you found me and brought me home is what Jesus tells us to do.' Our ministry is always open to refugees. They need protection and care. Olivia counsels them and our teams provide houses, food and language study."

The men finished their breakfast and Levi began cleaning up. "Go get a few hours of sleep. I'm going to relook at the missing parts of our puzzle concerning Ibrahim. Does anybody need anything else?"

Fournier said, "Thanks, Levi, for everything. I'll get another cup of coffee and help you clean up."

"That's appreciated, but you need sleep. I can handle this."

Fournier said, "No, I have energy left and I want to ask you a few more questions."

Alex got up and headed to his room. "Thanks for everything, Levi. We'll talk later today."

Fournier helped Levi clear the table. "I don't think it will surprise you to learn that Mrs. Pilon was a key player in all this for quite some time. On the day we arrested her, we went to get Ibrahim too, but he had disappeared. Our department gets anonymous tips all the time, and we actually try to keep up with them. Sometimes they pay off."

Levi said, "Alex and you were right on target, getting into her office and arresting her after Fauziah found the list of the past and future victims of Rami and Ibrahim. There are some distinguished people on that list, who were to be victims, but we also have another list — the curator list."

"So how many curators are on your list? You know we'have a few on ours," said Fournier.

Levi replied, "A few of the best-known museum curators from European capitals are guilty of purchasing stolen art works for their own personal collections or for their anonymous clients. Naturally, they're very tight-lipped about their sales, but some are only too glad to support the sale of confiscated art to any country, good or bad, if they can get the money they want. Dealers and buyers just want the art. World conflicts mean little to them, as long as they're safe themselves. Decadent souls will do anything for money. To get big money, somebody has to falsify the chain of possession documents, so the items can be legally sold.

Did the Paris Police Art Unit think Mrs. Pilon was more than a messenger for Ibrahim?"

"Oh, yes, we did. She was an excellent accountant and travel organizer. She made appointments with buyers to view certain pieces in the possession of Rami. She might show paintings or print information for previews for the sophisticated players in Paris. They would meet surreptitiously in a beautiful *appartement* and seal a deal. The buyer had to make the trip to the *Arts and Antiquities shop* in *Aix*, and if the buyer wanted it shipped anywhere in the world, Mrs. Pilon could certainly accommodate," said Fournier.

"Casseaux has a point about our working more closely. We could save on our resources, because in this case, we had almost the same information you had on Mrs. Pilon. You really helped us by getting into her office, along with the raiding the warehouse and capturing Ibrahim. We knew those rogues at the warehouse were hired by Ibrahim, but Rami knew them too." They finished drying the dishes and put them in the cupboards.

"I'm going back to Paris later today and I'll make sure the paintings are safe. Maya and Philippe should have a big bottle of champagne waiting for us. We'll stay in touch, Levi. I hope we work on some more cases together, although the art investigations are not usually my beat."

"I'm sure we will. By the way, I heard you have artistic talent, so it might turn out to be an assignment you will enjoy more than you think."

"We'll see. I'm heading to bed. See you later today." Fournier went to his bedroom and turned out the lights.

Levi turned off the small light in the kitchen, checked deadbolts, and picked up his gun and walked to his bedroom.

Chapter 45

Maya's Art

Alex and Lieutenant Fournier arrived at the elegant *appartement* of Philippe and Maya at 3:00 p.m. Claire-Lise opened the door and greeted them. Alex kissed her and gave her a big hug. "Meet Claire-Lise, the beautiful daughter of the Dalles," he said to Fournier.

"*Enchantée de faire votre connaissance,*" she said to Lieutenant Fournier.

"*Enchanté, aussi,*" said Lieutenant Fournier.

"So, are you replacing Mrs. Pilon here?" Alex asked.

"Yes, the management offered me a part-time job for a few weeks, until they find a replacement for Mrs. Pilon. I can't believe I'm in the manager's office where she collaborated with those thieves to steal my family's art. I couldn't resist looking around this office. I always thought she was an old crone and I never liked her. She's quite strange."

"She's been here more than twenty years, so you would never have thought she could do this, would you?" asked Alex.

"No, not really. I didn't think she was smart enough."

Fournier chimed in, "Well, she got under the influence of

some bad people."

"Sadly, she's gone now. We are excited to see you, Alex. We are grateful that you and Lieutenant Fournier masterminded an incredible recovery of the art. I'm just sorry I was not with you to follow your adventure," she said.

Fournier smiled and said, "I don't think Alex would call our experience an adventure, Claire-Lise."

"Oh, I'm sorry. I don't know all the details. Mom was stressed knowing that you put yourselves in danger for her art. I know what's in those packages you're carrying."

"I'm sure you do," said Alex.

"Mother is as excited to see you as she is to see the paintings. Go right on up in that shaky but elegant elevator."

Alex and Fournier rode the tiny elevator up to the Dalles' *appartement*, got out and rang the doorbell. A smiling Maya opened the door, embraced Alex and kissed him on the cheeks.

"Alex, just look at you. How wonderful it is to see you."

"Maya, let me present Lieutenant Fournier, my partner in the recovery of your paintings."

Maya extended her hand and then kissed his cheeks too. "*Enchantée. Merci, merci, merci.* I regret I couldn't do more to help, Alex. But here you are and I am very happy to see you. Come in. Come in. You two are my heroes."

Philippe joined them at the door. "Yes, yes, come on in. Welcome. You men did an incredible job."

Alex said, "Philippe, great to see you as always."

"But you two are the miracle workers!" exclaimed Philippe.

"Thank you, Philippe. You know that's not true."

"You did a great job. You rescued Amirah from her kidnappers and you found our art. That's two for one," said Philippe. "The newspapers are making you heroes. It's phenomenal really."

"We just did what we had to do," Alex said.

"All I did was keep an eye on Alex," said Fournier.

"Come, bring those precious packages over here and sit down on the sofa," she said. They all went into the living room and sat down. "We're going to open the packages."

Isabella appeared and set on the coffee table a tray with drinks, cheese, crackers and salmon on toast points. Maya handed each of them a napkin and a drink.

Isabella said, "Glad to see you back with your mission accomplished, Dr. Alex. I knew you would find the paintings. Congratulations."

"Thank you for your prayers and encouragement, Isabella." Alex handed the packaged paintings to Maya, who began to unwrap them. She embraced them, held them tightly and then looked at them with amazement.

"Alex, you know what these paintings mean to me, but I forbid you to risk your life for me ever again. It's too much. You and Lieutenant Fournier jeopardized your lives. I would never have been able to face your mother, if something had happened to you." She hugged Alex again and said a few "Hail Marys." As she marveled at the paintings she began to cry. "As much as I love these paintings, you are far more valuable than any of them."

"Maya, please, I did it because you have always been the most wonderful friend of my family and we all love you. I'm thankful God was with us and we succeeded in our mission."

"I cannot get over Mrs. Pilon being a member of a terrorist organization or a Mafia here right under my nose. How on earth could that nice poor lady get involved in such a mess?"

"Money, Maya. It's money most of the time," said Fournier.

"Alex and Lieutenant Fournier, I think we must have a celebration in your honor. Maya and I want to plan something special, but for now we want to promise you that you can always depend on us, and we will be there for you if you ever need us for anything," said Philippe.

Alex replied, "We wanted to do this for you. Please. If I enumerated all the gracious ways you two have blessed my family, we'd be here all afternoon. We love you. No more thanks needed."

Maya said, "I understand. Alex, I can't help but notice that unusual gold ring you're wearing. It looks vaguely familiar. What's the story?"

"Oh, it's kind of funny. I'm not a superstitious person, but this old gypsy lady has come to me several times outside the *Musée d'Orsay* since I've been coming to Paris. She's Romanian, and she continues to appear at certain times to give advice to me or share premonitions or even encouragement. At first, I thought she was crazy, but everything she's predicted has happened. She claims to be a Christian prophet with messages for me. I must have a real live guardian angel. There is indeed mystery in life in the oddest ways."

"Hmm, we have some people in Honduras whose advice and predictions have helped the local people find missing cows, jewelry and even children," commented Maya.

"I know it sounds weirdly supernatural, but long story short--she gave me this gold ring and predicted that I would find the paintings and solve the mystery surrounding them. I'll give it back to her the next time she finds me. It wasn't anything specific that she said, but more encouragement and assurance that things would end well."

"I'm not surprised. That's why I recognized it. She has something of a rare reputation. Here's something I've never told you, Alex, and you may find it interesting also, Lieutenant. I went to the *Musée d'Orsay* when I was about your age, Alex. A gypsy lady came to me, and I would bet my life she's the same one. She said she knew I would soon meet a man who would bring me peace and the greatest joy in life, and what do you know? That year I met and married Philippe."

Alex laughed, rubbed the ring and said, "The old gypsy lady surely gets around. She definitely has some kind of old soul, but it's surprising that you got a message too. Maybe it's a family connection."

Fournier chuckled, "You've kept that one from me, Alex. I've never had supernatural help on a case. It does sound strange."

"Now, regarding that celebration I mentioned, I'm thinking about one night this week. Maya and I would like to take you two to dinner in the city. When would it be convenient? Would Thursday work?"

Maya interjected, "We must go in the evening by the moonlight and the beautiful street lights. I have a favorite boatman on a little *bateau mouche* and we can relax, talk together and have dinner at a divine restaurant. How does that sound?

"You really don't need to entertain us," Alex said.

Maya insisted. "Nonsense. When can you go? Tonight? Tomorrow? You must bring your wife also, Lieutenant."

"Oh, that is very kind of you, Maya, but I doubt that I can go," said Fournier. "My wife would not want me to accept such gracious hospitality. Besides, I think she's planning a quiet weekend for us. And, anyway, recovering the paintings was all in the line of duty for me."

Maya says, "Aww, you must at least invite her to come with us. I promise you won't be disappointed. Alex, will Amirah be able to join us?"

"I know she would love to, but I will need to check with her. I should also clear it with Dr. Anna and Levi. Since Ibrahim and Rami have been captured, I feel that she is safe from harm. If all is well with Amirah and Lieutenant Fournier, let's say tomorrow evening," said Alex.

"I'll let Alex know if my wife is free."

"*Bien sur,*" said Maya. "From the bottom of my heart, *Merci! Merci!*" Maya hugged Lieutenant Fournier.

"I've got to get back to the station now, but I'm truly happy for you, Madame Dalle. Our art department at the police station will be in touch with you for follow-up."

"I've got to go too, Maya. You know I've got miles to go before I sleep," said Alex. "Besides, Fournier and I came together, so we'll leave together."

"If you must. Alex, I wish your parents could see how well you are handling things. If only they would move here for a few months each year, we would all love it. Philippe should have told me sooner about the paintings," she said.

"I was correct in keeping all the worry from you. You had enough on your mind," said Philippe, taking Maya's hand in his.

"Alex, I don't waste time worrying. Life is too short, because I have great faith in Saint Anthony and of course, I pray for you every day."

"Thank you, Maya. I really hope we can do dinner tomorrow night. I'll get back with you."

Isabella opened the door for Alex and Fournier. They got in the tiny elevator and pressed "lobby". Fournier said, "Look, Alex, you know I'm not one for fancy dinners. I like Maya and all, but you handle the regrets for my wife and me. You need to go because Maya is your godmother, but you and I see plenty of each other at the station."

"I don't think you can get out of this one, Fournier. Maya will insist. You must come."

"We'll see."

Claire-Lise got up when she saw them exit the elevator, walked to the front door to hold it open. "Have a great day. It's so good to see you, Alex, and nice to meet you, Lieutenant Fournier."

"Good to see you, Claire-Lise. Take care," Alex said, embracing her. Then they left the building.

Chapter 46

Celebration

The next evening at 7:30 P.M., Maya met Amirah, Alex, Lieutenant Fournier, and his wife Lizette in the lobby of her *appartement.* Maya greeted them with hugs. "I'm delighted you all could come and especially Amirah. I am so excited that we can see this beautiful city by night."

Lieutenant Fournier said, "Maya, let me present my wife Lizette."

Lizette and Maya replied together, "*Enchantée.*"

"Philippe sends his deepest regrets. He was called to Estonia last night to deliver a large supply of his confectionary boxes. There was no way he could get out of it. Since Claire-Lise loves to go with him, he let her go along. She sends her regrets," said Maya.

Alex said, "She may replace Philippe one day. You never can tell, but I'm sorry she's not with us tonight."

"Me too. Okay, come on, let's get into my limo." Maya and her guests went downstairs to the parking garage and she slid into the driver's seat of the black Mercedes SUV, opened the roof and off they went for their night tour.

Maya streamed Vivaldi as she drove. The *Eiffel Tower* was the starting point. "Everything looks so different at night," said Lizette. After passing the glittering *Eiffel Tower*, they approached the *Trocadero*, they then whizzed down the *Champs-Elysées*, rode around the *Arc de Triomphe* and parked near the Seine. "Okay, everyone out. Philippe arranged a private boat and captain for us to have the best river views of Paris tonight."

"What a surprise. I have never been on the Seine at night, Maya," said Amirah. "How lovely this will be."

The *bateau* captain greeted the entourage as they took their seats. "Welcome, welcome to each of you. My name is René. Monsieur Dalle has engaged my little boat and me for the evening to acquaint you with our lovely city by night. The *garçon* who is serving you champagne is André. If there is anything you need, please tell one of us. If you would like to stop at one of the sights for photos or if you have questions, please ask. Shall we begin?"

Everyone was so excited. René started the boat and the narrative. "You know, the Seine has been the hub for transporting goods since ancient times. The Roman empire used it as a major trading route. It's linked with the Loire, Rhine and Rhone Rivers of France and eventually flows into the English Channel. Tonight we'll cruise along the *Rive Droite* and the *Rive Gauche* in the city.

"This champagne is superb," and Alex added, "Maya, this is a yacht, not a boat. What a way to see the thirty-seven bridges and all the scenes along the Seine. Thanks to you and Philippe for thinking of this."

"My darling Alex, you and the Lieutenant have made me very happy. It is a small thing to give you this evening, after all you went through for us."

The boat sailed by the *Place de La Concorde*, the *Musée d'Orsay* and the *Louvre*. "Paris looks like lighted Christmas trees everywhere. It's pure magic," said Lizette, cozying up to Lieutenant Fournier. "We don't get to go on dates that much, and this is truly romantic." Alex was really enjoying watching Fournier give his wife all this attention. Obviously, she was loving this night on the town. Maybe it wasn't Fournier's cup of tea, but it was a hit with his wife.

"Oh," said Maya. "We're approaching the *Pont Neuf.* André, please take my camera and take several photos of the two couples in front of the bridge. Please ask René to stop there." The boat soon came to a stop and the couples posed in portrait style. Then Maya said, "Okay, let's have the crazy poses now. Come on, don't be shy."

The couples complied and struck their goofiest poses. By now everyone was laughing and feeling the effects of the champagne.

René began again, "The *Pont Neuf,* completed in 1607, is the oldest of the city's thirty-seven bridges, even though its name means "new bridge."

Amirah said, "Oh, there's the City Hall. I went ice-skating there the first year I arrived and had a ball. It's beautiful with all its lights. People were on the ferris wheel and the merry-go-round and, of course, people were strolling as the moon began to rise. I was so thankful to be here. I felt my circumstances had finally led me to a better life," as she smiled at Alex and squeezed his hand.

René asked, "Do you see the *Conciergerie,* once the splendid palace of Philip the Fair? It became a place of terror during the Revolution, when prisoners were held prior to being taken to the guillotine for beheading. I will add, the guillotine was invented by a doctor because he could not bear to see the cruel ways people were executed. He thought this would take away some of the drama, but he was wrong. People still came out again and again to witness its use. Ah, but moving on, we see the exquisite *No-*

tre-Dame in its reconstruction mode."

Amirah remembered how she felt seeing the *Notre-Dame* the first time and how it reminded her of the destruction of Aleppo. She knew her city was not being reconstructed and that it would be a long time before she would see the mosques of Aleppo returned to their magnificence.

René's voice interrupted her reverie, "And now look at the *Pont de la Tournelle*, where you see the dramatic modern statue of *Sainte Geneviève*, the patron saint of Paris. The statue is in front of the oldest and most expensive restaurant in Paris, *La Tour d'Argent*, which means the tower of money. There is also a lovely museum and a shop selling items from the restaurant like cooking utensils, plates, spices and seasonings. If you are still hungry after the roasted duck, the house specialty, then stop at the *Berthillon* on the *Ile St. Louis* for the best ice cream in Paris, right over there."

"Amirah, you must tell me when your next exhibition will be and what type of art you will present. I plan to invite all my friends to see your amazing work. It may take time before you feel like presenting, but whenever you're ready, we'll be there," said Maya.

"Thank you, Maya, I'm not sure when that will be, but I am preparing for it. I will give abstract expression to the recent experiences I've had coming from Syria to Paris. I often express my emotions through my art. I must paint to show all that I've been through," said Amirah.

"I know there is something primordial in these artistic expressions and as you paint more, you will continue to expand your style," said Maya. "You have your whole artistic life ahead of you. Let those feelings flow, Amirah."

"I would love to see your work, Amirah," said Lizette. "Please include us when you exhibit. You know, my husband is an amateur artist when he has time."

Lieutenant Fournier grimaced, "Yes, very amateur."

Maya interjected, "Really, I think that's incredible. You worked hard at protecting us and finding our stolen paintings, but I had no idea that you yourself have artistic talent. You must let us see your work sometime."

Fournier said, "No, I don't think you would really like my style of painting."

Maya spoke, "Nonsense. Of course, I must see it soon. I'm sure it's very original, because of the different experiences you've obviously had. And given the work you do, painting should provide an amazing outlet whenever you find time to do it."

"Madame Maya and guests, our boat tour is coming to an end. It has been my great pleasure to serve you this evening. I hope to see you again soon. Please enjoy your splendid dinner this evening and have fun in Paris," said René. "*Au revoir, mes amis.*"

Everyone thanked the tour hosts and disembarked.

They all got into the car and Maya drove them to her favorite restaurant, *Fouquet's*, where she had reserved the best table with the best view of an international mix of passers-by. As they entered, the staff recognized Maya and treated her and her guests as royalty.

"Who are the people in all these photographs?" asked Amirah, gazing at the walls.

"These are photos of famous guests associated with the arts, who have dined in this restaurant through the years. Opened in 1899, right here at the corner of *Avenue George V* and the *Champs-Elysées*, it has now been completely refurbished," said Maya. The smiling *Maître d'hôtel* approached the table, prepared to compliment the guests and recommend the specialties of the night.

The dishes were brought to the table and each one looked more perfect than the last. There was delicious onion soup, haddock, smoked salmon, sea bream, cucumber sour cream, grilled king prawns with a piperade of chorizo, veal rump steak flavored with oregano – so many delicious delights. The group savored each dish.

To top off the evening's dinner, the *pâtissier* brought several ravishing desserts to the table – raspberry and basil éclair; red currant jelly with black currant coulis and kirsch crème diplomate, and Vanilla Millefeuille with fig jam. After sampling the famous desserts, everyone was satisfied with a delightful evening of food and camaraderie.

As they were preparing to leave, the *maître d'hôtel* returned to the table to assist the ladies. Maya's group returned to her Mercedes for a cool night's ride back to her *appartement.*

At the end of the evening, Maya handed an envelope to Alex and Fournier. "I am indebted to you, and I hope this will at least give you a lovely vacation this summer."

"No, Maya," said Alex, handing the envelope back, but she refused.

"Absolutely not. This is a gift from me. No discussion."

"Maya, you know I can't accept this as a police officer, but I appreciate your offer," said Fournier.

"Well, I understand, but I'll think of something else for you, Lieutenant Fournier."

Everyone said good-night and departed, feeling euphoric by the generosity of Maya.

Chapter 47

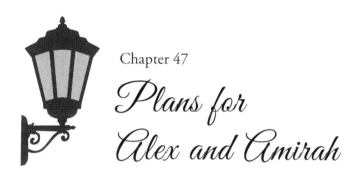

Plans for Alex and Amirah

One month later after the popular press lost interest in their harrowing experience, Alex and Amirah began to attend the International Church regularly. They were a stunning couple. It was obvious to anyone they were in love and cared deeply about each other. In addition to church, the weeks that followed were filled with discussions, romance, music, restaurants, friends and family. They were charmed by everything each did for the other.

One Sunday at the International Church, the pastor spoke on Matthew 8:23-27, the story of Jesus calming the storm. Amirah was spellbound as she heard the description of what she herself had felt that night on the Aegean Sea. The pastor read the words from the Bible, "A terrible storm suddenly struck the lake, and waves started splashing into their boat. The disciples said, 'Lord save us! We're going to drown!' But Jesus replied, 'Why are you so afraid? You surely don't have much faith.' Then He got up and ordered the wind and the waves to calm down. And everything was calm. The men in the boat were amazed and said, 'Who is this man? Even the wind and the waves obey him.'"

Amirah grasped Alex's hand and whispered, "I knew I was in a real storm on the sea and I was rescued that night by this man. I believe He was the Christ that the disciples knew and He extended His hand to me when I cried out to Him."

"You've faced many personal storms. I have too, but not as dramatic as yours."

"I think this Jesus made it possible for me to get to Paris and study at the Sorbonne, and especially to meet you, my love."

The pastor continued with the Bible lesson, "Placing your faith in people or things will not bring you genuine satisfaction in life and it certainly will not bring life eternal to you. Only faith in Jesus offers this." Amirah closed her eyes and laid her head gently on Alex's shoulder. He put his arm around her. Amirah whispered, "I don't know anything about the stories in the Bible, Alex. I hope you and I can read them together one day."

As they left the church, Alex said to Amirah, "How would you like to go to the Isabella Stewart Gardner Museum in Boston to see Rembrandt's *Christ in the Storm on the Sea of Galilee*? Rembrandt was my father's favorite artist. What do you think of him?"

"I know that particular scene is the only seascape ever painted by Rembrandt, and I would love to see it. As to your other question, I think Rembrandt is pure creative genius."

"We may have to wait a long time to see the original, because it was stolen in 2010 by two men disguised as police officers. It is still the largest property crime ever carried out in America, and guess what they're offering for the return of that masterpiece?"

"A million dollars?"

"Try ten million dollars."

"Do you think you could find that art as you found the Monet and Picasso? Maybe we should try together an extraordinary rescue," Amirah joked.

"It would definitely be a challenge, but we could have fun

thinking about it. And who knows, maybe, if we actually tried to find it, we might succeed and get the reward. I hope you won't stop loving me after we find the Rembrandt and receive the ten million dollars."

"Alex, let's see, could I ever leave someone as charming, kind, thoughtful, and loving as you? Hmm, maybe — no, I don't think so, so yes, I cannot stop loving you." He gave her a light hug and kiss.

They walked along in the *Quartier Latin* to a favorite Thai restaurant and ordered spicy curry soup and Roquefort cheese on romaine lettuce. "Why does meal time with you go so quickly, and why does everything taste so good when we're together?"

As they were eating, Alex remarked, "You know, Amirah, I want us to do everything that will help us stay passionate about our life together. I think we agree that we are not simply seeking to make a lot of money in this life, but are you sure you would want to commit to a vagabond life, if I end up traipsing all over the world as part of *Médicins sans Frontières*?"

Amirah touched his hand softly, "Alex, you shouldn't have to ask me that question. We will make our dreams come true together. As for my art, I see images everywhere, and therefore, I can create my art wherever we go."

"But you want to paint and have your exhibitions and maybe your own gallery. I'm concerned about how you can do that if I am working with *Médicins sans Frontières.* You know I love you and want to be with you forever, but I don't want you to miss your own calling that's been your destiny for a long time."

"Alex, I was homesick for Aleppo, but when you came into my life, you added a new dimension. Going with you is what I want to do — wherever it is. You know I want to go to Greece. I have faith we will find my mother and two brothers there. I don't trust Ibrahim to tell me anything anymore, and Imam Mansur hears nothing. Father is anxious, but he trusts you. I believe we will be able to locate them once we're settled in Greece."

"Amirah, Lesbos is a popular resort and the refugee camp is on the outskirts near the hospital, so if they're there, we will surely find them. Of course, they may already be on their way to Paris. I doubt that. But, regardless, we will find them even if they've moved somewhere else." Just then, the waitress appeared with the bill for the dinner. Alex paid and they left the restaurant.

"That was a lovely lunch. Do you think we can find a Thai restaurant as good as this one in Greece? I think we've become addicted to Thai food. Maybe I should learn to cook it."

"That's not a bad idea. I'm going to hold you to that. And I can make the salad." Walking along the *Rue de Rivoli*, they passed a jewelry shop. "Let's take a look inside," suggested Alex.

The two entered the boutique which was filled with antique French jewelry and heirloom pieces as well as some modern designs. Amirah examined some beautiful pieces. "Alex, what superb craftsmanship," she said, holding up a choker necklace of pearls and tiny diamonds.

"Go ahead, try it on. I want to see it on you."

The saleslady was only too pleased to fasten the lovely necklace on Amirah. Alex looked admiringly at her and spotted a matching bracelet under the glass. "May we please see this also?"

"For *mademoiselle* and *monsieur*, but of course. This is designed in the style of Vintage French." She lifted it from the case and fastened it on Amirah's arm.

"Yes, this is exquisite," said Amirah.

Alex said, "It is you, *ma chérie.*"

Amirah took off the bracelet and the saleslady removed the lovely necklace from her neck. "Will you take it with you?"

"Oh, no, not today," said Amirah. "Thank you," as she and Alex left the store. "That was fun, Alex. I love window shopping, but I don't usually go so far as to try on the jewelry."

"I'm telling you, it was you."

They strolled to the nearest boulevard and Alex hailed a taxi to *Sainte-Chapelle.* He knew it was one of Amirah's favorite chapels, dating back to 1150. Commissioned by King Louis IX, it housed Jesus Christ's crown of thorns, which the King brought back from the Crusades. The church featured gorgeous stained-glass windows in the elaborate Gothic interior from the 13th century. "Let there be light, the Bible says, and in this church the light pours in like God's grace to us," said Alex.

"We are so blessed, Alex. You know how much I admire these windows. Look, apparently they are set up for a concert here."

"Yes, they are and let me see," Alex reached into his pocket and pulled out two tickets. "What do you know? I have two tickets for the Vivaldi concert this afternoon. Will you be my guest?"

Amirah was laughing. "You're spoiling me. This is a wonderful day, but actually like every day with you, Alex. After last Sunday's concert at *St. Sulpice*, I am overwhelmed by the glorious music in Paris. The organist last week, what was his name?"

"That's the world-renowned Daniel Roth, who has been there in residence for the last twenty-seven years."

"Yes, Daniel Roth played the most incredible organ I've ever heard and so many people were there to hear his superb performance. And now you've brought me to this small, intimate chapel with the magnificent light streaming through the stained-glass windows. You're such a romantic, Alex. I love you."

Just then, as they took their seats, the performance by *Les Solistes Français* orchestra began with an amazing violinist. The Vivaldi Four Seasons concert reminded her of the new seasons of her life that she can anticipate with Alex. A powerful spirit surged within her.

After the concert concluded, Alex and Amirah left the church and strolled along the Seine. As they approached the bank where Alex first spotted Amirah, he took her hand and under the moon illuminating *Notre Dame*, he shared his deepest thoughts. "I want you to marry me and go with me to Greece and wherever else I go. I love you with all my heart. What do you say? Will you marry me?"

Amirah replied, "Our Lord is with us. You base your life on what is unchangeable and I long for that stability from God and you. You are like a candle to me, and I must have your light. Yes, yes, a thousand times yes. I will marry you and go with you to Greece. Together we will find our joy and contribute to the joy of others. I've already memorized the Christian wedding vows and I know my father will give his approval."

Author's Notes

The inspiration for this book started in Naples, Florida with a visit from a missionary couple, Stephanie and Levi. (Due to the sensitive nature of their work, I am using pseudonyms for those I met who work in the mission Life In Messiah.) After a Seder dinner, I mentioned that each year I do a mission of service in a foreign country, but this year I was undecided about what to do and where to go. "Why don't you do a mission in Paris, where we have lots of work taking place?" asked Stephanie.

I laughed and said, "Are you kidding? I don't think many people would think I was on a real mission field if I told them I was doing mission work in Paris." But they both assured me that Paris was in desperate need of solutions to the ongoing prejudice against Jews and Muslims, loss of traditional Christian faith and political unrest.

They told me about their ministry Life In Messiah International whose purpose is to build spiritual understanding among people of different faiths. They reach out to Christians, Muslims, Jews and others who have lost their faith in God and in cultures they no longer recognize. I was fascinated and said that I would love to help in any way I could. That summer a friend and I worked in Paris with their organization. It was an amazing experience. I promised them that I was going to write a book and donate proceeds to their ministry.

Since I taught English As a Second Language to many refugees from all over the world. I became fascinated with their stories of perseverance. They often risk their lives and give up everything to escape war, religious and political persecution, and imprisonment to arrive in a safe place. When thinking about the story I would write, I decided a refugee would be one of the main characters.

In March 2011 anti-regime protests erupted in Syria. Various rebel groups within the country tried to defeat the regime. This was primarily a war between two sects of Muslims, aided by other world leaders who took sides. Most of the rebels belonged to the Sunni majority, while the leading government families were members of the Alawite minority. Iran and Russia supported the Syrian government.

Censorship, surveillance, poisoning, and violence were perpetrated against any opposition to the government's leadership. Eventually the Syrian government used chemical weapons that killed a multitude of Syrians in 2013. Sanctions from the West were ineffective in stopping the slaughter. The rebels fought hard, but the governments of Syria and Russia continued to kill civilians, drop cluster bombs and target medical facilities, schools, civilian homes, and volunteer workers, as well as military fighters. Thousands of people were killed before millions of refugees fled on overcrowded boats or on foot in an effort to escape death and destruction. Diligently, I followed the news about Syria.

From this background comes Amirah, my fictional character, who escapes Aleppo with her father, leaving her mother and brothers to escape later. About 6.8 million Syrians are refugees and asylum-seekers, and another 6.7 million people are displaced within Syria. Indeed, Amirah, the heroine, continues to face multiple challenges after she makes it safely to Paris.

In the context of a suspense novel, I wanted to tell a story that not only examines possibilities of better understanding among people of different faiths, but also features a refugee who uses her faith both to overcome dreadful and dangerous circumstances and to grow as an artist and create a new life for herself.

Muslims, Christians and Jews are facing persecutions in many countries of the world. Europe's largest Jewish population is in France. However, many of them have been emigrating to Israel in the last few years because of the prejudices they've experienced.

I drove by an anti-Jew riot near the Eiffel Tower on one of my visits to Paris. It was a deplorable sight. In France, because of the terrorist attacks by Muslim extremists, there is often a certain hostile climate and discriminatory behavior towards all Muslims. At times French Christians also face discrimination for their views and evangelical practices.

Every day, an average of thirteen Christians worldwide is killed because of their faith. Twelve Christians are unjustly arrested or imprisoned, while another five are abducted. Moreover, twelve churches or Christian buildings are attacked daily, but most of the oppression of Christians does not occur in France and other Western countries. In this book I did not emphasize discrimination against Christians. Rather, I addressed discrimination against Muslims and Jews in France.

Dr. Anna Israel, who has recovered hundreds of works of art stolen from Holocaust victims in this story is a fictional investigator. However, there are Jewish investigators who continue to search for stolen masterworks and seek to bring the criminal perpetrators to justice. One of the great movies, "Monuments

Men," chronicles some of this history and the research concerning these paintings.

All accounts of raids, black apparitions, safe houses, *châteaux* and criminal activities are purely fictional. All of the events and names created in this book are fictional.

The *Pitié-Salpêtrière* is a very distinguished teaching hospital in the 13th arrondissement of Paris, but none of my book's characters is based on any staff or positions there.

As I mentioned earlier, I worked with a group of Messianic Jews in Paris. None of these workers has ever been involved with the Mossad or the Paris police on escapades to find and return stolen art.

As promised, proceeds from the sales of this book will help support Life in Messiah.

We all have stories to tell, and this is one of mine. I hope it encourages universal declaration of human rights and stops the cruelty of people hating and attacking each other the world over.

Thank you for purchasing this book. May it be a blessing to you.

Acknowledgements

First, I am eternally grateful to my dear long-time friend, Aubrey Neal, who enjoyed a distinguished career as a professor of history at the University of Manitoba. "A.M.", as he has always been known to me, spent hours from his Canadian office on the phone with me during this last year. He patiently and diligently read and re-read every word of my manuscript with me, painstakingly discussing content nuances, character development, time sequences, art, Middle East history and tradition, refugees and every subject my book touches. I would not have completed this manuscript with such richness of depth were it not for his immeasurable support, interest and encouragement.

I have been privileged to enjoy his friendship for many years and have been blessed to work with him on this incredible journey. I can never repay him for the hours we spent and the fun we had completing this manuscript.

I was ecstatic when my talented friend, Rouben Simonian, a brilliant artist, computer specialist and creative genius, agreed to create the cover for my book. His portrait of Amirah looking at the Eiffel Tower and the electrifying colors is amazing. He has captured the light and joy she will find in her new freedom in Paris. He and his wife Liz continue to inspire me with their exceptional creativity through the arts of photography, architecture, cuisine, painting and much more. Their discerning knowledge of Middle East history, particularly of the Armenian refugees, as well as present-day world politics has broadened my perception of the refugee crisis. I treasure their friendship and will frame the book cover to remind me to pray daily for refugees.

My good friend and lawyer, Denny Frey, who now spends his days enjoying The Villages in the Florida sun, was kind enough to use his eagle eyes to be my personal copy editor and make certain the text was grammatically correct. He wrote hundreds of briefs and other pleadings in his law career. In addition, he edited volumes of written witness testimonies. He pinpointed details with precision and edited any word misplacement and improved my sentences, often with the simplest changes. We worked at all hours of the night by phone from his Florida home. I thank him for his quick wit and sense of humor which gave us many good laughs, while working through the challenges of good writing.

I consulted hundreds of YouTube videos, and newspaper and magazine articles concerning the issues in this book. In fact, reading about the Syrian refugee crisis and the brutal killing of the civilians in Aleppo and other Syrian cities captured my attention daily. I could not stop reading, researching, conversing and praying about the state of these oppressed people. I am thankful for many excellent reporters who risked their lives to go to the frontlines and report the truth to us. When I began to write this book in 2015, I got up every morning and turned on YouTube to learn of the Syrian situation, reported by DW from Germany, Sky News from Britain and Australia, Gravitas from India, France 24, BBC from Britain and PBS from America. Now, I sadly follow this routine for information regarding Ukraine.

I am thankful for the many authors who have written of the Holocaust in each European country. Sadly, the horrors of the WWII Holocaust genocide continue to be repeated in many countries of this world.

I am thankful for the personal acquaintances and friendships I've made through the years with refugees from Vietnam, Cambodia, Laos, Cuba, Venezuela, Afghanistan, Sudan and others. They have enriched my life, expanded my worldview and brought me great joy.

Several individuals read the manuscript at various stages of writing and gave me valuable input: Genetta Adair, an excellent writer and teacher of writing; Georgeanne Daws, teacher, artist and compassionate community helper; Lyda Kaye Feree, a magazine editor and freelance writer; Beth Gooch, a newspaper editor, writer, journalist; Dr. Earl Davis, artist, pastor, writer and counselor; Alice M. Campbell, international investigator; Pamela Williams Hallin, former Pan American Airlines stewardess and excellent grammarian and her husband, Colonel David Hallin of the United States Marine Corps Retired. Their great gifts of time are immeasurably appreciated.

I also would like to thank members of several writing groups in which I have participated through the years: Collierville Writers; Central Church Writers; American Christian Fiction Writers; and Pelican Bay Naples Writers Group.

I deeply appreciate Ken Raney for formatting this book at

Raney Day Creative, LLC.

Thanks to Karen Sargent for the management of the *Alex and Amirah* Launch Team.

I have been blessed with family and friends who fill my life with love and laughter. Especially, I thank my grandchildren, who couldn't wait for me to finish the book because I gave three book characters their names.

Thank you to all who invited me to speak in churches, meetings, bookstores, book clubs and other venues. I especially want to thank my wonderful Alex and Amirah Launch Team who supported and encouraged me with love and outreach through this process. I thank them for their commitment to share this story and help Life in Messiah.

And thank you, Dear Reader, for buying the book and sharing it with your friends.

Cast of Characters

It's not the usual practice to list the characters in a novel, but I thought it might be helpful, since so many of the names are Arabic, French, Sudanese, Spanish and Hungarian, so here they are.

Doctor Alexander Winston
Amirah Hassan
Lieutenant Fournier
Nanian
Houssain al-Jabar
Ibrahim Soliman
Abdul
Doctor Reza
Mr. and Mrs. Bill Hertz
Fauziah
Maleeka Mansur
Sylvana
Olivia Israel
Jonathan

Yousif Hassan
Hilba
Mrs. Pilon
Senora Isabella
Maya Dalle
Philippe Dalle
Claire-Lise Dalle
Jean-Claude
Dr. Anna Israel
Sami Hassan
Rasheed Hassan
Mehri Hassan
Murad
Captain Casseaux
Egbert
Levi Israel
Jacques Israel
Farrokh Mustafa
Maslan
Dr. Jay
Iman Mansur
Rami
Ishtak
David
Antoinette
Madamn Brodeur
Lizette
Captain René
Andre

Tribute to Afghan Refugee, Anita Biriya

As I approached the final chapter of my novel, I had the privilege of meeting a beautiful young Afghan refugee whose artistic talent equaled that of my fictional ingenue Amirah.

She was presenting her portraits and abstracts in her first opening reception in America. Although she's young, beautiful, independent, and successful in her new country, she carries traumatic memories that will impact her life forever.

It has been an honor and blessing to learn more about her and her family's heart-wrenching escape from Afghanistan. I knew immediately I wanted to share a couple of her paintings in this book and provide her contact information to those who might be interested in viewing more of her work.

Anita Biriya welcomes commissions. Her contact is below.

I want to invite you to hear from Anita in her own words:

My name is Anita Biriya. My family and I left our homeland, Afghanistan in 2014. Our life, our job, our freedom, and our future were in danger. We fled to India where basic life as a refugee was extremely difficult. We faced many problems. After my father suffered several strokes, I became the one to care for and provide for my whole family. During this stormy time, my mind was racing, and worries ran wild. I picked up a pencil and began drawing in the late, silent hours of the night as I sat by my father's bedside. The deep emotions

I could not express in words came to life with each line and stroke of the pencil of each portrait. During those dark years, art was like therapy for me.

Finally, in 2021, we arrived in the United States in Memphis, Tennessee. I had my first solo art exhibition entitled: "Light in the Darkness". All the drawings that I did in India were on display and there I met an adorable lady, Kathy, the author of this book. We talked about my journey and about her book. Now it's my pleasure to be featured in her book. Here is my Instagram if you'd like to see more of my art.

Anita.b-art
My e-mail is Anita.biriya@gmail.com

Made in the USA
Columbia, SC
03 February 2023

11410437R00186